*"We are all in the gutter, but some of us are
looking at the stars"*
– Oscar Wilde

The House of Paris Le Grand

4

Contents

Prologue: Inconsequential

A dark heavy cloud descended and hung over the little girl. It was invisible to all, but she could feel its thick, oppressive weight push harder against her.

She remembered the blackness nipping at her from around the age of five. It was small then though, just a wisp of gloom, but it steadily grew into a dense smog that blocked out all light.

By the time the girl had grown into a young woman, it was a monstrous size and weighed over every aspect of life, making even the smallest of decisions difficult to make.

She soon became lost and latched onto whatever she thought hope looked and felt like, but the dark cloud always won and any glimmer of happiness in the young woman's life remained small before eventually being snuffed out.

The darkness soon carved out a void in her life. It was a giant lonely, bottomless pit that could seemingly never be filled. No matter what was thrown into it – family, friends or possessions – it remained dark, cold and empty.

While there was no physical effect, it made the young woman feel inconsequential, alone and in possession of a wasted life.

Everyday presented reminders that she was missing something. Pondering over people's lives on social media was something the now middle-aged woman would do religiously.

She'd study their happiest pictures and posts that had been proudly put out for all to see and try to translate the contentment into her own life. But the woman could never come up with an equivalent for herself.

Other people's colourful lives, happy faces and achievements zipped up her phone screen one after the other with a flick of the thumb. She couldn't help feeling that every one of the few people she followed on social media had made something of themselves. Their lives glowed with positivity and occurrences worthy of sharing with the world. Where was her sharable occurrence?

The thought of putting something of herself out there for all to see filled her with dread. As far as she was concerned, social media was worse than stepping out into the real world. She knew people laughed about her and talked behind her back. But at least that wasn't something in black and white on a screen that she could see.

And what people did see of her in real life wasn't much anyway. 'Cover it up so you and no one else can see it' had long been her philosophy. Why try to stand out and attempt to look or feel beautiful if there's nothing there to work with in the first place?

But this also made it tough to do what people considered as normal. Try going out and looking people in the eye when you don't possess even a drop of confidence. Smiling, laughing or anything jovial can only be done if you have a reason. Where was her reason to laugh and smile?

No, Sophie knew what she was now and that her place in the world had been decided. Ultimately, she would never be able to find whatever the missing thing was.

Chapter One: Typical Day

To most, Friday mornings signal the end of the humdrum working week and the beginning of two days of freedom to do with what you please. But for Sophie, who was sat alone at the kitchen table eating her usual breakfast of shop brand cereal and milk, Fridays just meant a weekend of staring at her living room's four walls lay ahead. But she didn't necessarily mind this.

Being alone was the only thing Sophie knew she was good at. If it was an Olympic sport, then she would be the highly decorated world champion of it without question. She could give even the hardiest of hermits a run for their money when it came to social evasion.

However, despite her best efforts to shut herself off from the world, there were people out there who felt the need to stop Sophie becoming better at being lonely.

For example, just as she'd finished breakfast and was preparing to leave for work at the call centre, where she had been fulltime for the past five years, the house phone rang. Sophie knew who it was.

Not only did she receive few calls, other than the odd one from a dodgy number or maybe her ex-husband Carl with an update on their youngest son Thomas, there was only one person who rang the almost forgotten phone that sat on a table in the sparse hallway.

"Hello mum," she said with a sigh on lifting the receiver to her ear.

"Darling! I've just been thinking how wonderful it would be if I came over this evening to have dinner and watch a film." This was typical of Beryl, who had always worried about Sophie's loneliness, like she was a pathetic divorcée who needed someone to sit with her.

"Well, mum, I was going to have a chilled one this weekend and maybe clean the house out. Thomas is staying at his dad's again and I thought I'd sort out the spare room," Sophie ventured, hoping it was enough to put her mum off the idea of coming around.

"Oh sweetie, darling! What a fabulous idea, we can make a whole weekend of it. Tell you what, I'll bring something over to cook for dinner and how about you get a bottle of wine in?"

Realising she hadn't managed to discourage the visit, Sophie relinquished with a sigh and agreed to have her mum over that evening for dinner. "Ok, I'll see you here at about six-ish. And... yes, I'll get a bottle of red," she sighed before her mother could chip in with a reminder about the wine.

Once she'd put the phone down, Sophie looked at herself in the round hallway mirror. She smoothed some wisps of chestnut hair and applied a little lipstick – the peachy tone of which wasn't too dissimilar to her natural lip colour and the reason she liked it – before picking up the keys to her car on the paved driveway and heading out.

She locked the front door and got into her Nissan Juke. While placing her phone and bag on the passenger seat, she made a mental note to be a little more enthusiastic about her mother's concern. Afterall, she was only trying to be helpful and, while some of Beryl's eccentricities could be a bit much, she was just trying to do good.

It was just a twenty-minute drive from home into the town centre where Sophie worked. She didn't like listening to foolish presenters on the radio and chose to play a self-help podcast through her phone instead.

Although none of the podcasts she listened to had actually proven to be any help, it had become a habit, just like the never-ending string of CDs, books and magazines she'd bought in a bid to subdue the biting feeling that had harangued her for as long as she could remember. Despite ultimately proving useless she would continue to tug at the string just in case one was eventually fruitful.

"Here's a little exercise for you," the whiny-voiced presenter of *A Meaning-FULL Life* told Sophie. "Count up everything you have in your life that can be seen as a positive. It could be your career, children, a partner or friends. You have a whole selection of things that others in the world would kill for. You are lucky. Now, I want you to say out loud, 'I am lucky' and then tell me why you are lucky."

"I am lucky, because I will soon be turning this podcast off," Sophie said to her empty car.

She wasn't entirely sure why she continued listening to the podcast after almost five months of arguing with the irritating presenter, whose words were about as helpful to her as a chocolate fireguard.

Counting her blessings wasn't going to achieve anything. Hers wasn't a math problem with an answer; she could tally up an infinite number of what the presenter called blessings and still end up with nothing.

Of course Sophie had love in her life, that wasn't the problem. Her mum loved her, her two sons did too, and she knew Carl adored her still, even after she'd divorced him. But no one, not even Sophie, could work out what the hollowness in her world was. She'd had forty-four years of it now and felt the battle to justify her existence was being lost.

Everything she did to cure it felt like throwing a pebble into a pool so deep you couldn't see the bottom. As soon as the ripples had stopped, it was as if nothing had ever disturbed the water.

It was a constant search for a missing jigsaw piece. Whenever Sophie thought she'd found a solution, eventually it became like trying to force the wrong shaped piece into the final hole of the picture, leading her to give up and let whatever it was she thought would help go.

As she pulled into the tarmacked work carpark, quickly reversing between the white lines of an empty space, Sophie tugged the USB cable from her phone, telling the podcast presenter to "shut it". She locked the car and hurried into the glass and steel office building where she worked.

Sophie's desk was in the middle of a busy floor full of other chattering call centre workers, who all sat in long rows.

The office was soulless, with white walls, big windows and modern black chairs that sat behind nondescript white and grey desks. She worked nine until five every Monday to Friday, which had been her routine since the boys were old enough to get to and from school themselves.

She sat down and put on a headset, ready to take the first berating from an irate customer about paying too much for their gas or electricity.

But, before she had logged on to the computer, Sophie could see Maurice – the boss who everyone called Morris just to annoy him – stomping over with his usual smarmy look across an open mouth that displayed two rows of crooked yellow teeth.

"Sophie," he said in a nasally voice that reminded her of a stereotypical busybody from a film. "I've had two complaints from customers about you this month and the company is not happy with you."

Looking up at Maurice as he spoke, Sophie thought it strange that two complaints could make a massive corporation annoyed. Surely the disgruntled complaints of a few grumpy people on the phone wouldn't be escalated to anyone higher than her boss. How could the 'company' be annoyed?

"Remember, you're on thin ice and very close to being put on performance management," a look of pleasure passed over his face as he spoke, making those jagged stained teeth of his more visible.

His short and fat frame was topped with greasy thinning black hair and a big red-tipped nose shone out from the middle of his face. He shuffled so close to Sophie that she could smell the bitter stink of his morning coffee and cigarette on his breath.

With gusto he told her that the divisional MD had already urged him to take action against Sophie for these complaints, but Maurice himself, the hero in all of this, had argued that she deserved another chance. His heroics were short-lived and with another breath he once again became the villain, threatening to involve HR if there was another complaint.

"I just don't see how I have a choice, really. This behaviour is intolerable, our customers deserve more," he huffed, struggling to catch a breath having made the long and arduous journey from one end of the office to where he stood next to Sophie.

"Look, Morris..."

"It's Maurice, Sophie," he said loud enough for everyone to hear, causing a few eavesdropping colleagues to snigger.

"Yes, sorry. Maurice, I don't know why people would complain," Sophie defended. "I'm doing my best. I've worked here for years and I only seem to have had complaints since...

"Since when, Sophie? I'd choose your words wisely right now."

"Sorry, Maurice. I'll try to be better." Sophie thought it best to admit defeat and not accuse Maurice of bullying. But, she had in fact only began receiving these so-called complaints since Maurice came in as the manager of her floor from another of the energy company's departments six months ago.

After her rotund manager retreated to his office where he spent much of his time clicking angrily at his computer's mouse and scratching himself, Sophie managed to make it through the morning with no further altercations.

On her lunch break, Sophie would usually venture into the town centre. Although there wasn't much there in the way of big-named shops, it had more than enough coffee houses and delis to buy something nice to eat.

The high street was typical of a Home Counties town. It wasn't massive, but not small either and there were lots of knickknack shops and lots of places to eat and drink, but otherwise very little else to do.

On Fridays she ate at El Fino's Café Bar, a small independent place that served salads and sandwiches and somewhere she knew her colleagues, who usually went to the pub for lunch at the end of the week, wouldn't see her. After ordering a cheese panini and coffee, she took a table which she thought was out of sight near the back and checked her phone while eating.

"Sophie Alexandra Defoy, is that really you!?"

Sophie looked up from her phone, taking a few seconds to place who was standing over her. It was Amanda Barnes, who she'd known as a neighbour while still married to Carl over a decade ago.

"Well, how are you doing stranger?"

"Oh, Amanda, I hardly recognised you. You look so..."

"I know, I get my lips and cheeks done now, don't you think I look like a reality TV star or one of those social media influencers?"

The leggy peroxide blonde thing, who must now be approaching fifty, was just as tall and scrawny as Sophie remembered her to be. But now her face looked like it had been stung by a hive of wasps and her hair was dry and wispy at the ends where it had been over-dyed.

"Amanda, you look, err, amazing. You haven't aged a bit. How's the family?"

"You know, the girls are doing their own things now they're at uni and David sold his packaging business to a corporate, which means we're pretty much set for life. I'm not usually in the country, we have houses in Italy, France, Spain and, well, almost everywhere now, you know."

"Oh yeah, I know," Sophie said with a half-smile. Amanda wasn't known for being subtle about her financial status. She'd made many comments to Sophie in the past about the things she and Carl owned. They weren't direct insults in the way someone would say "that's rubbish and cheap", but Amanda had an ability of dressing up her scorn.

When Sophie and Carl had bought new living room furniture, Amanda's review of it when she was over one time was: "It's fabulous, really it is. I think I saw it on that programme where those poor people swap lives with the rich. It was definitely in the poor person's house and I remember saying to David how different it was."

Amanda was still rambling on about something or other, Sophie wasn't fully listening and got something about her parents moving into sheltered housing.

"How's your life then, Sophie?"

Sophie looked down and scowled at her panini, which was now oozing its melted cheddar. She wished she'd sat in a less noticeable place. It was the most loathsome question anyone could ask her. Especially from someone who so freely gloated about having it all.

"Well, it sounds like things are wonderful. I'm really happy for you," Sophie said through almost gritted teeth. It was taking a colossal amount of energy to maintain a friendly voice and keep her face from exposing the contempt she had for the odious Amanda. "I'm just plodding along as normal. The boys are fine, and work is great. Speaking of which, I really need to get back. Bye."

"Ok. Ciao! We must have lunch one day while I'm over," Amanda shouted. But Sophie pretended she didn't hear and scampered out the café's door without looking back.

It had been tough enough to feign interest in this woman's life when they were next door neighbours. Having lunch together would be torture and was not going to happen.

Sophie always had a million excuses ready to get herself out of any sort of social engagement. A ream of lies lay waiting in her mind to be effortlessly pulled out to save her from any situation involving people, especially those she didn't like.

After making her quick exit, leaving the rest of her lunch and coffee behind, Sophie fumed over people like Amanda who had it all without even trying. "Bimbo and a rich husband," she said to herself while sitting back at her desk, causing a few nearby colleagues to look up.

She managed to get through the rest of the day without another visit from Morris. So, at the end of her shift, Sophie shut down the computer and quietly shuffled away without saying bye to anyone. Although she'd worked there for years, Sophie had made a point of talking to as few people at the company as possible. She knew hardly anyone's name and preferred to keep it that way. There was always the risk that, if she built up even a small friendly relationship with someone at the office, they'd quickly see how pathetic she was and expose her to everyone else. It was easier this way. There was no point in making friends if they were just going to eventually stop talking to her.

A road accident had disrupted her drive home, which meant she had to take the winding country roads. With the extra traffic and the additional distance she had to drive, Sophie pulled her car into the small drive of her semi-detached four-bed yellow-bricked house half-an-hour later than usual.

The lights were on in the house, which meant Beryl had let herself in and had probably started mixing together a medley of ingredients that no one other than her mother would think worked together. It was half-past six and near pitch-black. When Sophie got out of the car, she could feel the evening was cool and quiet, with the smell of chimney smoke in the air. It was the kind of night Sophie liked most.

"Darling! I've been expecting you for ages, are you ok?" Beryl moved quickly from the kitchen and into the hallway so she was just a breath away from Sophie before she'd even had chance to take off her coat and put the keys into the bowl on the table below the hallway mirror.

"There was a bit of traffic, sorry mum."

"Not to worry, sweetie. I've started dinner anyway and I see it's a good job I brought the wine too," she said looking down at Sophie's empty hands.

"Ahh. Yeah. I completely forgot to go to the shop. I guess I'll just…"

"No harm done," Beryl interrupted as Sophie turned back towards the door to go back out. "Now go and sit down and tell me about your day while I finish off cooking my Malibu chicken."

"Ooh, Malibu chicken," she humoured her mother, knowing whatever crazy concoction was in the pan on the cooker would be foul, but hopefully not as bad as some of the dishes she'd been forced to eat out of politeness in the past.

Chapter Two: Eccentric

"Oh Christ, what's she doing now?" the neighbours would say, twitching at their blinds to see what eccentric seventy-year-old Beryl was up to.

Many believed Beryl laboured to be different, while others would say she was just going senile. However, Beryl's eccentricities were completely natural, yet had certainly become more prominent with age.

When she was a young mum and her husband, Sophie's dad, was alive, she would dress smartly, but always with a standout feature. Leaving the house without an accessory such as a sparkly pair of half-moon glasses or garishly coloured shoes was out of the question.

However, when her husband Bernard died thirty years ago, at the age of forty, Beryl steadily began to let the butterfly of colours inside her out in full force.

She now had large, thick-rimmed black glasses, would often wear metallic Dr Martens and her clothes were mostly purple. Her short, straight steel-grey hair was usually covered by a turban the colour of which, she would say, represented whatever mood she was in.

Just to make sure her kooky appearance was loud enough, Beryl chose to wear voluminous capes and shawls that would billow out behind her in summer breezes and winter gales alike, giving her a majestic and almost magical appearance.

It was difficult to say what Beryl would be up to next. One day it would be yoga in the front garden for all the neighbours to see, while the next she could be scaling and twirling at a pole dancing fitness class. On quieter occasions though, Beryl would be content with singing and dancing for passers-by in the town centre – "just to brighten up their day". She was the woman in purple, "just living my best life, that's what the kids these days say, isn't it?".

To some she may appear lunatic, but Beryl had all of her marbles and well-rounded reasons for doing whatever it was she turned her hand to. However, it was, at times, embarrassing for Sophie and her two boys.

Beryl was well known in the town, which meant most people knew who she was related to. Despite her daughter and grandchildren's best efforts to discourage the maverick behaviour, Beryl would just shrug her shoulders and point out that she was causing no harm to anyone, saying flatly "you've got one life and you must live it to its fullest".

Such a sentiment was how Beryl had always led her life, most especially before she met her husband and had their first and only child Sophie. Prior to those two milestones, though, the erratic older lady people now saw had led an exciting life, even by today's standards.

At the age of 16 she left home to see the world. There was no doubt in her mind that she would one day marry and have children, but until that point Beryl would have as many experiences as she possibly could. It wasn't what the posh youth these days called a "gap yarr", Beryl told her two grandchildren and anyone who would listen. No, this was a real adventure – "untamed and gritty, full of excitement and danger".

She first ran away to join a travelling circus and became a snake charmer's assistant, wearing Egyptian-style costumes that hung loose and showed off her midriff, "quite the scandal in my day", she'd laugh. To her, the snakes were like puppies or kittens and she'd handle them as such, cooing over her smooth friends while tending to their needs.

After the snakes, Beryl trained elephants, lions and tigers. She then became a trapeze artist, scaling ropes all the way to the top of the circus tent before gliding freely back and forth through the air, encouraging rounds of thunderous applause from gasping punters hundreds of feet below. As a child, Sophie would be regaled with Beryl's tales of the circus and her other travels. The young girl wished that one day she would also lead such an exhilarating life. There were romances too, many of them, but those stories weren't shared with her daughter. They were secret memories, just for her own private joy.

When Beryl had experienced all the circus could offer, she travelled to India and worked from job to job, including one in a rice paddy field where she'd succumbed to a nasty case of malaria.

It was then that she was forced to return home to be cared for by doctor Bernard Chase, who she fell in love with. She married this man who always laughed and joked – he kept the fire that she'd lit in herself alive. He was the perfect father, too, and was involved in Sophie's life from the day she was born. She was the love of his life and he hers.

Bernard was, in a way, Sophie's hero. He would come home every day with a surprise for his smiley and happy daughter. But then Sophie's mood changed, and so the smiles and laughs stopped. While he made many attempts to lift his daughter's spirits, Bernard also respected she was different from others. Sophie wasn't an extrovert like her mum, nor was she ambitious like him.

Although life wasn't by any means perfect, it was as close to it for the small family. The trio, however, turned duo when Bernard was diagnosed with cancer and died after a short battle, leaving devastation in his wake.

After his death, Beryl's number one priority was her child and then her grandchildren when they came along. She'd forever tried to help Sophie from her solitary shell. But, without the persuasion of her husband, it became a struggle to prevent Sophie from falling into an even darker place. Her daughter was lost in the world and couldn't find a place to fit.

When Sophie met Carl and gave birth to Beryl's two beautiful grandsons, she thought her daughter was complete. However, Beryl soon noticed it was just a quick fix as Sophie began to return to her old reclusive and regimented ways. Whatever had been filling the void was gone.

Sophie wouldn't meet people, she had no friends to speak of and didn't seem to enjoy anything. It was as though her daughter had become a robot by the time she was in her mid-thirties, completing core tasks essential for survival, rather than living or relishing in any part of life.

Beryl, however, had always lived in the moment and got as much from life as possible. She could remember smiling and laughing throughout her childhood, adulthood and motherhood. Even when her husband died, Beryl soon found a way to tackle the grief and isolation that followed. She found a way to have fun again, "it's what your father would have wanted," she told a scandalised Sophie, who was hurt to see her mother relishing in life again.

Spending as much time with her daughter, especially after she'd decided to divorce Carl, was the only way Beryl thought she could help. There was no question that Sophie's behaviour was worrying. It was as though a dark cloud always followed closely behind her daughter.

On more than one occasion, Sophie had confided in Beryl that things would have been better if she wasn't here at all, gut-wrenching words for a mother to hear. Bernard's mum, she knew, had suffered with mental health problems all her life until she killed herself when her son was just twelve. This fact about Sophie's paternal grandmother had always lingered in Beryl's mind. It was a dark cloud of her own.

She thought Sophie was more like her dad's side of the family in that sense, but she had also inherited the looks and figure of the women from the Defoys. Sophie's shape was just like Beryl's when she was younger and, going further back, her mum's too – not slender, but not fat. "You're curvy, darling, you can wear almost anything and in any colour. Stop wearing those drab draping clothes," Beryl would plead at her daughter.

But Sophie didn't see it, she always told her mother that her bottom was fat, and clothes were not made to look beautiful on her body. But at least baggy jeans and jumpers covered everything up. Sophie didn't even think she was a looker, despite having a beautifully shaped face, dark eyes and long eyelashes. She was a catch and didn't know it, yet even now in her mid-forties', men looked at her with hunger.

***

"So, darling. Have you thought about dating again? You've been single for a long time now," she asked in Sophie's modern kitchen while stirring a pan of what Sophie assumed was the Malibu Chicken she'd promised to make on her return home from work that day.

Her love life was a topic Beryl would often bring up to Sophie's annoyance. It was frustrating because she knew a man was not the missing piece. That lesson had been learned the hard way and had ended up with two children and a divorce.

"Mum, really. I'm fine on my own. It wasn't right with Carl and I don't think it will be right with anyone else either."

"But you didn't give things with Carl a proper go, not really. You divorced when the boys were so young. You hadn't had chance to live your lives together properly, had you?"

It was Beryl's biggest concern that, as soon as Sophie felt a little uncomfortable with something, she'd give up on it without thinking things through.

"Are you a lesbian, sweetie?"

"Mother! Stop."

"It's fine if you are. Mavis from yoga is a lesbian now. She, what is it *they* say? Ah yes, she 'came out' last week, but said she always misunderstood something about herself and until her husband Archie died, she couldn't put her finger on it. But it seems she has now."

"Look, mum. I'm not a lesbian and I don't need a man either. It doesn't really have anything to do with you. Carl and I had some happy times together, but I just wasn't in it. I thought it was what I wanted, but it just didn't work out. He knows that and I know that, now please stop talking about it."

Sophie didn't like being hard on her mum, but she was tired of hearing that she hadn't given it a real go with Carl and that she should be searching for another man or love of any kind.

"I appreciate you coming around to keep me company, but I really don't need you to babysit me."

"Oh, sweetie, I just thought it would be nice to have a girls' weekend in. A nice meal, film and some popcorn, like those girls in the films." She carried on stirring the mixture in the pan, which was steaming off a curious scent and Sophie couldn't decide whether it was delicious or repugnant. "I know you don't need looking after, sweetie. Don't worry, I'll be out of your hair in the morning."

Once they'd eaten what turned out to be a foul mixture of coconut rum, tinned tomatoes and pan-fried chicken breast, the pair sat down to watch what her mother called a girly film before Sophie made up the guest bedroom for Beryl and then went to bed herself.

It was around seven the next morning when Sophie woke to a strange humming noise and tinkling bells. She pulled on her jogging pants and a baggy old woollen jumper before going downstairs to see what it was. Her mother had probably been up in the night and left the tele or radio on.

When she went into the living room, Beryl was resting on her head, upside down and with her legs crossed in the air. She was breathing slowing and producing a deep "ummmmmmmmm" with every exhale. What Sophie least expected to see was a strange man sat opposite her. His eyes were closed and he too was humming and tapping a small bell with a wooden stick.

He was bald and dressed in shawls woven with what looked like Aztec prints in the shape of lizards and other desert animals.

"Mum! What on earth are you doing up so early on a Saturday morning... and who the hell is this?" she shouted, but then felt embarrassed as the stranger snorted and opened his eyes which were now alarmed and looked Sophie curiously up and down.

The sharp, loud yap from Sophie also sent a wave of shock through the room which hit an unsuspecting Beryl who was then sent tumbling to the ground. Her legs straightened out in an attempt to break her fall, but instead kicked the television and sent it tumbling from its stand, causing it to crash on top of her mother's companion with a thick and painful wallop.

Sophie's hand involuntarily raised to her mouth, pitifully stifling her loud swearing about the fact the television was now likely to be broken. But the groans of the flailing man soon snapped her concern in a different direction. He was about the same age as her mother and was tangled in his silly garments and trapped beneath the wide, flat screen tele.

While her mum just laid there laughing at what had happened, Sophie flew into a panic over the distressed, oddly dressed stranger. "I'm sorry. Are you ok? I didn't think she'd end up pushing a TV on to you. Help me lift it off, mum!"

They released the man and stood him up, checking to see if he'd been injured. He was fine and Beryl, as though this sort of situation was quite normal, introduced him as Derrick, her Shaman spiritual guide. After allowing him a few moments to catch his breath, Beryl sent him on his way with nothing bruised but his pride.

"Mum. You really need to stop doing stupid things like this. Headstands at your age, it's just nonsense. You could hurt yourself," Sophie scolded her mother once the old man had been shown out and driven away in his noisy old car.

"Darling, Shaman Derrick has been helping me stay centred for years and I don't intend on stopping any time soon. You could do with a little centring yourself, sweetie. You're uptight."

"For the last time, I'm fine. Now please, can you get ready to leave because I have things planned."

"What exactly do you have planned, Sophie? Because you don't do anything other than go to work, come home and sit on your own. It's not healthy, your life has no meaning and you've given up trying to find any."

Anger rose up inside Sophie from her stomach and out of her mouth like hot, stinging sick. She knew her mum was right and admitting that, even in her mind, was infuriating. To her, it was a fact this was all she would amount to. She wouldn't reach the upper echelons of energy company management, nor would she have a rich husband like Amanda.

"Mum, for God's sake. I just..." but with those six words the venom that had bubbled up from Sophie's gut soon dissipated and she couldn't think of anything to say to the truth. "I think you should go now."

"Ok sweetie, but please do something with your life. Don't waste it being miserable."

Chapter Three: Accident

After her mum had left on Saturday, the next day Sophie decided to gut the house. Cleaning it from top to bottom always gave her some sort of clarity and was sure to help scrub away the sticky words her mother had said to her.

Being called out by her own mum about one of her biggest insecurities was painful, with the directness of them so cutting Sophie felt she was in physical pain. Never had Beryl been so blatant about Sophie's circumstances. It was more common for her mother to skirt around the subject, suggesting this or that would be lovely to do. And while Sophie always knew what she was getting at, not saying it sort of made it ok for Sophie to continue plodding along.

But those words had been let out into the room and no matter how hard Sophie scrubbed the floors, teased black mould from the grouting in the tiles or made the stainless-steel cooker hob shine, they stuck like a permanent stain. she had wasted her life and she still didn't know why or how. She had wasted her life, despite the efforts to gains some sort of meaning – getting married, having kids and getting a divorce. Although, the divorce did feel right.

Sophie had made her peace with the fact that she would never accomplish anything. She would be miserable and alone until the end.

The final days of her life played through Sophie's mind as she was down on the bathroom floor bleaching the non-existent dirt from the lino. If she ever had grandchildren, they wouldn't want to visit 'Moody Nanny Sophie'.

She'd spend her last few hours on the planet alone, sitting in a well-used chair in a care home filled with other forgotten elderly people.

A bottle-and-a-half of bleach later, Sophie decided to clear out some boxes that had been stored away in the guest bedroom wardrobe. They'd been there since she'd moved into the newbuild house after divorcing Carl.

Getting the house hadn't been easy; she and Carl were by no means well off, but they had scrimped and saved all their married life and Sophie had done prior, which was easy since she'd never had a need to spend on frivolity.

She'd left Carl and moved into Beryl's with the boys for a year. The sale of the marital home had given her and Carl a decent lump sum each to buy new homes and then her savings allowed her to splash for a bigger place on a new estate.

The boxes were stacked high above Sophie's head when she opened the wardrobe door. She pulled them out one at a time and stacked them into a leaning tower on the bedroom floor. A piece of paper fell from one and silently glided under the bed, causing Sophie to tut and make a mental note to get it when she was done.

Each box was filled with useless junk. Ornaments and knickknacks that harboured no sentimentality or feelings, it was just tat that had been accumulated over the years – old ornaments that were out of fashion and bits and bobs that her mother had bought her from television shopping channels for birthdays and Christmases over the years.

There was no need to sort things into a keep box and a charity box, everything was going, so she dragged each one down the stairs and placed them in the hallway to be put in the car for the next morning. She'd drop them off at the charity shop on her way to work on Monday morning.

She went back into the bedroom to straighten things up and noticed the piece of folded paper under the bed. Sophie reached down, picked it up and opened it. The writing was hers, but it took her a while to register what it was the words that had been written neatly on the lined paper meant.

It was a list of things she'd written down to do in her life when she was divorcing Carl. The desperation she'd felt at the time of writing it came flooding back.

She remembered being huddled on the bedroom floor of their marital home, restrained by the grief of the fact she'd shattered the relationship. She hadn't been able to make it work, it was a massive risk to go into it in the first place, based only on a small shard of hope that she'd grow to love Carl as he did her. The remains of her sadness still marked the page of the list, which was puckered with untidy round dots where her tears had dried.

It was headed with 'Bucket List', which she snorted at because a lot of the things on it would probably seem mundane to a normal person.

Yet, even now, the thought of each one seemed no different to climbing the world's tallest and gruelling mountains. There was no way Sophie would have the drive to do any of them.

Some of the things she'd wanted to do included:

- Adopt a dog
- Find a best friend
- Ride a bucking bronco without looking stupid or peeing myself
- Shear a sheep

- Have a girly shopping trip
- Have a makeover
- Tour Europe
- Have a whirlwind romance
- Have a one-night stand
- Go on a date
- Go dog sledding
- Smoke a joint
- Have dinner in a restaurant on my own
- Join a gym
- Find a hobby
- Learn to cook at cooking classes
- Go to a life drawing class
- Run a marathon (or a half)
- Go to a drag club
- Learn how to do DIY
- Have a city break in Edinburgh

Sophie looked at the list again and again, tracing some of the more mundane items with her finger, each one she touched shooting a jolt of embarrassment from the page through her finger.

"Pathetic," she said to herself, crumpling up the list and throwing it into one of the boxes when she made her way back downstairs.

***

Sophie woke earlier than usual the next morning so she could load the car and drive to the charity shop before going into work. Monday was as cold and clear as the weekend had been, and just like most early winter mornings, she began by scraping ice from the windscreen of her car before driving the twenty-minutes into town.

She'd decided to give her usual self-help podcast a miss and switched the radio on to one of the local stations. An excitable presenter told her the road where the accident had occurred on Friday was to remain closed while the police and the Highways Agency investigated it further and carried out repairs, which meant Sophie had to drive down country lanes into town.

It had just gone half-past seven, so the roads were quiet and void of the hundreds of commuters who would soon be cluttering them up. She drove as carefully as she could on the tight, icy lanes, trying to admire the twinkling frosty tree branches and grass verges.

At a particularly tight bend, Sophie slowed the car to a near crawl and slipped it into second gear. These roads weren't that familiar to her, she'd always felt at risk taking quieter routes in case she broke down or needed help.

The ice was also making her drive with extra caution, her wariness increasing each time she tapped the brakes or shifted her gears down. She was managing it though and soon she began to feel at ease and almost started to enjoy the quiet journey as well as the music on the radio, only occasionally interrupted by the presenter whose excitement still hadn't dulled.

The ease soon rushed out of her when the back of the car lurched violently to one side and then the other.

Sophie tried to think what she'd read about skidding and couldn't remember whether she was to turn into it or away. Braking, she knew, was out of the question, but her right foot instinctively smashed into the middle peddle.

The car let out a high-pitched squeal, as though she'd stepped on a dog's foot rather than the brake. Her body filled with a tingling panic that sent her numb and made her head feel light and blurry.

So many decisions and actions had happened in mere seconds, but nothing was stopping the car which, at this moment, had a life of its own. It hurtled straight, towards the densely wooded edge of the road, then spun into a slide towards the trees before catching the curb at the edge of the road with enough force to tip it onto its left-hand side and then into a roll.

Metal, plastic and glass all crunched together making terrible noises as though she was listening to music from some sick orchestra as Sophie's car tumbled over and over, shaking and knocking her about.

She couldn't do anything but sit, fastened in place by the seatbelt. The boxes in the boot and on the back seat added their unique notes to the terrifying medley, spilling out their contents which crashed into Sophie's face and body as the car continued to summersault.

And then it all went quiet and still. The hideous ornaments were no longer attacking Sophie, the crunching had stopped, and the world wasn't spinning. A quiet hissing from the car's engine broke the silence for a second, but then died away like someone's deep breath during sleep.

Sophie whimpered, she could smell blood and she felt woozy. A thick, sticky stream of red slowly dripped from her head onto the windscreen with each drop falling faster than the last. The seatbelt cut into her chest and hips, but it was causing her no more pain than when she was being hit by porcelain figurines and the other tat from the boxes during the crash. She was hanging upside down, unable to move and bleeding. This is all she thought before closing her eyes.

It was cold when Sophie opened her eyes again. She knew where she was and had remembered what had happened. It was still light outside, so she hadn't been asleep for long. Her body was aching, and she could feel bruises begin to swell up all over her.

She thought about undoing the seatbelt, but even if she could, she'd fall into the windscreen and potentially do more damage to herself. She tried to take in a deep breath to scream, but quickly whimpered after filling her lungs only a little. It felt like knives were being jabbed between every one of her ribs.

Whenever Sophie had heard people talk about near death experiences on the tele, she'd always rolled her eyes at the "my life flashed before my eyes" part. But, to her shock and disgust, Sophie couldn't help but let the last forty-four years of her life play out in her mind.

It was boring. There was nothing she'd achieved. When had she smiled, laughed or cried with happiness? What was it that they would say at her funeral? "Here lies Sophie Defoy, the most interesting thing that happened to her was the way she died."

She had allowed everything to get sucked into a big black, vacuous hole. Even on days most women would note down as their happiest – the first time a man said I love you; getting married; having kids; and watching your child's first steps – she'd let everything disappear into a vacuum. She'd always felt numb.

Whether it was the shock of the accident now settling in or the fact her pathetic existence had just played itself out, Sophie's eyes were filling with tears. Great big, agonising sobs left her mouth. She'd never cried like this before.

It was a mixture of physical and emotional pain that had joined forces to create a desperate mess. But then, finally, she could hear sirens from somewhere on the road and only hoped they were for her.

She looked down around her to see if there was anything that could be used to help attract attention. There was a small ball of paper, not useful. But before Sophie realised, the paper was tightly in her hands.

When she next woke, the room around her was unrecognisable. It took Sophie a while to recall what had happened and understand that she was in a hospital bed. On the bedside table there was a bunch of flowers with a card on them with Carl's and both of her boys' names on. At the bottom of the vase the ball of paper she'd managed to swipe up was there. It was the pitiful bucket list.

The room was clinical, with pictures of daisies on the wall. Under the crisp white sheets of the hospital bed, Sophie could see that she was wearing a hospital gown. Lifting the sheets made her arms and back ache, so quickly she put them down and reached up to feel her head, which was wrapped in a thick bandage that covered most of her skull.

It had been a lucky escape, she knew that. As melodramatic as it sounded in her mind, she could have died. Yet, the thought of dying wasn't the upsetting thing. What haunted her most was the thought of continuing to live the way she had done over the years and so she fixed the ball of paper on the bedside table with a stare and promised herself that her death wouldn't be the most interesting thing about her.

At that moment, a doctor walked into the room told Sophie she was indeed lucky to be alive, as a tree branch had pierced through the side of the car and had almost impaled her. He also let Sophie know that her family was in the waiting room ready to come in once she was conscious.

He recorded a few vitals, such as her temperature, blood pressure and pupil dilation, before letting her know what they had done to her. It had taken the fire crew almost an hour to free her from the upside-down car, doing so while she was mostly unconscious.

Once in the ambulance, Sophie was losing blood quickly from an injury to her right thigh, while she'd also suffered a concussion and bruising to her spine and minor fractures to her ribs.

It had taken several hours of surgery to deal with some internal bleeding, relieve pressure on her spine and brain and to restore the blood she'd lost. However, the doctor continued, while the accident had caused serious injuries to Sophie, she was now likely to make a full recovery and would she like him to send her family through?

"Mum!" Ralph and Thomas shouted as they launched into the room ahead of Beryl and Carl. "Dad called me and I came on the train from uni as soon as I could. Are you ok, you look terrible," said her eldest son Ralph.

"I feel like I probably look," Sophie said with a smile, feeling genuinely happy to see her family.

"There's something different about you", said Carl curiously. "Did you bang your head, have the doctors ruled out any brain damage?" he asked with real concern.

"I wouldn't worry. I feel like things have been pushed into perspective a little more today," Sophie said to Carl.

"It was probably one of the scariest moments of my life when the car spun off the road," she told the four of them. "It was very close and for a moment all I could think about was how boring it's all been so far. How agitated, moody and depressing I've been all my life. There isn't one thing, other than you two, boys, that I am proud of achieving. There's nothing that I can look back on and think, that is how I'd like to be remembered when it is actually my time."

Beryl had tears in her eyes and was wiping the corners of them with a small tissue. "I was worried that the last things we'd set to each other were in anger," she wailed dramatically. "I thought I was going to lose my baby, it's not right that a mother should outlive her child."

"Oh, mum, really. It's not you lying in a hospital bed after skidding from an icy road, having been nearly speared by a tree branch."

***

It was now Thursday, and Sophie was preparing to leave the next morning, packing up the few things that she'd accumulated or had been brought to her over the past ten days.

Books, magazines, spare pyjamas and other bits and bobs were all put into a suitcase her mum had wheeled to the hospital for her.

The doctors had told her that she was able to go home by the end of the week, but only if someone was able to care for her.

As she was laying out her clothes on the bed ready to wear the next day, Carl knocked on the door of the private room she was in. Sophie turned and gave him a little smile before gesturing with her head for him to come in.

"You're not going to be weirded out by me staying at yours for the next couple of days, are you? I know you've enjoyed your independence and doing your own thing, but I'm just going to be there to help you out, that's all. The boys said they'd feel better this way."

"No. I think it will be quite nice to have someone around the house for a little bit. I know Thomas stays with you because it's closer to his college, but it can get quite lonely when he only comes home on the odd weekend.

Carl's face lit up at her answer. He'd never wanted their marriage to end. He'd fallen in love with Sophie almost from the moment he'd knocked into her when he was on a night out in a bar with friends.

After only a handful of dates, he was infatuated with her quiet and self-deprecating nature. Deep down, he'd always felt that she didn't feel the same way about him as he did her but believed that she did love him in some way.

When Sophie had sat him down in their living room to tell him she wanted a divorce one night when the boys were staying with their Gran, the world had crashed down around him. Everything he'd known and come to love was being taken away and there was nothing he could do.

He remembered sitting there, in a stunned silence. There was nothing he could say while Sophie was telling him that her heart just wasn't in it. She'd felt like it shortly into their relationship, but kept thinking that, because he loved her so much, she could grow to love him.

Every time she'd gone to break up with him, there was another thing she felt she should try to make sure that it wasn't just her being silly – their first holiday away, saying yes to getting engaged, getting married, having their first son Ralph and then Thomas.

But she couldn't go on any longer and wanted to make sure they were both still young enough, in their thirties, to make another go at life. Sophie knew another relationship wasn't on the cards for her, but since Carl was a few years younger than she was anyway, he stood more of a chance at starting out fresh.

"But, then I do like my space, so I think I'll be looking forward to having the house back to myself by the end of your stay," Sophie piped up to make sure Carl wasn't getting the wrong idea about things.

This snapped her ex-husband out of his little daydream and he quickly removed whatever happy expression was on his face. "Don't worry. I'm not getting any funny ideas."

She smiled at him and then made sure the tattered list saved from the car accident was safely tucked in one of her magazines.

Chapter Four: Paris Le Grand

Nearly a month had passed since Sophie came home from hospital with Carl. The two of them had cohabited amicably, considering they had been divorced for over a decade.

Having him around didn't make Sophie feel as claustrophobic as she thought it would. Actually, it was nice to have someone else in the house to talk to and do things for her. While it was obvious Carl wanted to start things up again, there was no doubt in Sophie's mind it was something that would stay in the past.

That didn't stop Carl, though, who launched himself into an assault of relationship redemption. He would wake early every morning to prepare Sophie's breakfast, bringing it up to her bedroom on a tray with a single carnation in a small glass vase.

For the rest of the day he would busy himself with jobs around the house – cleaning, ironing and fixing things that Sophie had forgotten about our grown accustomed to being broken.

During half of Carl's stay, Sophie was unable to get out of bed once he and Ralph had helped her upstairs. Nineteen-year-old Ralph had returned to university in Manchester where he was studying English. Thomas had gone back to Carl's to look after the house – promising he wouldn't throw parties and agreeing to regular visits from Beryl who would make sure he was looking after himself.

One evening, as Carl's stay was coming to an end and Sophie was fully recovered and ready to go back to work the next week, he again broached the subject of two of them once more becoming an item.

"There has only been you, Sophie," he said sheepishly, knowing he was already fighting a lost battle. But he carried on, fixing Sophie with his green eyes, while nervously running a hand through his coppery hair.

Much of the furniture in the living room was what they had bought together for their marital home. The navy sofa and brown leather armchair along with the television stand and the countryside paintings. Sophie had even used neutral coloured paint for the walls, which she'd insisted on doing in their first family home.

"I just wanted you to know that I was in this from the moment I almost knocked you over in the bar and I am still in it now. It wouldn't be difficult to pick up where we left off or even to start all over again. We have two wonderful boys who are almost grown up. It could be our time to..." he trailed off as Sophie held up her hand and spoke in a soft voice.

It was hard to have this conversation with Carl again. The last time they had talked about their feelings for each other was when Sophie had sat him down and shattered his life. It was possibly the worst moment of hers, but continuing with their marriage would have been unbearable.

"In a way, Carl, I do love you but it's not how you want me to love you and not in the way you deserve to be loved either," she said, willing the conviction in her voice to get through the thick skin of hope he'd been harbouring for years.

"After the accident I have decided to do the things that I have never let myself do. I haven't allowed myself to live my life and unfortunately, you too have fallen victim to whatever my issues are. You don't know how sorry I am about that. But that's what it is and we both need to move on."

For the second time in her life, Sophie saw hopelessness in Carl's eyes. She had torn this poor man in two asking for a divorce all those years ago and she was again dashing his hopes by attempting to close the book on there ever again being a Mr and Mrs Stapleton.

A new woman was now trying to break through the darkness she'd lived with all her life. She could sense a tiny blip of some unrecognisable feeling bubbling to the surface and knew, however sorry she felt for him, living a lie with Carl was wrong.

***

Monday morning came unwelcomingly quick. Carl had gone back home on Friday and Sophie was once again alone having breakfast at the round kitchen table.

The radio was on and female pop artist who she'd never heard of was singing a song about not letting your no-good ex back into your life. It wasn't exactly the same sentiment Sophie had for Carl, but all the while it was refreshing to have someone reinforce her principle. The pair had come closer together during her recovery, but it was better to be friends.

The beginning of the eight o'clock news signalled the end of breakfast and time for work. Usually Beryl would call each morning to see if Sophie was well, but yesterday she had left town for a month-long mindfulness retreat somewhere in the countryside and phones were banned.

Picking up the keys to the loan car from the insurance company, Sophie caught sight of herself in the hallway mirror. The gash on her head had healed over and the hair was growing back through.

She made sure the rest of her hair was covering the stubble properly and left the house.

It was the first time since the accident that she'd driven. Although she was able to avoid the country road where it had happened, Sophie felt a little nervous about the journey and tried to push it out of her mind.

A Meaning-FULL Life's tepid host was telling Sophie that things were going to be great for her. Life was full of surprises and now was the time to embrace every single one of them. Usually this sort of encouraging comment would make Sophie scoff and mock wretch, but this time she took the words in, listening attentively to the advice of how to find happiness.

On entering the soulless glass and steel building, Sophie nodded in response to the receptionist's smile and offer of "good morning" and made her way up to human resources, where she was to have a back-to-work meeting.

She got out of the lift on the sixth floor and could see Maurice in a glass-fronted meeting room chatting animatedly to a pretty HR woman who was nodding politely and taking notes. Sophie knocked on the door and heard a muffled "come in" from her greasy boss.

"Ahh, you've finally decided to come back to work have you?" said Maurice with what Sophie took to be a mix of fake concern and humour. It made the HR woman, who introduced herself as Lynda, nervously cut in quickly with "you're looking very well and we're happy to see you on your feet".

"I'm feeling well, thank you. My doctor has said I have made a full recovery and will be able to come back to work as normal. Morris...

"It's Maurice."

"You're looking well," Sophie said as sincerely as she could.

"Sophie, we're here today to make sure that you are able to come back to work and to see if there's anything that you will need from the business to make sure you transition in the best possible way," said Lynda with the sterile tone HR advisers seemed to adopt with worrying ease.

As HR Lynda spoke, her curly hair bobbing up and down while attempting to bring the company's mundane technicalities to life with animated hand gestures, Sophie looked around the cold room, empty of personality.

She wondered how many people had been brought up to the white box with its glass wall facing onto the HR team to be told they no longer had a job or that they were underperforming and needed to buck up their ideas or else face the chop.

She'd spent years here, purely to earn money to pay the bills, buy food and help Ralph and Thomas out where she could. Surely, the new Sophie who was bubbling up from the depths of the void wasn't the sort of person who would want this.

Although this unknown person inside Sophie had yet to show herself, it was unlikely she'd willingly allow strangers to yell at her down the phone about the cost of their gas bills. More so, would she let tubby unwashed Morris threaten her with the sack on an almost daily basis? Probably not.

"Sophie. Sophie are you listening to Lynda?!" Maurice spat, a clump of greasy hair sliding over his forehead.

"Actually Morris, I'm not listening. No. I couldn't think of anything worse than sitting here listening to the things HR Lynda here and you have planned to help me transition back into a job that, quite frankly, is mind numbingly boring. I believe the phrase I'd rather watch paint dry is quite an apt response."

Maurice and HR Lynda sat in stunned silence with their mouths open as Sophie let rip the truth about the company and how she could think of nothing worse than returning to work for such a detestable man.

"Morris you're possibly one of the most disgusting, unhygienic little men I've ever met. A good shampoo and a toothbrush wouldn't go amiss once in a while. And did you know that, when you talk, you spit. A lot. Lynda, perhaps you and the rest of the HR department could work on a solution to the biohazard risk greasy, tubby Morris here poses."

Too far, Sophie thought, but it was impossible to stop. It was as though a fire had sparked to life in her belly and someone was blowing on it, making it burn bigger and brighter.

"It's Maurice, Sophie, but I guess that doesn't really matter now does it. You've overstepped the mark little lady. Lynda, please tell Sophie that she is dismissed with immediate effect and should leave the premises."

"Uhm, errrr..." flabbergasted HR Lynda began.

"It doesn't matter, Lynda. You can stuff your job, Morris. I don't want it."

With that, Sophie stormed out of the little white box. She could hear Maurice shouting after her as she opened a door onto the stairs and took them two at a time until she was on the ground floor and out of the building.

She got into the car and was shaking, the adrenaline from her uncharacteristic outburst still pumping through her veins. Where had it come from? She threw her handbag onto the passenger seat, but it missed and fell to the floor, spilling out its contents. The magazine she'd put the bucket list into slid out and Sophie reached down into the footwell to pick it up. She opened it and pulled out the list, reading over the words again and again before pointing at random to one of the tasks. 'Go to a drag club', it read.

After a quick Google on her phone, she found the address of a local gay bar called Sophisticats and decided she would go there when it opened that evening.

On her drive home, the reality of what had happened with Maurice and HR Lynda began to sink in. Sophie was now jobless. She had never been jobless.

In the heat of the moment she didn't think about paying bills or even buying food. When she was going hell for leather, it all didn't matter but now Sophie was calming down, her stomach tightened, and she began to panic. It was a feeling she'd never had before – like someone was piling great big heavy bags of sand on to her chest, making it increasingly difficult to breath.

She pulled onto her drive and went quickly into the house before slamming the door and sliding into a pile on the floor behind it. "Shit! You bloody idiot!" She cursed to herself. "What the bloody bugger are you going to do now without a job?"

After a little while on the hallway floor, Sophie began to pull herself together, and started to justify what she'd done. The energy company was a dank, soulless and mundane place to work. Morris was a miserable self-righteous, greasy swine and, let's face it, Lynda from HR was just as bad as everyone else there. She had liberated herself. If she was going to starve or be made homeless, then at least she'd got a good story out of it.

There was more than enough money in her savings to survive for three or four months before she'd have to look for work or consider something else, she reasoned and commended herself, for the first time, for not having a life.

If the savings ran out before she found a new job, then perhaps she'd just sell the house. It was almost paid off; both boys had a room at Carl's, and she could just move in with her mum. Living with Beryl, though, would have to be her last resort, she told herself with a gulp.

Once fully calmed down, Sophie walked into the kitchen and sat at the table with a cup of tea. She'd pulled out the list, which had been stuffed into her pocket, and began copying every point into a notebook with a rainbow pattern on it she'd grabbed from the kitchen drawer.

There were things on the list that seemed impossible, like have a whirlwind romance. But she was determined to carry out every task she could. And, instead of just copying out the tasks that were on the crumpled piece of paper, she added others that had popped into her head, giving each one a page to itself so she could make notes as she ticked them off.

It ended up finally reading:

- Adopt a dog
- Find a best friend
- Ride a bucking bronco without looking stupid or peeing myself
- Shear a sheep
- Have a girly shopping trip
- Have a makeover
- Tour Europe
- Have a whirlwind romance
- Have a one-night stand
- Go on a date
- Go dog sledding
- Smoke a joint
- Have dinner in a restaurant on my own

- Join a gym
- Find a hobby
- Learn to cook at cooking classes
- Go to a life drawing class
- Run a marathon (or a half)
- Go to a drag club
- Learn how to do DIY
- Have a city break abroad
- Skydive
- Self-defence classes
- Go horse riding

When she was done, she drew a circle around the task she was going to tick off that day and thought on it. Who would she go to the gay bar with? What would she wear? And why would a drag club be on a bucket list? Finding something to wear would be a good start, she thought and left the kitchen and went up to her bedroom.

Upstairs, Sophie's wardrobe was a depressing sight. There were folded piles of loose-fitting jeans in various shades of blue. Hung above them were drab jumpers in shades of grey, black and the odd one with a flash of colour. She'd never had to dress in anything other than casual clothes for work and the last time she'd gone out anywhere that could ever be deemed fancy was for an anniversary meal with Carl.

Determined to look like anything other than the woman who she saw in the mirror in front of her, Sophie pulled out every item of clothing from the drawers and wardrobes. By the time she was finished, the room looked like a stall at a car boot sale. The bed, floor and every available surface were polluted with her pitiful garments, until at last, stuffed down the very back of the wardrobe, Sophie hit gold.

What she found wasn't something that would be seen on the cover of *Vogue*, nor would a catwalk model strut down a runway wearing it. However, the black dress was so far removed from anything she'd worn for the past decade, that to Sophie it felt as though she was holding a piece of couture fashion.

There was little makeup in Sophie's bathroom. Other than her trusted peach lipstick and an old tube of crusty mascara, she couldn't remember ever owning makeup. After an unfruitful search of the rest of the bathroom, Sophie remember her mum kept a stash of toiletries in the spare room from previous visits.

The room was bright and airy, with dreamcatchers and crystals dotted around the place, making Sophie realise the room was no longer the spare room, but had been overtaken by Beryl. In the top drawer of the white painted dresser, she struck gold again.

All kinds of glittery makeup had been left there, and after some routing around, Sophie settled on a deep red lipstick, a dark dusty gold eyeshadow as well as a tinted moisturiser and a fresh tube of mascara.

She showered and then went back into her own bedroom where the mini makeover began. With the precision of a small child testing out their mother's makeup, Sophie massaged her freshly washed face with the tinted moisturiser and applied a thin coat of the shimmery eye makeup.

To most, this wouldn't have been a transformation, but to Sophie, the woman looking back at her was almost unrecognisable. It wasn't the inch-thick makeup she'd seen others on the street and in social media pictures wear, but it was a start.

"Baby steps," she told herself before pulling the mascara brush through her eyelashes, which were longer and darker than she'd expected them to be, having never studied her face in much detail. The look was finished with a swish of red across her lips, making them pop as though she were a burlesque dancer ready to perform or someone about to head out on a hot date.

Makeup done, she stepped into the black dress and zipped it up at the back, twisting around in the mirror to make sure it was done all the way. Sophie examined herself in the full-length mirror that was on the inside of her wardrobe door – so she didn't catch a daily sight of herself. Standing there wasn't the person she'd come to know over the past 40 years.

This woman stood out and looked confident. Her bosom was high, and the dress fit close to her waist and over her curvy bottom and legs.

Although tighter fitting than she'd usually be comfortable with, Sophie thought the dress could synch a little close to her waist and so fastened a shiny black belt from her mother's room around her middle, before choosing a pair of black patent leather court shoes, with a low heel. She was ready.

While waiting for a taxi downstairs to take her to Sophisticats, Sophie dug out a bottle of gin from the kitchen and poured herself a large G&T, which she drank in four gulps. This was it, Sophie had never felt so nervous. What was she going to do alone at a gay bar? The flicker of fear in her mind would easily grow into a full-blown argument against going out if she didn't stop thinking negatively.

There was no reason to go. What exactly would she do, surely she should be looking for a job now. Anyone who came across her would have a right laugh at this fat old woman looking like a slug struggling to stay in its skin. But, several blasts of a car horn from outside snapped her out of it and soon she was safely in the taxi en-route, for the first time in her life, to the unknown.

"Girls' night out is it?"

"Uh. Oh, something like that," Sophie replied to taxi driver's eyes which she could see in the rear-view mirror.

"Monday night is usually a quiet one, but I've been quite busy dropping people off into town. You're going to that gay bar, Sophisticats? My son's there all the time, loves it. Says it's the best night out in town."

"Great. I've never been before. I don't really know what to expect."

"They'll treat a stunner such as you like a queen."

Sophie didn't know what to say. She'd never felt comfortable with compliments and rolled the taxi driver's words over in her mind, trying to find the hidden nasty meaning that was likely to be lurking somewhere in them. Her face flushed when she realised he was being sincere and she gave a small laugh a minute or two later.

She paid the driver and stood outside the club. Her legs were wobbly and any courage she'd been able to conjure before the journey into town was quickly dissipating. Now was the opportunity to push through the red wood and glass door in to the unknown or else head back home.

Before the last drips of confidence leaked out of her, Sophie barged through the door at just past ten o'clock and didn't know what to make of the scene in front of her. It was a long dark room full of young men no older than 25, along with a few girls around the same age.

The room was the length of an Olympic-sized swimming pool and had a bar that ran almost all the way down the left side of it. Dotted around were tables and chairs, booths and high stools next to posing tables. At the very end of the room there was well-lit stage with disco lights and a stunning woman singing an exceptional version of Whitney Houston's *I Want to Dance With Somebody*.

She kept her head down and walked over to the black marble bar and ordered a vodka and tonic from an extremely attractive topless barman. She paid, said thanks and then found herself a table in a dark corner on the righthand side of the stage.

The performer was coming to the end of the Whitney Houston song and Sophie realised she wasn't a *she* at all, but a man dressed as a woman. Not only that, the words to the song weren't coming from her mouth either, but instead she was giving a convincing lip-synced performance.

As the room broke into applause, the drag artist, who announced her name was Mya Ding-a-Ling, stepped carefully from the stage, allowing Sophie to see her voluptuous curves and plummeting cleavage, before disappearing to the back of the room.

A bodyless voice commanded the attention of the room, introducing the next act as Paris Le Grand. Sophie gasped as a goddess mounted the stage in black high heeled leather boots, from which a pair of shapely thighs emerged that in turn supported curvy hips, a synched waist and two convincing large pert breasts.

Paris's face was painted in a way that conveyed both femininity and power. She wore a similar shade of red lipstick to Sophie, but her eyes and cheekbones were dark and smoky.

Music to a Beyoncé song filled the room loudly, to which Paris began a seductive dance, moving across the stage with both elegance and swagger. She squatted, laid on her back with her legs in the air and crawled across the stage like a pussycat. Sophie knew she was watching a man perform as a woman, but she'd never seen something so empowering.

At the end of the song, Sophie stood and clapped with everyone else in the room, tears spilling from her eyes at the sight of someone exuding the confidence and personality she wished to possess.

The performer left the stage and pop music played from the club's speakers, signalling to the people in the room that their attention was no longer needed, and they could make their own entertainment. As Paris was stepping down from the stage, she noticed a woman with red lips and watery eyes was still standing and staring at her. It piqued her curiosity enough to have a closer look.

"It's rare I get such a long-standing ovation from a lone woman in a crowded gay bar," Paris said to a now stunned Sophie. The voice that addressed her was neither camp nor typically masculine. But it was such a juxtaposition from the stunning creature it came from, that it rendered Sophie speechless for a few seconds.

"I've just never seen anything like that," was Sophie's stuttered reply.

"Well hun, I'm flattered, but it's nothing special considering the rest of the battered and beaten hags in the show can do exactly the same thing."

"I disagree. That one before you didn't have the grace you do and when she got off the stage you could tell she was a man. You, on the other hand, look like a woman, even this close."

"Shady...

"Sorry?" asked Sophie not sure what Paris had said.

"You're being shady to one of my sisters. It means you're being a bit of a bitch."

"Oh. I didn't realise she was your sister and I hope I haven't offended you," Sophie began, now feeling itchy with embarrassment.

But Paris just laughed, making the big dirty blonde wig on her head wobble and shake. "I'm a fishy queen, which means I paint my face to look as womanly as possible. Mya, however, is more of a comedy queen and beats her face with as much makeup as it will hold to make it look clownlike."

Sophie still didn't quite understand what the drag queen in front of her was saying, so nodded and waited for Paris to continue.

"Are you here on you own then, hun? It's usually only the creepy, older, married men who come alone to try and bag themselves a twink for a one-night stand behind their wives' backs. You know, closet cases?" Paris said in response to the quizzical look on Sophie's face.

"Don't strain yourself thinking about it too much, hun, you might do yourself a mischief. Anyway. What are you doing here alone?"

In just a few minutes, Sophie managed to spill a garbled everything that had happened to her over the past few months; the crash, how her ex-husband had helped her, the bucket list, quitting her job, and how she had decided to live her life differently.

Paris, a stoic and unsympathetic sort, stood in silence as the middle-aged mess of a woman continued to vent her life story. The things Sophie told her weren't really that unusual, but the idea of someone like Sophie ticking things off a bucket list had grabbed her attention. She was interested.

"Well, hun, if you need somewhere to work, we've got a sort of stage manager job going. It's nothing exciting, taxing or challenging – just making sure the queens are on stage on time. But it's yours if you want it."

Before Sophie gave an answer, Paris swished off into the crowded club, leaving an open-mouthed Sophie unsure about what had just happened. She'd done something completely out of character. Not only did a stranger now know the ins and outs of her recent life, she felt like there had been some sort of a connection. And had she just been offered a job?

Still standing, Sophie thought on the offer. It wasn't exactly the sort of place she'd imagined working. This was the first time she'd even spoken to a drag queen, having never been in a gay bar. It wasn't something the old Sophie would do, she thought and before she knew it, Sophie was in pursuit of Paris who had now disappeared into a crowd.

Weaving in and out of the tables, between groups of chatting and gyrating men, finally Paris was in her sights. In touching distance of her, Sophie lunged forwards between two kissing men and grabbed Paris on the shoulder.

However, in her excitement, she was moving too fast. Then, to Paris's and her shock, almost brought the two of them to the floor as she lost her balance – thanks in part to having had two strong drinks, but mostly because she wasn't used to wearing heels, even small ones.

Paris swore loudly, causing the kissing couple and a few other revellers to stop and look at her and Sophie. "What in the hell do you think you're doing sneaking up on a queen like that," she blasted loud enough for those in the vicinity to hear.

Now flustered, Paris wiggled her wig to check it was still in place, patted her fake boobs and continued to scold Sophie. "Don't you know what I could have done? I could have smacked you right in the face, or worse, I could have broken a nail."

Sophie looked at the thunderous Paris, whose composure was slowly returning, and laughed so hard she thought Paris would certainly take a swipe at her this time. There was no stopping it, the absurdity of chasing down a drag queen in the middle of a club to take her up on a job offer was incomprehensible. It was all just a bit too much.

"What on earth are you laughing at?" Paris's face was again clouded with fury.

"I'm really sorry, I don't know what happened. I think it's these shoes and I don't' usually drink this much. If you knew me, then you'd understand."

Paris said nothing. Her face was still stiff and etched with anger.

"I'd like to have that job you offered, if it's still going?"

Sophie waited a few seconds for a reply and then followed up with a: "Well?"

"Well what? You want me to give you a job here, so you can attack more queens? Once in a lifetime is enough for both you and I," she said but now with some humour cracking across her face and in her voice. There was something about this tragic woman in front of her that interested Paris.

"I'm really sorry. I didn't mean to. I was just excited I guess, and I really do need this job."

"Come back at five tomorrow afternoon and try not to maim or kill any queens between now and then. Ok hun?"

Just as Sophie started to ask for more details about the job, Paris turned and marched away, moving around the men in a cat-like way, sliding her hands gently over their shoulders and backs so they'd move out of her way. Men cheered and embraced her caresses as she went along, before a Britney Spears song conjured a crowd of writhing men around her, eventually enveloping her so Sophie could no longer see the curious creature.

But now, standing alone in the middle of a gay bar filled with men dropping to the floor in squats and dancing together closely, Sophie once again felt self-conscious. It was nearly midnight and probably time to leave, she thought.

In the taxi home, the same driver who had dropped her off regaled her with stories of his evening. He'd picked up a few girls who'd drunk too much and had to kick them out of his cab after one of them threw up out of the window. "Don't worry though, I made sure one of their parents collected them," he said to an uninterested Sophie.

She'd got a job. Sophie Defoy, a sad forty-four-year-old divorcée with two grown-up children and an eccentric widowed mother, was going to be working in a gay bar. With drag queens.

Chapter Five: Drag Queens

Beryl was digging around in her handbag outside the front door trying to find the keys to Sophie's house. She'd just come back from her mindfulness retreat in the countryside where phones weren't allowed, but even if they were, she couldn't remember where hers was anyway.

The keys were right at the bottom of her deep carpet bag which she used anytime she stayed away from home. Once through the door, the house in a strangely gloomy state. None of the sunlight from the bright and clear winter's day outside was making its way into the hallway from the kitchen windows ahead of her or the living room door to the right.

It was not like Sophie to leave the house for work without opening the curtains and blinds, Beryl thought. Come to think of it, the car outside on the drive didn't look like her daughter's. Something was wrong.

There was also a musty smell in the house, but Beryl couldn't quite work out what it was. It reminded her of the parties she went to as a young woman. It smelled of stale alcohol. But it couldn't be that, because Sophie didn't drink much, if anything.

The lounge on the right was decorated just as it had always been since her daughter moved in – dull, neutral colours with a navy sofa, scrubbed pine furniture and flowery pictures on the walls. She sniffed the air and wrinkled her nose as the pungent stench strengthened.

The living room was at the front of the house and had the dining room straight off behind it in one open plan space. On the table there were takeaway cartons and an empty glass with red lipstick on it. At first, Beryl thought perhaps one of her grandchildren had had a party, but that couldn't be right. Sophie never went anywhere, and she certainly wouldn't have allowed Thomas or Ralph to have a group of friends over and leave the house in such a tip.

As she looked closer at the mess on the table, there was a shuffle from somewhere upstairs. Damn, why do I always lose my phone? Beryl thought to herself, her heart thumping at the pending danger. There was someone in the house. What if Sophie had been abducted and there were now squatters living here? Or, worse, what if they had bound and gagged Sophie upstairs and she was about to meet the same fate?

Someone was walking down the stairs, trying to be soft and quiet because they could hear a person snooping around. Beryl picked up the white porcelain dog she'd bought Sophie for fifty pence from a charity shop a few years back and readied herself to belt someone with it. She'd then make a run for it out the house and call the police.

Waiting quietly behind the living room door, she held her breath for so long the sound of her heart was thumping in her ears.

A nest of matted and ratty chestnut hair slowly edged around the door, which was followed by a screech of "I know you're in here and I've got a weapon!".

"Oh, you bugger. Sophie, it's me. I was about ready to whack you. What are you doing home so late? And look at the state of you and this house."

"Mother. Why are you sneaking around? What if I walloped you?"

"Sweetie, darling. I hardly think you'd cause me much damage with that kitten heel, now what are you doing home still, are you ill?"

Sophie had forgotten her mum was returning today and even if she had remembered, it didn't occur to her that Beryl's first stop would be here. As usual, her thick steel-coloured short hair was nearly all tucked away beneath a turban, this time an emerald green one. She was wearing her trademark purple floaty clothes and thick black rimmed glasses, which made her eyes bigger than normal.

"I err... well, that's a question. I'm not at the call centre anymore. I quit yesterday and I have a new job now."

"Wonderful darling! I always thought that job sounded dull. What are you doing now? Have you started your own business, or have you finally followed my advice and decided to retrain as something more exciting, like a travel writer or something that gets you out of the house more?"

"Actually, I'm a stage manager at Sophisticats..."

"The gay bar in town, darling? Oh, sweetie, that's wonderful, I knew you'd come to terms with it sooner or later. So, what's her name, or are you still finding the right woman?"

"Mother, for the last time, I'm not a lesbian. I just went to the bar last night on a whim. I'd had a strange day and thought I'd do something a bit different. I'm kind of trying new things at the moment."

"A whim, darling? I didn't think you knew what that word meant," but Beryl stopped talking as Sophie's brow narrowed crossly. "What I mean to say, sweetie, is that's magnificent. I do like that Mya Ding-a-Ling, such a convincing woman, dear. She could teach you a trick or two about make up... she taught me a few things and I always get looks on the street."

Sophie smirked, as she remembered what Paris had told her about Mya's look being extreme and comedic rather than feminine and could now see a little of that in her mum's make up.

"You've been to the drag bar?" she said, the surprise in her question fading at the last words. Of course her mother had been to Sophisticats.

"Darling, you know I like to have as many experiences as possible. Now let's get this mess sorted out," Beryl said with a flourish of her hand, which pointed at the state of the living room

Once Sophie had tidied the mess of last night's takeaway – a Chinese meal from the restaurant where she asked the taxi driver to drop her – the curtains and blinds were then opened, as well as a few windows to let the stale air out.

Everything was still sinking in. It was hard to believe there was no nine-to-five job; no dull office to go back to and that Morris would never again threaten her with the sack. For the first time, she felt there was a little control and direction in her life, and she was surprised to find there was a small part of her looking forward to the unknown.

"Coffee, sweetie? I've only been drinking dandelion stuff at my mindfulness retreat and all I've been thinking about is having a cup of the real thing. Or something stronger, if you have it?"

"No, it's too early for that," Sophie interjected before her mother made her way to the lonely gin bottle that had been sat under the kitchen sink for years.

While her mum searched through the cupboards for some coffee beans to grind, Sophie sat at the kitchen table and looked at the bucket list she'd left there the night before. She flicked through the pages, going backwards and forwards, trying to decide what would be easy to tick off next.

Going to the drag bar seemed such a simple task now, but everything else looked less achievable and more out of reach. Things like touring Europe would cost a lot of money and take her away from home and any form of income for too long. While a whirlwind romance was laughable and tacky and the thought of a one-night stand, well, that was just outrageous. Sophie would never invite a stranger into her bed. Even worse was the thought of sleeping in someone else's.

Coffee was plonked down in front of her, the noise of it breaking her attention from the book. It was a welcome drink and would help sort Sophie's increasingly painful headache. Her mum sat next to her, looked around the kitchen, pointing out the things that could be changed now she would have some extra time around the house.

But Sophie wasn't the sort to give great consideration to interior design. She'd watched programmes on the tele where experts would go into a home, tut and laugh at the simplicity of it all before turning into something from a show home or magazine.

Her kitchen was basic. Magnolia walls, baby blue coffee, tea and sugar canteens with matching kettle, microwave and breadbin. It was practical to buy everything matching. The cupboards, worktops and all the whitegoods, as well as the stainless-steel cooker and hob, came with the house and were fitted into the kitchen, so she'd never needed to change them.

"Perhaps a splash of colour here and there wouldn't hurt," she admitted to her mum. "But I'll sort it when I get time."

"Marvellous, but I've got an eye for these things you know, sweetie. So, when you go paint shopping, make sure you bring me along. I've got some wonderful ideas for you. And once we've tackled the kitchen, maybe we could look at the living room, it looks like you're in rented accommodation and the furniture all came with the house."

After humouring her mother for a little longer, Sophie wondered what sort of a house this new woman who was emerging would live in. Would it be a showy, sleek home with lots of expensive ornaments, or perhaps a simplistic modern space with white walls and clean surfaces?

"What's that you've got there on that pad? It looks like a list."

Sophie saw her mother craning her neck to get a better look at the book, so she closed it and put her coffee mug on top. "It's just a bit of a shopping list, nothing special. Just a few things I've decided to get sorted."

After another hour or two, Beryl eventually decided to go home and unpack, giving Sophie time to think about her first shift at Sophisticats. Last night didn't feel real and looking at her reflection in the hallway mirror, it was a nothing short of a shock to see the person looking back.

Mascara was smeared across her eyelids and under them. Her lipstick was smudged around her mouth and chin, making her look a little like the Joker from Batman, and there were dark bags under her eyes from the late night. The whites of her eyes had thin red veins creeping out from the edges. This must be what hungover looks like, she thought.

There was no makeup remover in the house, since it was possible to wash her trusted peach lipstick off with a bit of warm water and a flannel. And her usual minimum of eight hours' sleep had meant she'd never seen such dark circles under her eyes before.

Her skin, which had never seen much sunlight or suffered years of caked on foundation and other products, was usually smooth and blemish free. It was a shade darker than milky white and had no deep wrinkles, but there were a few lines across the forehead, if you looked close enough. Not that anyone ever got chance to look that close.

The tatty mess of hair, however, was something new. Big tufts rose up from the top of her head in the shape of bird's nests and there were frizzy strands sticking out like spun sugar. Adding to the rough effect were pieces of egg-fried rice and god knows what nestled in various parts of the mound. She didn't feel that drunk when she'd gone to bed, but then she hadn't eaten since breakfast that day.

"Right! In the shower and then time to find something to wear for tonight," she told the strange raggedy woman in the mirror, who, to her surprise, was smiling. The woman she'd caught short glances of over the years had rarely, if ever, done that.

After showering and making herself feel more presentable, Sophie sat on the end of the bed in her towel, staring at her wardrobe. Without having to look, she knew there wasn't anything in there other than her jeans and jumpers. The dress that had been found out of desperation the day before was the only jewel waiting to be discovered.

A pair of straight-cut, more tightly fitting, dark denim jeans and what looked like one of Carl's old white shirts was decided on, which, she told herself, looked fine with the white Converse-style trainers she'd bought from a supermarket a few years ago.

Hair dried and back to normal, as well as some light makeup applied, Sophie trotted downstairs to make a late lunch and see if Ralph would pick up his phone at university. It rang about two dozen times and just as she was about to give up, it crackled into life at the other end.

"Hello?" a gravelly voice questioned.

"Are you still in bed? It's almost three o'clock, what have you been doing all day?"

"Mum?"

"Yes, it's mum. Why are you still in bed?" she asked, thinking she'd heard another boy's voice in the background asking what time it was.

Her son's voice sounded louder now: "It ended up being a late one last night. A few of us went into Manchester and things got a little messy. But I went to class today, so don't worry."

"Well, that's a relief. At least you're not drinking away your education." Silence followed as Ralph tried to work out if it was his mum on the other end of the line. Perhaps it was a trick. It wasn't the type of conversation they'd normally have in this situation. Hearing that Ralph was still in bed after a drunken night out would usually warrant a lecture about not taking things seriously and wasting money on alcohol.

"Are you ok, mum? I was kind of expecting a bit of an ear bashing. I mean, don't get me wrong, I'm grateful you're not shouting at me, having a hangover and all."

"Everything is fine. I'm actually just about to head out for work and thought I'd give you a quick ring to see how things were." She wasn't going to tell him her evening and morning had been similar to his. Nor would she admit that she too was also suffering from a mild hangover. "Your gran is back from her mindfulness retreat, although I'm not entirely sure what the result was supposed to be. She tried to attack me with that disgusting charity shop dog she bought me."

"I don't get it. What's going on and why are you only just going to work?"

"Nothing to worry about Ralph. I quit the energy company and started working at the gay bar in town as a stage manager. It's my first shift tonight. Anyway, wish me luck and I'll speak to you soon."

Ralph's stunned silence before she'd hung up was the reaction Sophie had wanted. It told her she was doing something unexpected and forced her lips into a wide, almost painful, grin. Although, what had happened in the past twenty-four hours still seemed alien, and even less familiar was telling people about it, but also being excited at the thought of working in a gay club.

Once she'd eaten a microwaved pasta bake and wiped down the kitchen, Sophie got into the blue Fiesta courtesy car, reminding herself to get in touch with the insurance company about paying out so she could buy a new one of her own.

It only took fifteen minutes to drive into town, as she was going in the opposite direction to the rest of the traffic which was leaving the centre. There was nowhere to leave the car outside the bar, so she carefully drove up and down the streets at the back of Sophisticats, before parallel parking between some cars next to the back door.

The front of the club was painted black, its windows were coloured with rainbows and scenes of men kissing men and women kissing women with love hearts all around them. Sophisticats' sign was a metal sculpture of an elegant feline figure wearing a black top hat on its head and a bowtie around its neck, finished off with a rainbow square sticking out from a pocket on its chest.

It was now five minutes to five and Sophie couldn't get in. She'd tried the door, but it was locked. Knocking didn't seem to do anything, and she hadn't taken Paris's phone number before leaving the club last night. "Bugger."

Just as she was about to search for a doorbell or another way in, loud cackles and shouts of "yahhs queen" broke the silence on the darkening street she was standing on. It was the middle of February, so nightfall wasn't coming as quickly as it did in the dead of winter, but it was still too dark to see who was making the noises.

"Did you see how she looked at me? I can't believe she tried to come for me. I tell you what, if I hadn't just had my nails done, I would have been right up in that ugly mush of hers. Oh, what's this?"

A group of five men, who were all dressed flamboyantly and heading towards the doorway she was standing in, were the source of the noises. On spotting Sophie, waiting with a nervous look on her face by the front door of the club, the conversation ended abruptly. They eyed her playfully, like five bored cats would view a spider.

"We don't open until nine tonight, hun. Maybe come back later," the man who was telling the story said Sophie with a hand on his hip.

"I know," Sophie began timidly. "I actually work here, Paris offered me the stage manager job last night and I've been waiting outside for ten minutes now."

"Ooooh! So, you're the mess she's hired," another of the group, this time one with short pink hair, said in a high-pitched squeal. "You don't look as bad as he made out. Paris, you said she was dowdier than this."

"I didn't say she was dowdy, just a little lacking in the style department," said another, this time familiar, voice from behind the group. He was walking up behind them and moved through the middle to the front. He stood, with his arms folded across his chest and eyed Sophie. "Hun, I didn't think you'd actually take me up on the offer of a job. Remember me? I'm Paris, well, Ben when I look like this."

The man standing in the middle of the others was easily the youngest, no older than 27, Sophie guessed. He had big brown eyes and short brown hair that stuck out in purposeful peaks from his scalp. He was also one of the skinniest men Sophie had ever seen, with long legs and a slender waist.

He looked so petite and nothing like the ferocious feminine creature that had owned every part of last night's stage. Where had the curves she'd seen last night gone?

Now it was apparently Sophie's turn to speak as the six of them stared at her in silence, waiting. But they'd all just insulted her and Paris himself had said he hadn't expected her to come. She was so excited about the job this morning and now all she felt was foolish. She really was a desperate idiot.

"Hun, we're only joking. Remember, it's just shade. I taught you that last night. You'll have to get used to it if you're going to be one of the family," Paris said, breaking the silence which interrupted Sophie's thoughts of making a run for it.

"Well, you'd better show me what I'll be doing then, before I decide to ditch the lot of you ugly old hags." It might have been too far, but Sophie wanted to see what she was capable of giving back.

"Well, there's certainly a bit of a spark in this one, Paris," said the pink-haired one. "Only thing is, hun, don't call Mya old. She'll skin you and wear you – anything to look younger, isn't that right Mya?"

"Bitch! I will sit on that runner bean boy body of yours," the man standing at the back of the group shouted back. He was bigger than the others and looked older too, almost 40 Sophie thought. His face was round, but it had happy eyes that mirrored the smile on his face and as a deep laughter roared from the pit of his stomach, the rolls of fat on his chest and stomach jiggled. "Let's get off the street before someone asks us for business... Again." he said, which was met with loud cackles and whoops from the others.

"You'd have to pay them, Mya," the one with pink hair shouted before being chased into the club by Mya, who was pretending to be annoyed.

Sophisticats looked nothing like it did the night before. It was now lit by harsh floodlights and had been cleaned with disinfectant, a smell that reminded Sophie of her recent stay in hospital. The floors were dark wood and the tables and chairs in the middle of the room had a Parisian café look to them.

The banquette seats around the sides were covered in mostly ripped dark green leather and looked as though they'd seen better days. The walls had been painted a deep blood red and had framed posters of glamourous pinup girls from the 1950s on them, as well as neon lights in the shapes of lips, boobs and legs that flickered on and off.

"You'll be working backstage tonight, Sophie, but we'll want to get you out front at some point because it gets too busy for the girls to handle on their own. Don't look scared, everyone's friendly in here and it will do you good," Paris said to the shocked look on Sophie's face.

Backstage was a web of wires and ropes, all connected to buttons and levers. Sophie didn't have a clue what they all did but was told she needn't worry. Further behind the stage was a large room with what looked like a kitchen worktop running along one wall with six large mirrors spread equally out above it and the same number of mismatching chairs sitting in front of them.

"This is the dressing room where all the girls get ready. You'll need to make sure we're out of here and at the stage on time. Give the girls a once over to make sure they look loved and then send them out." Sophie was trying to take in everything Paris was telling her. But, so far, it seemed simple.

"There are only five queens on tonight, so it shouldn't be too much trouble. We'll start with Mya, then Loxie, the boy with the pink hair who you met, followed by Fischer and Lady Diamond. I'll go on last so I can help you wrangle them," Paris said, now with the authority of an army sergeant.

Just like that, four hours had passed, and it was time for the girls, as Paris called them, to start their shows one at a time. When the club opened at nine, just one-hundred people came in, but it was expected to get much busier, so Sophie was extra cautious to get her job right.

She sent the girls on stage in the order Paris had said to, making sure they were ready just before the thirty-minute set of the previous queen was over. They seemed compliant and when she'd suggested a bit more lipstick or noticed a wig wasn't on properly, they thanked her and fixed themselves up.

After Paris's one-hour set, which involved several lip syncs and ended with a striptease, the night came to an end and once again Sophie was surrounded by the six men she'd met at the front of the club.

The bar staff had cleaned up and left at around one in the morning, leaving Sophie and the queens sitting on the leather banquettes at two o'clock. "You did good tonight," said Mya whose lips were still tainted purple from her makeup. "But we need to do something about that wardrobe of yours."

Anyone else sitting at the table would have taken it as an empty insult, probably even laughed at it. But to Sophie it felt like a slap in the face. She hadn't felt self-conscious since coming inside the club and the girls had made her feel safe. But had they been laughing behind her back after thanking her for helping them?

"What Mya means," Paris began, "is we'll need to have you dressed for the front-of-house next week.

We're doing a big promotion with some queens from London who have national followings and you're going to be out front helping. We'll sort it hun, don't worry."

"But I don't have anything. I live most of my life in jeans and jumpers."

"That sounds like my kind of challenge. Let's get home for a couple of hours sleep and I'll pick you up at your house before lunch."

Reluctantly, Sophie gave Paris her address and agreed to be ready in less than nine hours' time at eleven. But Paris wouldn't say where they were going.

Chapter Six: Shopping Trip

The house was cold when Sophie woke in her bed later that morning. After a short and uneventful drive back from the bar, she made herself a small gin and tonic before washing her makeup off and going to sleep just before four.

Her first shift at the club was excitedly whirring round her head, making it hard to sleep. Thinking about it gave her a tickling feeling in her head and tummy. Surely this couldn't be her life now, she was obviously still unconscious in the hospital after the car crash.

Everything replayed through her mind, including what Paris had said to her about sorting out her wardrobe and how kind the girls had been.

She still couldn't settle and took out the pad with the bucket list and studied it under the light from the lamp on the bedside table. How long would she wait before getting some of the bigger tasks on it ticked off? Perhaps she didn't need to carry on with it, now she'd already made such a big change to her life. Before deciding though, she was fast asleep.

It was now nine and she was sat at the kitchen table wondering what the day ahead with Paris might look like. Would he take her to a clothes shop used by drag queens and what sort of clothes would he make her buy?

These weren't the sorts of questions Sophie had asked herself before. Questions usually stopped her from doing anything other than what she had to – going to work, the food shop (which she'd been doing online since it had become a thing) as well as taking and collecting the boys to and from school until they were old enough to do it themselves.

The nagging in her mind began to speak to her once again. There really wasn't any need to go and buy new clothes. The ones in the wardrobe upstairs were fine, and anyway, as soon as Paris and the other drag queens got to know Sophie a little more, they'd quickly realise she was no good for the bar and she'd be back working in a call centre again. Back to just existing.

Her hand twitched next to her mobile, the goblin at the centre of the now blazing doubt in her mind was willing her to text Paris and tell him not to come. She should just tell him that she wouldn't be working at the bar anymore.

But the phone vibrated into life before she'd even touched it. Sophie had decided it was Paris calling to cancel on her – he'd realised there was no point investing any time in the pathetic middle-aged woman he'd found in Sophisticats.

"Hello, Paris. I was just about to text and call today off."

"Mum, what are you talking about? Who is Paris?"

It wasn't Paris. She felt a little relief, but still also a desire to call things off with the drag queen and return to what she was used to. At least she knew it was safe and there was no risk of getting hurt or being the centre of any jokes.

"Thomas, is everything ok? You don't usually call."

"Ralph told dad about your new job and I wanted to say that it sounds better than the call centre, maybe a bit weird having my mum work at a gay bar, but it does sound fun."

"Thank you. That means a lot to me. How's college going and is your dad feeding you some decent meals?"

Not having the boys around the house much now was a bit of a relief for Sophie. It meant she didn't have to worry about disappointing them. But she still liked to mother them in her own way by making sure they had everything they needed.

"Yeah, everything's fine, thanks. Just been revising for some exams and chilling with my friends. Dad's feeding me fine. Gran comes around every now and then with some food for us, but you know what that's like. It tends to go in the bin. Have you tried her Malibu chicken?"

They both laughed at Beryl's cooking as Sophie caught Thomas up on what had been going on with the night club, as well as an edited version of how she quit her job. But she didn't mention the list. This was something she wanted to keep to herself for now.

After half-an-hour on the phone to her youngest, Sophie hurried upstairs to shower and get dressed. There was no use in trying to find something decent to wear, so she went with a grey jersey hoodie and some light blue jeans. That's the best I can do, she thought without looking in the mirror. She went downstairs, makeup-free and leaving her hair do whatever it wanted.

Moments later, just before eleven, there was a knock on the door. It was Paris, or Ben, she decided, as he wasn't in drag. His brown hair was coiffed up in a flick at the front and looked very smart. In fact, he looked just as elegant and stylish as he did in drag, considering it was just a shopping trip. He wore light brown brogues, straight cut dark blue jeans, with a white shirt tucked into them and a tailored tweed blazer over the top.

"Don't you look, er... well. Are you ready to go? We've got a bit of a drive until we get there," he said to Sophie with a smirk when she opened the door.

Ben was clearly unimpressed with what she was wearing, but Sophie knew there was no point in trying. He wouldn't have liked whatever she pulled out of her wardrobe anyway. Although this was only their third conversation, he came across as a bit of a snob, she thought.

After locking up, she followed Ben down the driveway to his car which was on the side of the road. Sophie hadn't given any thought to Ben or what his life was like when he wasn't Paris. But parked in front of the house was a huge black four-by-four with tinted windows and gleaming chrome accents. It was a luxurious beast of a vehicle.

The interior was just as suave. Its cream leather oozed class and felt more impressive and expensive than everything in Sophie's house combined. The only thing that linked it to the Ben she knew from Sophisticats was the pink fluffy dice hanging from the rear-view mirror.

"You need to have a bit of fabulousness somewhere," he said, clocking Sophie's gaze. As the car roared to life, so too did Dolly Parton from the car's speakers, which Ben turned down so they could talk.

After half-an-hour of conversation about nothing in particular, they were on the M25 and heading towards London. "I didn't want to tell you where we were going last night in case you thought it would be a bit much. But we're going to Oxford Street where I've got a good friend at Selfridges who is going to take care of us."

"But..."

"I don't want to hear it," he shot over Sophie before she could tell him no. "You don't have to buy anything you don't feel comfortable with and if something's too expensive we can shop around. But you're doing this, because I can't think of anything worse than seeing you walk around in those clothes for a moment longer."

Rather than argue, Sophie kept quiet. In truth, there was no reason why she couldn't spend a little money on herself. She had a large sum saved in the bank, and as she was now working at the club, there was no need to scrimp and scrape to make it last. Instead of fighting against the trip, she thought it best to ask Ben about himself; was he seeing anyone (no), how long had he been doing drag (for almost ten years); if there were any holidays coming up (no, he was too busy at the club); and did he prefer being called Ben or Paris (the latter was fine).

Traffic in London was just as bad as Sophie had imagined it would be. This was her second trip to the city in her life. Being in such a busy place, surrounded by so many strange and unpredictable people had never been appealing.

She didn't know how someone could drive on the cramped, hostile roads either. Thinking about it made her feel hot and itchy. But Paris didn't bat an eyelid. He moved in and out of traffic quickly and decisively, before driving round the back of the giant Victorian building into a car park, which was filled with so many expensive cars, Sophie didn't know where to look first.

It was all the more impressive inside the department store. There were rows upon rows of makeup counters in one room and dozens of brands that she hadn't heard of. As they walked through to the next room, fogs of perfume and aftershave hit her nose, making Sophie wince and cough as it caught her throat. But Paris continued to weave in and out of the people, searching for whoever it was he'd arranged to meet.

Milling around the counters were busy shop assistants, working like ants to try and please the hundreds of customers who were busily dashing this way and that way, hands and arms laden with bags. They were gawking at shelves of expensive accessories and perfumes and stopping assistants with questions of where various departments in the store were located, or if they could try on some scent or have a sample of this or that.

It was noisy and Sophie felt uncomfortable. The entire shop was full of uptight people, who clearly had too much money. Every woman was pretty and perfectly made-up, wearing the latest designer clothes and showcasing colourful bags with big labels and logos on them. Yet here was Sophie, looking like a homeless woman in baggy jeans and a scruffy grey hoodie. They would look at her and question why a poor bag lady was walking around the shop with a young, attractive fabulous thing like Paris.

"Ahh, here he is," squealed Paris as a tall and elegant man dressed in tight-fitting black clothes approached them. "Sophie, this is James. We go way back. James, this is Sophie who I told you about in the text. She needs some help... and yes, we've got all day before you ask."

After the introductions were made, Sophie was swept upstairs to the personal shopping department and seated in a private room with Champagne and nibbles. It was nothing like buying clothes in the supermarket, surrounded by people from all walks of life, which is what she was used to.

Here, she began to feel like someone special, although that thought quickly dissolved as she began telling herself James and the other assistants were probably poking fun at the frumpy woman, clearly so desperate for attention that she had to convince a gay man to bring her shopping.

"Now, let's take a look at you. Stand up," James ordered before slowly twirling Sophie around, looking at every inch of her body. He grabbed her jeans and pulled them tight so he could see the shape of her legs and did the same with the hoodie, making a growling noise at the size of her boobs.

"We've got a lot of good things to work with here," he said to Paris, continuing to pull Sophie's dowdy clothes tight as though she was some sort of a mannequin. "I'm going to get some of my assistants to pull a few bits and bobs together for us, do you have a favourite designer?"

"Well…"

"How about a least favourite?"

"I erm…"

"I've got just the thing for you. Wait there. I'll be back in a mo. Make yourself at home."

Before Sophie could answer any of the questions, he'd rapped at her like a flamboyant machine gun, James was off, out of the room and lost in the noisy sea of people on the shop floor outside hers and Paris's sanctuary.

"Paris, how do you know James and what the hell am I doing in a place like this? You drive a car that costs more than my house and we've only known each other for the best part of forty-eight hours. What's going on?"

"Don't hold back, hun. I wouldn't."

"I'm sorry, but it's just all very strange. We don't know each other, yet you offer me a job, which I am grateful for... and then you offer to take me shopping and introduce me to James and none of it makes sense."

"Look, when you poured your sad, pathetic life out to me in the club and mentioned your little bucket list, all I could think about was myself. I'd been given a rotten start in life. My parents weren't happy when I came out as gay, but it was a step too far when they found out I was doing drag. They kicked me out. But someone had the heart to take me in and help me. Then my Nan died and left me a chunk of money. I'd always been close to her, but she was in a care home and lost her marbles, so she couldn't help me out until she died."

Just like Sophie had to him in Sophisticats, out poured Paris's life. He'd spent years working in whatever dodgy nightclubs he could, saving every bit of spare cash to open his own place. He'd done a set at what was to be Sophisticats a few years before buying the place. He felt safe in the town, made friends – or a family as he called them – and when his Nana had died, he finally had enough money to buy the place outright.

Ever since, he'd been building up its reputation, gathered a strong group of talented girls to work at Sophisticats and used the network of drag queens he'd built up while working all over the UK to spread the word about the club. Sophisticats had become synonymous with drag in the UK over the years thanks to him and his friends, he assured her.

"Now I want to pay it back. I pitied you when you told me your story, but I also felt admiration and saw something in you that you clearly don't see in yourself. I know it's there and I will help you find it. I think you've seen it yourself, maybe just for a moment or two, but it's in there and..."

"You hoo. I'm back. And don't I have just the thing for you two," said James waltzing into the room, without a care that he'd cut Paris and Sophie off mid-conversation. Behind him stood a line of assistants, each pushing a rail of clothes with dozens of brightly coloured garments hanging from them; or holding piles of accessories and shoes in shapes and designs Sophie had never seen before.

The aim of the game, according to James and Paris, was to find staple pieces for Sophie's wardrobe that could be dressed up or down or partnered with other items to create new outfits. So followed hours of Sophie parading up and down the room in dresses, skirts, trousers, designer jeans, tops and heels. The latter, she was told after some wobbly steps, Paris would teach her to walk in.

Bags, scarves, gloves and belts were wrapped around her or perched over the crook of her arm, before being put into a keep pile or sent away with one of the assistants. Thirty or so items of clothes were selected as basics that would last her the rest of winter and into spring/summer, James said. They would be taken away to be carefully wrapped and bagged for home.

Exhausted, Sophie and Paris were then whisked up to the rooftop restaurant for afternoon tea. Over a glass of Champagne each and a selection of tiny sandwiches and cakes, the point of which Sophie didn't see, as she was still starving once they'd finished, she apologised to Paris.

He was right. There was something in her that had been waiting to get out, she agreed. But for too long, she explained, it had been buried away, bullied by a gremlin in Sophie's mind, too tough and stubborn for her to ignore it or stop herself yielding to its dark charms.

"You make it sound very dark, but you do realise that it's just a case of making yourself do something?" was Paris's reply.

"Well, I don't think it's as simple as that. I mean…" but he jumped in before she could say anything else.

"How about a bit of pampering and we can sort your makeup out while we're here too?" He suggested, a cheeky glint in his eye. "You can't have a new wardrobe and leave with the same makeup you came in wearing… and a new hairstyle too," he said almost too himself and with a devious smile.

It was all getting to be a bit much for Sophie. But she tried to repeat in her mind what Paris had said to her when they were waiting for James to return with the rails of clothes earlier. She was beginning to trust him and stopped herself from saying no to a new hairstyle and makeup.

"Fine. But I don't want to come out of here looking like Mya. My mother would be too happy about that, it seems she is her makeup idol."

Once Paris, despite Sophie's insistence on grabbing the bill, had paid for tea, they went downstairs to the hair salon. A young stylist called Katie, who had bright red hair and arms full of tattoos, agreed not to change Sophie's hair too much.

A lighter shade of brown and a new, shorter cut with a bit more style was settled on and once the hairdresser was done, Sophie quite liked the result. Her hair was lighter and shiny. It looked healthy and had a shape to it that she would never have considered or asked for herself. It was bouncy and feminine and nicely complimented her almond-shaped face.

Now it was time to head down to the ground floor where Paris had already arranged for one of the men on the makeup counters to talk Sophie through her skincare regime, as well as how to make up her face. He was kind and patient and had some brilliant, according to Paris, but simple ideas for Sophie to try at home.

The artist said her skin was beautiful and clear, so she wouldn't need any foundation or other products like that. Keeping it simple with coppery and autumnal shimmers, eyeshadows and lip products would be the best thing to do and easy for Sophie to replicate.

Sophie was also advised to throw out her peachy lipstick and was given other, darker, richer and warmer tones as alternatives. Her day makeup, as the stylist called it, should be simple, with just a bit of mascara and subtle highlights on her face. Going out for dates, drinks or even at work, she could apply a little more and perhaps go for a smoky eye too.

Nearly two-hundred pounds later and a heavy bag of makeup to show for it, Sophie and Paris headed back upstairs to collect her things from James.

"And who is this radiant goddess?" the personal shopper playfully questioned, thrusting an arm out and pawing at the air in front of Sophie with a limp hand. Sophie knew full well he was being overly nice, but tried to enjoy it anyway. "Jamillah. Jamillah! Come and look at this. You won't recognise her." Sophie was becoming embarrassed at the attention James was encouraging, but she endured the oohs and ahs from him and the assistants, shyly thanking them for noticing.

"So, that will be five-thousand and sixty-six pounds," the sales assistant said at the till, as though it was a perfectly normal amount to spend. Sophie's knees almost buckled. She felt dizzy. How could she spend this much on clothes? It wasn't a question of whether she could afford it. There was plenty of money in her account, as she'd never really spent anything. But surely it was frivolous?

"Just think of it as ten years' of clothes you owe yourself," Paris whispered and grabbed hold of her elbow, as though he was worried she was about to slump to the floor in shock. "You've never spent anything on yourself and, after this, you'll only need to add a few pieces every now and then. What's here is classic and won't go out of style. You've just bought really good quality, which means it will last longer too."

Despite still being unsure, Sophie handed over her card and reluctantly agreed with Paris. At least she could tick girly shopping trip off her list. Afterall, Paris was kind of like a girl.

Chapter Seven: One Night Stand

"Sweetie, darling! You look incredible. I hardly recognised you. Did you say it was a gay friend who convinced you to do this to yourself? That man deserves a medal." Beryl was standing on Sophie's doorstep, having, for the first time rang the bell and waited for her daughter to answer, rather than letting herself in as she would usually do.

"Mum, thank you," her daughter replied bemused. "Yes, Paris and I went to Selfridges on a little shopping trip and one thing led to another and, well, this is what I ended up looking like. I'm glad you like it. But why aren't you using your key?"

"Well, sweetie, I wanted to see what you looked like in the daylight. You told me on the phone that you'd had a bit of a makeover, but I didn't think it would have been as much as an overhaul as this, so thought the natural light would have helped me see whatever miniscule change you'd made."

"Lovely. Come on in mum, before you freeze and all of the heat gets out."

Although the weather was trying to shift into spring, it was still chilly. Sophie had been conscious about saving energy and money after blowing thousands of pounds on a new wardrobe. Since the shopping trip last week, she'd also been quite frugal with her spending, which had made her feel better about the big purchase.

"Darling, I'm made of strong stuff you know. A boring little chill isn't going to kill me. When I do go, it will be because my body has failed me and I'm too frail to get out and do things, which was something that made me worry about you. Not now, though, since you got involved with that fabulous lot at Sophisticats, I think you're having more fun than I am."

"I don't think that's necessarily true; you seem to have fun doing the most mundane things but thank you. I am enjoying my time with the girls at the club. Tonight will be my first time front-of-house. Paris has asked me to seat people this evening. It's a special night with some queens coming over from London and they've sold it by the table or something."

She couldn't quite remember what Paris had told her, since the fact being front-of-house had caused her to panic. All Sophie knew was she'd have to be happy and smiley and make a good impression on the punters, Paris had told her.

The thought of being responsible for the club's reputation made her nervous. She'd also have to make sure people were seated in the right places and that the wait staff, who had been hired especially for the evening, were aware their guests were sitting and ready to be served.

This was a major night for the club, Paris had told her and the other girls. Some of the biggest names in UK drag were coming from London, as well as one who had been on a show in America.

There was also a stag party for a gay bachelor coming in, the groom being a rich well-to-do type from one of the affluent areas outside London. He'd made his money in the events space and was very influential, so it was important he had the night of his life. He was apparently selective of the people he worked with and Paris wanted him to work with Sophisticats.

In the run up to the big event, Paris, Sophie and the other girls had closed the bar on the previous Sunday to paint and decorate it. Any shabby furniture had been patched up or replaced, the walls repainted, and every inch of the club had been scrubbed. There was even some money spent on the dressing room, so the American drag star and the big names from London would feel more at home, and not like they were in some dive bar in a nowhere town.

The week whizzed by with all the sprucing up they'd been doing to the club and it felt like Friday had arrived quicker than normal. The club was fully booked and, as well as feeling anxious about the evening ahead, Sophie was also happy to see Paris fizzing with excitement.

"It's a make or break night for us, girls," he would say each time there was an update on the acts or a guest's booking. "This could really set us up for the next few years. We'd be fully booked for the foreseeable future, so we need to make sure it goes off with a bang."

Before the doors opened at nine, the girls were all dressed in the most extravagant outfits made and bought specially for the evening. Paris and Sophie had briefed the team and, other than a few hiccups like ice machines breaking or late alcohol deliveries, everything had gone to plan.

Sophie's wardrobe, too, had played in her favour, and received so many of what she was happy to believe were genuine compliments from the girls and bar staff. She had been wearing the clothes Paris and James had chosen for her on the London shopping trip. It was amazing how great she felt about herself, how a pencil skirt and silk jewel-coloured blouse with a pair of patent leather heels could make her feel so different – elevated, sophisticated and elegant, she thought when looking in the mirror.

But tonight, things had been stepped up another level. Because all the girls were able to expense new outfits to the club for the big event, Paris insisted Sophie should have a showstopper too. For her, he'd selected an oily black sequin dress with dark green tones that appeared with various intensity depending on the light and how she moved.

The dress was tight over Sophie's hips, giving her an hourglass figure, before cutting off just below the knee to reveal calves given shape by a pair of high heeled (high for Sophie anyway), pointed shoes. She felt sexy, and even more so after a vodka and tonic, which she drank to help relax before the evening began. Paris had even helped with her makeup and had, in his words, toned down one of his own looks by painting Sophie's eyes like dark green clouds.

"You really are now part of the House of Paris Le Grand," he said to Sophie with a hand on her shoulder as he finished her makeup.

"Err, that's so sweet?" she replied with a quizzical look on her face.

Paris interrupted and explained: "Well, some drag queens, especially those who've had a rough start in life, kind of make their own family," Paris explained while giving some final touches to Sophie's face. "It's known as a house or a family and they bring other queens and people who they like and can trust into it. They might also help other acts start out by giving them advice and guidance. These people are called drag daughters and will take on the same surname as their drag mothers."

It was a little overwhelming for Sophie to be told she was considered to be part of a family like this after so little time. She'd never really had friends or been close enough to anyone to be given such a label. But there was no time to dwell on it, the night was about to begin.

The bouncers on the door started letting people through to the club and Sophie took names of important guests at a VIP, glittery gold check-in pedestal that had been set up for the evening. Nearly all of the VIPs had been seated and were waiting for the show to start at ten with a comedy set from Mya.

Sophie was double checking which tables they were waiting on when she heard a commotion firing up in the entrance to the club. She couldn't hear much over the loud music and chattering punters, but someone was furiously shouting "don't you know who I am", interjected with swearwords and what Sophie thought were threats.

Just as Sophie had plucked up the courage to see what was going on, Paris stormed past. He was wearing a floor-length rose gold gown studded with sparkling diamantes, which glittered ferociously under the club's lights. It had a huge slit on the right side, which separated to reveal Paris's long legs and the highest midnight blue stilettoes Sophie had ever seen.

"Come on Sophie. He's here," Paris shouted as he quickly slipped past her and out into the reception area.

Doing as she was told, Sophie followed Paris into the entrance of Sophisticats and saw a group of ten men and women, at the centre of which was a short bald man who was staring up at one of the club's largest bouncers, poking at his chest with a sharp pointing finger.

"Felix! Felix, you made it. Please, leave my doorman be and let's get you seated," giggled Paris. The short man stopped harassing the bouncer when he caught sight of who was addressing him. "Come on, let's get you and your group sat down, we're about to start."

"He has an attitude problem," Felix, who was again pointing at the annoyed bouncer, snapped at Paris. "He said I had to provide an invite otherwise I couldn't get in. I want him fired. He'll never work in this business again."

"Hun, let me deal with this and all of you can pop along to your table with Sophie here... we've got oodles of complimentary drinks waiting for you," he finished as a final temptation for the diva of a man who'd managed to cause such a big scene.

Bald, short and angry he may have been, but even Sophie could see the man of the hour was well dressed. An expensive sumptuous scent billowed from his body, on which designer clothes were fitted and styled. From the top down Felix reeked of money, but not necessarily class. He wore a blazer with punk art motifs on it, ripped jeans and a pair of crocodile skin boots with a heel almost as high as Sophie's.

"Mr Geller…" Sophie began.

"It's Felix," he barked back with a look of disgust. "Now do your job, girl and get us seated."

"Of course. Felix, if you and your party would like to follow me this way, your waiters are prepared and ready to serve you."

Sophie was quite proud of herself. Usually in confrontational situations she would have stuttered and tried to flee as quickly as possible. There had only been two displays of strength in her life – the first was when she divorced Carl and the second when she quit her job at the call centre.

For some reason, working with Paris and the girls had made her feel a little more capable and in control. It may have been the faith Paris had put in Sophie tonight, or perhaps it was just the fact she was wearing the costume of a confident woman. Either way, she grabbed on to it, hoping she could keep hold of it for the rest of her life.

Once the stag party was in place, the evening could start. Lights and music all sprung to life as Mya walked onto the stage ready to poke fun at the crowd before the other acts would dance, sing and lip sync. Everyone looked like they were having a great time, even Sophie began to relax.

As she was looking around the room to make sure the VIP tables were being serviced, a man sat on Felix's table in the middle of the room caught Sophie's eye. He was staring at her. Her stomach flipped at the thought of it, but then she remembered he was part of a gay man's stag party and decided he must need a drink.

"Hello, do you have everything you need?" Sophie asked after walking over to the table. Up close the man was more attractive than Sophie had first realised. He had brown eyes and hair and designer stubble. He was wearing a thin material V-neck jumper in teal that hugged muscly arms and pecks. His jeans, although smart, didn't match the showy style the rest of the group was decked out in.

"I was hoping you could maybe get me an Old Fashioned, Champagne isn't really for me," he said with a nod towards the ice bucket on the table. Sophie didn't know what an Old Fashioned was, but didn't say so and instead asked for one at the bar and brought it back.

"Thanks. I'm Josh. I just wanted to say sorry for the way my brother behaved earlier. I'd like to say it's pre-wedding jitters, but I'd be lying. He's just always a bit of a prat."

"There's really no need to apologise," Sophie said, thankful she was wearing a thicker than usual layer of makeup so he couldn't see her cheeks going red.

She'd never thought about men since divorcing Carl – or even before or while she was with him, if she was honest with herself. But Josh had certainly stirred up something inside her. Probably just the vodka and tonic earlier, she thought and said: "If there's anything else you need, the wait staff will be more than happy to help," and walked off back to the safety of her gold pedestal.

That's certainly something new, Sophie thought to herself while pretending to check something off a list, trying to avoid another glance at the man on the other side of the room. But it was too tempting not to look at him and again their eyes met, this time causing Sophie's stomach to almost flip inside out.

While she pretended to be busy again Josh had walked up to the pedestal without her realising. "Bugger! What are you trying to do to me?" she shouted over the music, steadying her golden workstation which had wobbled dangerously after the shock of being sneaked up on.

"I'm sorry. This really isn't my kind of thing. I mean, the drag queens are great and the club is lovely, but I can't stand my brother's friends. I only agreed to come because I'm his best man and he would have thrown the biggest hissy fit if I didn't."

Sophie stared at him, watching his mouth as he spoke and trying to take in what he was saying, but the music was quite loud and she was feeling nervous too, so just nodded.

"I wondered if I could buy you a drink?"

"What? Oh, that's very kind of you, but I can't, I'm at work." He must be kidding, she thought. This must have been one of those cruel games she'd heard about people playing on stag and hen parties, where each member of the group has a card with a task to complete. Josh had clearly been challenged to flirt with an older woman, after all, he had to be in his mid- to late-thirties.

"No you're not, Sophie," said Paris who had just snuck up behind her. "You can go and enjoy yourself; we've got it all covered now." He was saying it with raised eyebrows and a flirty look on his face. "My name is Paris, I own this club. If you promise to be a gentleman, then I'll let you buy Sophie a drink."

"I will be a saint. I promise," Josh replied with a wink to Paris.

Nervously, Sophie led Josh to the seats at the end of the bar and asked for a vodka tonic and Josh ordered another Old Fashioned. If he was taking part in a dare, then sitting at the bar she would be able to laugh it off and start a conversation with one of the bartenders before making a run for it, mortified that she'd been the butt of a joke.

He asked Sophie how long she'd worked at the bar and what she'd been doing before then. Josh didn't seem bothered about the fact she had two grown up children and didn't ask her age.

There wasn't much for her to tell him, but she found out that he worked for Felix as an operations manager for the events company and had done that for as long as he could remember. He was 38 and wanted to settle down with someone, but not necessarily have kids "what will be will be, it's about finding the right person", he told Sophie.

After a few more drinks, Sophie felt a little drunk and was glad Paris suggested she leave the car at home for tonight.

"I'm staying at a hotel in the next town along with that lot. I can't really be bothered with their drama anymore to be honest," Josh said rather genuinely.

"Oh, they seem like a fun bunch," said Sophie, watching the group, who clearly had too much money, popping Champagne corks and soaking the tables and floor around them. The thought of going home with Josh had crept into her mind a few times over the course of their conversation, but she'd only just met him. She was forty-four, divorced and this wasn't the sort of thing a woman like her would do.

But the bucket list that she hadn't looked at since crossing off girly shopping list kept popping into her mind. She remembered how pathetic and cringy it was to see the words 'have a one-night stand' on it. But, fuelled by vodka tonic and wearing what she considered a disguise, because she'd never dressed like this before, the words came out of her mouth before she could even stop herself.

"Why don't you stay at mine? I've got a spare room..."

"I promised your friend over there that I'd be a gentleman though," Josh said with a grin that told Sophie this wasn't a no.

"I'm saying you can come over and sleep in the spare room, not for you to share my bed. I just feel bad for you having to spend time with those over there," said a firm, but surprisingly seductive voice from Sophie's lips, which were now just inches away from Josh's.

"Well, how could I say no to an offer like that," he replied with a smile before covering the remaining space between their faces and gently kissing her on the lips for a split second.

Whether it was the vodka, the fact she'd been awake and at the club since the early morning or because she'd been kissed for the first time in god knows how long, the room began to spin around Sophie. Her body tingled, as though thousands of feathers were being brushed up and down every bit of her skin.

She found Paris to ask if it was ok for her to go home. Paris looked over Sophie's shoulder at Josh who was waiting for her near the club's exit. "Hun, you go home and enjoy yourself. How long did you say it had been? You might need to give it a good dusting before..."

"He's staying in the spare room. Don't make me feel cheap."

"Oh, there's nothing cheap about that one. But whatever you say." A wink followed his words and then Paris trotted off to sit with Felix and the other guests, leaving Sophie to lead Josh from the club and into a taxi that was waiting outside.

The journey back to Sophie's was quiet, but involved some kissing and what her mother would call 'petting'. Once in the house, though, her mind raced and she began to panic. Oh god. Oh god. I'm not ready for this. A man hasn't seen my body in well over a decade. I can't do this. Sod the list, started a debate in her head.

It was true, things with Carl were never that spicy. There weren't that many occasions of intimacy and the last time they'd gotten close like that was about fifteen years ago. She hadn't prepared for this. Why would she? She wasn't exactly going out on the pull. Things hadn't been shaved and even if they had, Josh would run a mile at the sight of her body once the beautiful clothes and makeup were removed.

"Right, the guest bedroom is upstairs. Third door on the left. Can I get you a drink of something," she pointedly asked without looking at Josh.

He didn't reply, but moved closer to Sophie until he was able to wrap one arm around her waist and pull her close enough to kiss her more firmly than he had done all evening. "Oh to hell with it," Sophie whispered, turning her head to meet his gaze and relaxing into whatever it was she was allowing to happen.

Chapter Eight: Naked

A stranger's soft breathing and a chink of sunlight woke Sophie the next day. Her mouth was dry and still tasted of alcohol, a sensation made all the worse by a headache that was trying to punch a hole through her skull. The first effort to turn over and face the person breathing lightly next to her made Sophie's mouth fill with saliva and her stomach contract, taking all her effort to not throw up.

Her second attempt at movement was more successful, and she was met with a broad pale back that was smooth and dappled with faint freckles. She groaned at what had happened last night, she'd let herself go and was now overcome with regret. Why had she allowed this stranger into her bed?

It took a herculean amount of energy to sit up, move her legs out of the bed and crawl as quietly as possible to the bathroom at the other end of the upstairs hallway, navigating last night's discarded clothes as she went.

Finally, the cool tiled bathroom floor felt amazing on her skin and took Sophie's mind off the splitting headache and nausea for a moment, giving her time to think of what to do about the houseguest. Could she hide in the bathroom and wait for Josh to get the message and leave? Probably not. Perhaps he'd look at her, sober and in the daylight, and flee without another word. That was probably a more likely outcome. Whatever the solution, and however it was going to happen, she needed him to leave.

"Sophie," a voice called curiously from outside the door. "Are you in there? I really need to take a leak... are you ok?"

"Don't come in!" she yapped louder and more forcefully than was intended as the door handle was tried. "I'll be out in a second... I'm just taking out my contacts." Sophie didn't wear contacts, but thought it was better to say that rather than 'I'm on the loo' or the more accurate 'just give me a couple more hours while I die from this horrendous hangover and mortification of having slept with a stranger'.

But no. Now was the time to be brave. Maybe she could channel the idiot confident woman who she thought she was last night. Where was *she* now? Unfortunately, it was just plain old regular Sophie cowering on the bathroom floor.

"Sorry, I think I should have taken them out last night," were the words she chose to say quickly while rushing past the naked man still standing outside the door and into her bedroom, where she got dressed before going downstairs to make coffee and a proper plan.

Clothes littered the hallway, kitchen and living room. How could two people wear so much, she thought. Now wasn't the time to clean up though, she needed a good excuse to get Josh to leave before working out how to feel about last night.

"Ahhh, I could murder a cup of coffee, is it fresh?" a voice asked from behind Sophie who was looking in one of the cupboards for a cup. She looked up. "Oh god! Why are you still naked! Please, put some clothes on," demanded Sophie in a high-pitched squeak, going red and turning around quickly so her back was to Josh who was standing nude in her kitchen, as though it was normal.

If that wasn't enough, she heard the lock on the front door turn. "Quick. Please, go upstairs and get dressed," Sophie now pleaded, knowing who was about to come in.

"Sweetie, darling," the singsong voice of her eccentric mother rang out through the house. "Darling? I think you've dropped some clothes here on your way to the washing machine. Oh, my. Are you doing your delicates, dear?"

"Mother. Please could you go into the living room for a moment," was her quivering response. But it was too late. Everything moved in slow motion as Sophie saw her mum's eyes, magnified by her thick black-rimmed glasses, playfully look the naked man in the kitchen up and down.

"I didn't know you had company, darling. He reminds me of your father."

"Oh god. Mother! Please get out," she screeched as Josh held out a hand ready to introduce himself to Beryl.

"Go and put some clothes on," Sophie again turned red and told him through gritted teeth, "and mother, I'm taking your key off you. Please sit down at the table and be quiet while I clear this mess up."

She gathered the discarded clothes, shoving Josh's at him and retreating upstairs to the spare room with a bundle of her own. Her mother was still sitting downstairs at the kitchen table. Sophie worried about what to say to her. But why would she have to explain anything?

It was Sophie who seemed to be upset about this. Not Josh or her mother. Everything that had led to the moment had been out of character for her. She did this because of some words written years ago on a crumpled piece of paper.

Was this who she really wanted to be? A forty-four-year-old divorced woman having one-night stands with men she picked up at gay bars? But berating herself hadn't given her a happy life so far either.

The old Sophie would be livid about this morning's situation. Yet, alone in the spare bedroom, she could now see the funny side and began to giggle.

"This is where you're hiding? I'm really sorry if I've caused some sort of problem for you this morning," offered a now fully clothed Josh, poking his head around the door. But Sophie was still cracking up, tears now running down her face as she hiccupped with laughter.

"You tried to shake my mum's hand while you were naked… in my kitchen," she snorted. "I've never had a naked man in my kitchen before. Hell, I haven't slept with anyone in nearly fifteen years."

There was no comeback from Josh. Instead, he stared at her, bemused. He hadn't had a serious relationship in his life, just hopped from bed to bed with beautiful women, not really thinking about his future. But before him now was a sparkling woman who, in her baggy pyjamas and with terrible bedhead, looked even more beautiful than the one he'd met at his brother's stag party last night.

"I've called a taxi and it should be outside now. Look, could I have your number, maybe we could do something a little more traditional, like go for a drink and something to eat one night?"

"You don't need to, honestly it's fine. What happened last night was wrong. So wrong. I've never done anything like it before and I don't expect you to be chivalrous."

Stung and not entirely happy with the answer, Josh leaned in, took Sophie's hand and gave her a peck on the cheek and then turned to leave. Sophie heard the door downstairs open, followed by her mother shouting, "it was lovely to meet you", then it banged shut.

Josh had placed a scrap of paper with a mobile number on it in Sophie's hand, which she crumpled up and threw into the wire bin near the bedroom door.

"He's gone sweetie," Beryl said from the bottom of the stairs.

When Sophie walked into the kitchen, the table had been set with a fresh pot of coffee, slices of toast, butter and jam. Beryl's elbows were on the table, her fingers were knotted together with her chin resting on top. She looked Sophie up and down with a straight face and asked sympathetically if her daughter was ok.

"I'm not sure. I don't know what came over me," Sophie began. "This time last month my life was a schedule, I knew what I was doing and when I was doing it. Now it feels as though I'm someone else, completely different to who I thought I had to be."

"Sweetie, darling," Beryl replied so softly it sounded like a purr. "No one is prescribed a certain way of living. You don't have to explain your decisions or choices to anyone, not to me and especially not to yourself. How you were living before was not a life and over the past few weeks, I've seen you smile and laugh more than you ever have. You may think that what you've been doing recently isn't right, that it's unnatural to you. But what is more natural than being happy?"

Sophie thought on her mother's words in silence for a minute and found herself, possibly for the first time, agreeing with them.

"I don't really have to give my key back do I, sweetie?"

"No, mum. You don't. But you can help me with something, I guess it's what started all this madness."

Over the next couple of hours and another pot of coffee, Sophie told her mum about the list, what was on it and that she was going to tick as much of it off as she could over rest of the year.

When Beryl left, Sophie stripped her bed, bleached the kitchen and had a shower. By the time she'd settled down with a magazine in the living room, feeling fresher, it was two in the afternoon.

As she flicked through the glossy pages of *Country Living*, her mobile phone started to vibrate.

"Hey hun, what did you end up doing last night?" a rough sounding Paris asked.

She told him what had happened, including the kitchen encounter with Beryl, which made him unable to speak through his deep belly laughs for several minutes.

"If that isn't the most hilarious one-night stand story I've ever heard, then I don't know what is," he finally said, still chuckling and waiting for a reply from the other end of the phone.

"Shush, it's not funny. I've never done anything like this before. The only person I've slept with is Carl and the last time that happened was so long ago I can't remember," she said, finally allowing herself to laugh a little with Paris.

"Well, it must have been like riding a bike for you, because whatever you did or said to Josh, I think it's helped us bag Felix as a consultant. He called me this morning and he's in. This is going to change everything."

Chapter Nine: Gay?

Several weeks had passed since Sophisticats' big event and the bar was the talk of the drag world. Gaining Felix's services as a consultant to the business had already begun to take effect and for seven days a week over the past month, the building had been full to capacity.

Sophie didn't really understand what Felix had done or why he was so important and influential, but things had changed. The events guru had secured coverage for the club on national websites that hailed it as the best drag venue in the UK.

A public relations agency had also been brought in to enter the club into awards as well as encourage more press coverage. It all resulted in Paris being invited to an interview with BBC Breakfast to talk about the drag scene, the club and why the culture was so important in the UK.

Sophie and the queens who regularly worked at Sophisticats were invited to sit on the sofa with Paris at the BBC's Manchester studio. Paris also suggested that, while they were in the city, he and Sophie should spend the evening there to scout out some new talent to bring back south with them now the club was at the height of its popularity. It was also a good opportunity for Sophie to catch up with her eldest son Ralph, who she hadn't seen since he visited her at hospital following the car accident a few months back.

Paris and the girls were great on the breakfast show. They were already in their drag when Paris picked them up in his car at three that morning and remained beautifully presented until they changed after the interview.

Each was quizzed by the two BBC presenters about drag queens, if it was something a person did as a fulltime job and whether people's interest in them would be short-lived, driven only by the current popularity of television shows about the drag queens.

"Listen, hun," Paris cut across the male presenter. "Collectively on this sofa there's nearly one hundred years' of drag experience – most of which comes from Mya here."

Mya spluttered at the friendly insult but didn't have chance to respond as Paris quickly continued his rebuttal. "And long ago before us, thousands of other men dressed as women for the entertainment of the paying public. This is not a recent trend and it's not something that will go away either."

The interview done and the other three girls safely on a train back home, Paris and Sophie drove over to Ralph's flat, which he shared with three other students. Sophie had planned on cleaning the flat, as well as buying Ralph some food shopping and taking him out for something to eat before going to Canal Street with Paris for the evening.

A flatmate had let them in after Ralph called to say he would be late back from a lecture. "Hun, this place is disgusting. I'm not touching a thing," Paris, who had de-dragged at the television studio, moaned before placing his coat between his bottom and the sofa before he sat down.

While Paris lounged around, engrossed in whatever was on his phone screen, Sophie started cleaning in the kitchen. She filled a bucket with bleach and water and gave everything a good hard scrub, then vacuumed and did the same in the bathroom.

Ralph's room was relatively tidy, but she quickly ran the hoover around it anyway, changed his bed and folded the clean laundry that was piled on his desk and put it away. What she didn't notice fall from the clothes, however, until she stepped on it, was a glossy magazine featuring a semi-naked man on the front.

She picked it up and read the title "*Gay Today*" out loud. The coverlines were telling her which celebrities had come out recently, how to find the right partner without using dating apps and what the latest gay hotspots in the UK were.

"Paris!" She yelled in a panic. But she didn't know what the panic was about. Ralph had never said anything to her about girlfriends or boyfriends. Was her son gay and hadn't told her?

"Yes hun," said Paris only looking up from his phone as he came through the door. "This is a clean room. What's that you're holding... oh."

Spotting the magazine in Sophie's hand, both sides of Paris's mouth moved up at the corners into a wide grin, before a loud fit of giggles burst from his lips.

"What are you laughing at," Sophie demanded. "My son is gay, and he hasn't told me. What does that mean?"

"Well, hun. Let's not jump to conclusions, he might not be gay, although his room is freakishly clean and I can see he has a lot of shoes...

"This is not funny, Paris. Ralph is hiding the fact that he's gay from me. Why would he do that?"

As Paris began to think of an answer, the lock on the flat door rattled before Ralph called out his return.

"Quick, hide it," Sophie whispered and flung the magazine to Paris.

"I don't know where to bloody put it," he snapped back.

"Throw it under the bed and get out before he find us."

Just as Sophie kicked the magazine beneath Ralph's bed, he walked in and looked curiously at Sophie and the stranger stood next to her. "Mum, what are you doing in my room and who is this?" He asked with a frown to his mother and a smile for Paris.

"Oh. Me? Well, I was just giving it a once over with the hoover and a duster. You know, doing my motherly duties and I, err, this is Paris my boss who came in to look at your, err. Your, erm...

"Your mum said you might have jumper I could borrow because I'm a little chilly," Paris jumped in. "You know what us southerners are like when it comes to the colder northern air. But I feel ok now, must have been a passing chill." he finished with a forced, nervous titter.

"Right," said Ralph, now looking confused. "I guess we should go out for something to eat then, as long as you're not too cold, Paris, was it?

"Really it's Ben, Paris is my drag name but most people still call me Paris, so I guess you can too. Lunch sounds great, doesn't it, Sophie," he babbled.

"Oh, yes. Lovely. Where would you suggest we go, Ralph?"

Ralph moved aside to let his mum and her friend leave the room, but peered in before he closed the door, a surge of panic in his stomach as he wondered how long his mother had been in there for and what she might have found.

After about half-an-hour of walking around the streets near Ralph's flat, which was a ten-minute bus ride from the centre of Manchester, the trio decided to have lunch in a vegetarian café. Inside the furniture was mismatched, what Sophie guessed some people would call shabby chic, but to her it just looked dirty and unordered. They each ordered coffees, as well as salads and sandwiches, while a jug of tap water and three glasses, translucent from being over washed, were placed on a doily in the centre of the old, round mahogany table they were sat at.

"What's new with you then, Ralph. Is Uni going ok?" Sophie asked as she poured them all a glass of water.

"Nothing really. First year is just about finding what you like about the course and deciding what you're going to specialise in."

Ralph was studying art, having always had a talent for the subject since primary school. His mum, however, didn't see it as something that would ever gain someone many opportunities, financially or otherwise. She didn't want her children to be anything like her. At the same time, she wasn't a pushy parent and knew how uncomfortable it was to be persuaded to do things you didn't want to.

"Have you met any special people while you've been up here then," she pushed further and was about to specify boys or girls, but Paris jabbed her in the shin with his booted foot, the shock of which caused her to yelp and jump, knocking one of the water glasses over.

"Sorry, hun. My foot slipped," said Paris, his eyes wide with warning. "Actually Sophie, could I just see you over here for a moment?"

Awkwardly, Paris marched Sophie through the front door of the café and to the street outside where he berated her, "what do you think you're doing?"

"What do you mean, I'm just asking my son if he has anyone special in his life."

"You know what I mean. You found that magazine and he could very well like men. If he has something to tell you, then he'll do it when he is ready. Leave him be," finished Paris, before swishing back through the door to his seat.

Sophie stood outside for a little longer, thinking about what Paris had said. Why wouldn't her son tell her that he was gay? Had she been such a terrible mother to him that he was uncomfortable sharing something like this?

The questions she had weren't just about why he hadn't told her, though. She wondered what having a gay son meant about her. If the way she was as a parent had warped or tainted him in any way and whether her attitude to life had made him like this. But she pushed it all to the back of her mind and went back into the café to join the group.

Once lunch was over, Paris drove her and Ralph to the supermarket so Sophie could stock his cupboards and fridge up with some food.

Back in the flat, she packed away the food and tried to give some suggestions on what to do with it. But Sophie's cooking skills weren't much stronger than her mother's and all she could suggest was mixing a jar of pesto with some cooked pasta. Nonetheless, it was some motherly advice, she felt, and once her job was done, she and Paris went to a hotel he had booked for them to stay in that night.

The hotel was a short walk away from Canal Street and was, as Paris described it, ultra-trendy and hipster. The walls and floors were all made of polished concrete and music constantly thumped at a low volume as trendy bearded men, and women wearing baggy high-waisted jeans, sat on chairs in the lobby with their faces glued to fancy laptops.

Although she wasn't dressed like the hotel guests and staff, Sophie didn't feel out of place. She was wearing what Paris had suggested for the television interview that morning – a black A-line pleated skirt in a light floaty material that fell to her ankles. She had this on with a white cotton, short-sleeved t-shirt and three-quarter length denim jacket.

Room keys collected, they went up to the suite. It was one of the most beautiful places Sophie had seen. She'd never stayed in a hotel before, as she'd never left her hometown for more than a day.

The walls were painted in dark sumptuous blues and teals with gold accents and decorations. Off a main sitting area there were two bedrooms with ensuite bathrooms. The beds were covered in expensive fabrics and looked so comfortable Sophie thought she could snuggle up in the duvet and sleep for a year.

"Have a quick shower and get ready," Paris shouted from his room. "I've rang down for some Champagne and nibbles to keep us going until we're ready. And make sure you don't overdress, we're only bar hopping."

This was the first time someone had asked Sophie not to overdress and she snorted at the special request, as well as the fact she hadn't bothered packing anything fancy anyway.

She unzipped her overnight bag and hung up a long cotton black dress with a tiny polka dot print on it, which she'd wear with her denim jacket and a pair of white lace-up Vans Paris had convinced her to buy, even though she'd argued the style was too young for her.

Showered, hair dried and face made up, Sophie returned to the sitting area and poured herself a glass of Champagne from a bottle that was sat in an ice bucket on a side table. She plonked herself down and waited for Paris to finish getting ready.

"Hun?" she heard Paris shout from the other side of his bedroom door. "Are you there, hun?"

"I'm here. What do you want," she said with a giggle, wondering what he was up to.

"Will you announce me?"

"What do you mean?"

"Announce me into the room. I can't come out until you announce me."

Sophie began to laugh harder this time, but did as Paris had asked and said in what she thought was a regal voice, "ladies and gentlemen, please welcome the one and only, the drag queen extraordinaire, the beauty with a little secret, Paris Le Grande."

This was followed by Sophie putting her glass down, standing to attention and welcoming Paris into the room with the loudest clapping and cheering she could muster. He was wearing black jeans that were so tight they looked like leggings, a long see through black and white shirt and some patent leather, pointed boots.

"Right, let's down this," he said pointing to the Champagne, "and we'll see how much of Manchester we can paint pink."

***

They finally got to Canal Street at around ten that evening – after waiting for a taxi because Paris refused to walk ten minutes as his shoes were already hurting him.

The street was teaming with all kinds of people out to enjoy themselves on a Friday night. There were groups of women on hen parties, shrieking at the tops of their voices; men of all ages, sizes and colours milling around or standing waiting for people; and there were dozens of drag queens working the long street, trying to get as many punters into their bars as possible.

"Let's try in here first," said Paris pointing to the first bar on his left. "I've heard this is the best place for drag queen bingo, but I think that's only during the week."

Sophie followed Paris through a dark doorway with thumping music streaming out of it. He led her up a small set of sticky steps and into a main bar area that was packed tight with men all vying for the bartenders' attention.

All eight of the servers behind the bar were young men, no older than twenty-five she guessed, and wearing nothing other than a pair of denim shorts each. "Oooh," Paris hooted. "I think I've got a few ideas already," he said eyeing up a brunette bartender.

"Shush, you big floozy," said Sophie with a playful nudge to his ribs. "I can't imagine our bar team making it through the night alive if you had them dressed like that. Go find us a seat and I'll get us some drinks – vodka and Diet Coke ok?"

With Paris now on a mission to find some seats, Sophie jostled to the front of the bar, confident after having drunk half a bottle of Champagne, and ordered the drinks. She found Paris sat in a small booth near the front doors where they could see people coming in, but couldn't be seen themselves. He was chatting to an extremely tall woman with a large blonde beehive hairstyle.

"Thanks," said Paris as Sophie put the drinks down on the table. "Hun, this is The Duchess, she's hosting here tonight."

"Lovely to meet you, I love your hair," said Sophie to the person in front of her, now obviously a drag queen.

"Don't you look darling in your little pumps," said The Duchess looking Sophie up and down, who was now self-conscious because of the compliment.

"When did you come out to your parents?" Sophie blurted.

The drag queen was taken aback by the abrupt question and stared at Sophie for a few seconds. "How do you know I'm gay," she squawked.

"I'm sorry, I didn't mean to pry. But you are, erm, you know, gay, aren't you?"

The Duchess threw back her head and laughed, which made her hairdo wobble precariously on top of her head. She then confirmed that yes, she's gay, and her parents had known she was gay from a young age.

"I couldn't really keep it a secret any longer, I was leaving the house dressed like this most weekends to work here," she finished after a few minutes of explaining. Why do you ask?"

"No reason, I'm just curious about how it all works. It's just a bit strange to me that you have to announce to the world who you are if you don't fit into the box everyone expects you to."

"That was quite deep of you, Sophie," Paris said, knowing his friend was looking for confirmation that if her son was like him and The Duchess, then perhaps there would be some sort of time limit before the truth came out. But he also knew that wasn't the case, and if Ralph had something to tell his mum, then he would do it when he was ready and without feeling pressured.

After chatting with a few of the staff working that night, Paris and Sophie had agreed to move on to a second venue on finishing their drinks.

Once Paris had convinced her to quickly down the last quarter of her vodka and tonic, Paris recognised someone among a large group who he recognised. It was Sophie's son Ralph, and he was very close to one of the boys he'd walked into the club with. He then saw Ralph lean in to kiss the boy, making Paris's eyes widen as he knew Sophie would soon see them.

"What are you looking at?" she asked, turning to follow his gaze. "Oh. I see," Sophie said quietly, facing Paris again.

"I don't think you should go over and make a…" Paris started, but it was too late. Sophie was already halfway towards the bar before he could finish his sentence. Instead, he got up and followed her as quickly as he could and when he got to the bar, Sophie was already tapping Ralph on the shoulder.

"Mum, what are you doing here? I'm… these are my friends who I come out with here sometimes, you know, just for a bit of fun."

"I can see the sort of fun you're having, Ralph. What I want to know is why you couldn't be honest. Why you've been hiding who you really are from all this time. Have I really been such a terrible mother that you thought I wouldn't accept this? For heaven's sake, I work in a gay bar."

Sophie could feel a lump form in her throat and tears begin to fill her eyes. She was angry that her son was going around, kissing boys, and hiding it from her. But she wasn't sure who she was more annoyed with – Ralph or herself. Had she really been such a cold, unloving person that her own son felt like he had to hide big things like this from her?

"Mum, it's not like that. It's only since I've been here that things have started to happen really. I didn't want to say anything yet, because nothing has really happened. I've only been…"

But as Ralph tried to explain, Sophie turned and sternly walked out, tears now falling in streams down her cheeks. Paris mouthed "it's ok" to Ralph before following Sophie out, where he found her sobbing in an alley next to the bar.

"Why wouldn't he tell me?" she whispered through snotty sobs. "I'm his mother and he couldn't be honest with me."

"Hun," Paris began and handed his friend, who was now sitting on the floor, makeup running down her face, a tissue. "Believe me, it's not just about whether or not he felt comfortable telling you. It's not necessarily like he's been lying either. These things are more complicated than saying 'I am' or 'I'm not'. I don't understand why 'coming out' is a thing anyway, I mean, did you come out as straight?"

Sophie half snorted and half hiccupped a laugh. "I didn't exactly come out as anything, I've really only just started to understand who I am over the past couple of months."

"Well there you go. Imagine how difficult it is for Ralph to understand who he is and to tell you something when he probably doesn't even know what it is he needs to tell you. Hun, he's not trying to hurt you and I don't know what things were like for him growing up. But the fact you're upset that he didn't tell you and not about the fact that *he is* or could be tells me you're probably very good mother. I wish this is what my parents were most upset about when I was his age."

Sophie was beginning to calm down as Paris's words sank in. She was sure it wasn't the fact that her son was gay that was upsetting her, and she would hate to make Ralph feel like Paris's parents made him feel. Although he hadn't told her much about them, Sophie knew they'd been rotten and all but disowned Paris when he came out to them.

"I should probably go back in and apologise," said Sophie, standing up and straightening her clothes. She'd managed to sit on some cigarette butts, which Paris helped her to flick from her polka dot dress.

"Mum, what are you doing round here?" Ralph had found them and was taken aback at seeing his usually emotionless mother looking dishevelled. "I didn't mean to upset you," he continued after seeing the tears on her cheeks.

"I don't know what I would have told you or when, but I would have told you."

"You don't have to tell me anything," she said, thinking about Paris's words. "If you like boys, girls or both, you don't have to tell me. I just want you to be happy and to be comfortable being who you are. I've only just started to understand what that means myself. So please don't feel like you must put a label on it or announce anything to me or the world – unless you want to, then that's ok too. I should come in and apologise to your friends."

"No," said Ralph with a fast and forcefully. "I mean, it's fine. I'd rather we just left it here for now. We can talk about it when I'm home for Easter."

Although she was a little offended that he didn't want her to meet his friends, Sophie was also relieved she didn't have to go back into the club after making a show of herself. She told Paris she was tired and asked if it would be ok to go back to the hotel, even though they hadn't really seen much of Canal Street. But Paris agreed it had been quite an eventful evening anyway and that it would be best to call it a night.

Back at the hotel, they had a nightcap and a chat about what they'd discovered about Ralph that day. Paris assured Sophie that she had done the right thing and that although her reaction had been a little dramatic, it had come from the right place. But he warned her not to press the subject with her son.

Chapter Ten: Cooking

Sophie woke the next day to Madonna's Vogue being played loudly from the suite's sitting area. She looked at the alarm clock next to the bed and could see it was almost nine. Although she hadn't drank much while she and Paris were out on Canal Street the night before, they'd decided it would be a good idea to take another bottle of Champagne upstairs and Sophie was now feeling results.

Her head was aching and her eyes were sore, but it wasn't the worst she'd felt after drinking, she told herself thinking back to her encounter with Josh at Sophisticats. But now it was time to get up if she and Paris were to make it south in time to have an afternoon briefing with Felix about the next steps for the club.

"Good morning, don't you look a sight for... well, don't you look a sight," Paris laughed as Sophie walked into the sitting area. "I told you another bottle of Champers wasn't a good idea."

"I think I told you it wasn't a good idea, actually. But you insisted it would make me feel better. It did at the time, but now I'm regretting it."

They quickly got ready and checked out of the hotel, which was filled with a fresh hit of hipsters in the lobby, all working on laptops while funky music played quietly in the background. Were they paid to sit there, did they work there? Sophie didn't know, but thought it was strange they all seemed to be working from there.

Before they went to bed last night, Paris and Sophie talked more about Ralph and what it meant that he hadn't told Sophie. She knew Paris was right about it not being personal, but it was hard to shake away the guilt that her child couldn't talk to her about something she considered to be such a big and important part of his life.

But Paris had again told her there was nothing more she could or needed to do, other than wait and let Ralph do his own thing. She decided not to talk about it anymore and so the pair of them spent most of the four-hour journey back to Sophisticats talking about the club.

"You've been doing so much more than when you first started with me," Paris said as they left the M25 to join one of the country roads that would take them back to town. "I've been thinking about your future with Sophisticats and what that looks like."

Sophie had been pondering her next steps too. She was happy managing the girls backstage and doing the odd shift front-of-house, but she didn't know how long it would be possible to keep up with the late nights and couldn't imagine herself doing it for the rest of her working life. Had Paris considered the same thing and thought about ditching her for someone younger? The idea shot panic up her spine.

"What do you mean? I'm really happy doing what I'm doing, and I think I've made things run better than they were before," she defended with a raised voice as her body became rigid with angst. "I do enjoy working with the girls and working front-of-house is a lot of fun too."

"I know, but it's not really something you can do forever, I think you've got a lot more to offer."

Sophie was really worried now. It was exactly what she'd expected to happen after taking the job, Paris had realised who she was. A nothing. A nobody. And now he was sticking the boot in and letting her down gently by saying how wasted her talents were working for him. A sob was about to let itself out of Sophie's mouth as she thought on everything she'd learnt about herself at Sophisticats and all the fun she'd had too.

"Why are you looking so worried," Paris asked, a cheeky glint in his eye. "If you don't want to be more involved in the club and are happy carrying on doing what you are, then I'm good with that."

"You're not letting me go?" Sophie asked with relief, trying to stop the swollen sob passing her lips. "I thought you were going to fire me."

"Why on earth would I do that? You've helped to make Sophisticats a bigger and better business. If it wasn't for you, we wouldn't have landed Felix and we certainly wouldn't be as successful as we are now. What I want, if it's ok, is for you to be my right-hand woman. Things are getting so busy I can hardly keep up and now I need someone to move into a general manager role."

An overwhelming sensation of relief now stopped Sophie from replying to her boss's kind gesture. She'd never thought anyone could put that kind of faith in her. Years of plodding along in minor roles, clocking in and leaving at the end of her shift without a second thought, had left little room to consider herself as being able to have a positive impact on something like Sophisticats.

"Yes. Please. I'd love to be more involved," she said without a thought. "I'd really love to be more involved."

"Good. We can talk about the finer details after our meeting with Felix today and of course there will be a pay rise. There's no question about that, I wouldn't be able to afford a general manager if it wasn't for you, so it's only right you have a better salary."

For the rest of the journey home, Sophie was buzzing with pride and her tummy felt as though it was a washing machine on a spin cycle. But then her mind turned back to the thing that led to the opportunity in the first place – the bucket list. If she had a career, there was no way she'd find time to tick things off it.

Once Paris dropped her back home in the early evening, after their meeting with Felix, she sat down at the kitchen table and again studied the list of activities she still wanted to complete. She still thought most normal people would consider them mundane and boring, but to her they were experiences she'd never afforded herself. It was exciting.

After flicking the pages between her fingers for a little, listening as the edges rapped past her thumb, she settled on the one task, cooking. It would be easiest to achieve with little research and effort, she thought. But going alone didn't appeal to her, she wasn't brave enough for that. Asking Paris or one of the other girls from the club also wasn't an option, it just wasn't the sort of thing they'd be up for. 'Drag queens don't cook, hun,' Paris would probably say if asked. Who could she go with?

As she continued pondering, realising that she really hadn't made any connections that had resulted in something close to friendship, the familiar rattle of the front door, followed by her mother's singsong greeting, ended her fruitless thoughts.

"Yoo-hoo. Sweetie darling, how was Manchester? Do I have a new son-in-law?"

"In here mum," Sophie said loudly from the kitchen. "I told you, I'm not looking for a husband right now, I'm focusing on other things."

"Ahh yes darling, that little list of yours. What else have you managed to cross off it... I'm assuming that lovely man I met in the kitchen was something to tick off, yes?"

Sophie was trying to forget about the naked man in the kitchen incident and wished her mother would stop bringing it up, so she ignored the comment and instead offered Beryl a coffee.

"That would be wonderful, sweetie. I'm parched. I've not stopped all day today between yoga and a little trip into town for some shopping, this is the first time I've sat down."

A fresh pot of coffee now made, Sophie placed two full cups onto the round pine kitchen table and told her mum what had happened in Manchester with

Ralph, asking if she'd known anything about it and what she should do.

"Oh, it will be wonderful to finally have a gay in the family sweetie. I always thought Ralph had something special about him, but no, I didn't think this was the sort of thing. And I don't understand what it is you think you should do. Being a homosexual these days is very normal, so if I were you I would just treat Ralph as if nothing's happened."

"But what about him not telling me about it, why couldn't he confide in me?" Sophie asked, expecting a different perspective from her mother to Paris's.

"Well," said Beryl with a look of deep thought on her face. "Darling, I don't think there is anything to tell. 'Coming out'," she said with air quotes, "isn't really a thing these days. If Ralph came home with a boyfriend, then that should be as normal to us as if he came home with a girl. He shouldn't have to announce whether he likes willies, hoo-hoos or both. Now, what's next on your list?"

Sophie wondered how her mother was so wise to the modern world. She knew of people from previous jobs around her own age being confused and almost repelled when they told stories of their children being gay. She knew that, traditionally, people her mother's age would also usually be repulsed, finding it a sin or unnatural. But she was satisfied with what her mother told her and moved on.

"Well, I've been looking at the things I can do quite quickly, easily and cheaply and have decided on taking up a cookery course. I've just Googled and there's a beginners' class tomorrow night for adults at Thomas's college. Maybe you should come with me."

When she'd decided to focus on ticking this next task off her list, Sophie was thinking of the wrong kind of person to take with her. She didn't need a friend, but someone who was just as bad a cook, if not worse, than her.

"Me?" gasped Beryl with a hand to her chest and a look of genuine shock on her face. "You think I need to go to a cookery class? Sweetie, I've been cooking for nearly all my years on this planet and you think I could learn some lessons at a beginners' cookery class?"

Clearly disillusioned, thought Sophie, before adding: "No, mum, I don't think you need to learn to cook. I just need someone to go with me and I thought it might be nice for us to spend some time together."

"Well, that's different. Of course I'd love to come and spend some time with you. What a wonderful idea," said a now excited Beryl. "But you usually work in the evenings. You haven't gotten yourself fired, have you?"

After explaining that she was now working shifts during the day in a general manager role at the club, news of which made Beryl chirrup with congratulations, Sophie arranged to meet her mother at the car park down the road from the club the next day, following which she'd drive them both to the college.

***

Her first shift as Sophisticats' general manager meant quickly learning to deal with numbers, stock ordering and all other kinds of strategy work, which was difficult. So at the end of the day, Sophie was ready to leave and meet her mum to go to the cookery class.

When she got to the door of the club, her mother was stood outside, visible through the glass. She wasn't a tall woman, and Sophie gave a half chuckle at the sight of Beryl peeping through her big black-rimmed glasses at her, waving as though they'd been separated for years and this was some sort of a reunion.

"Mother," said Sophie rather firmly, "I thought you were meeting me at the car."

"Oh, I couldn't remember if you said bar or car, sweetie. I've been standing here for almost an hour; didn't you hear me knocking?"

In hindsight, Sophie had heard something but put it down to the wind or perhaps someone just using the doorway to smoke or make a phone call in. "But I told you I'd be finished at five."

"I know, sweetie, but I thought it would be wonderful to see you in action in your new career and I also thought that perhaps I'd catch a glimpse of Mya or one of the other girls out of drag. I've never seen one as a man before."

"They're not aliens, mother," laughed Sophie as Beryl rose to her tiptoes to get a better look inside the club over her daughter's shoulder. "And anyway, they don't usually start turning up until a little later. If you like, though, I can work late one night this month and you can come down and meet them all out of drag."

"I wouldn't want to cramp your style, sweetie. But if you insist. How does next Wednesday work for you, say around six?"

Sophie rolled her eyes and agreed Beryl could come to the club then. Her mother was wearing a dark blue turban today and had, as her daughter warned her, toned down her attire so she wasn't wearing anything too floaty. Had she turned up in billowing clothes, Sophie was sure they would either catch light or cause some other drama.

She, on the other hand, was wearing a pair of navy-blue tailored trousers that cut off just above her ankle, which she'd paired with a cream t-shirt with thin blue stripes and a pair of pumps. She felt it was smart enough for a general manager, but also causal enough to go to the first class she'd taken since leaving school.

The college was a post-war concrete building constructed in the brutalist style that wouldn't look out of place in many other towns or cities across the UK. By now it was approaching six in the evening and there were a few teenagers milling around outside the building.

After Sophie had parked her car – a new Mini Cooper which the insurance firm had finally paid out for – she and Beryl walked up a small set of steps to the front door and entered the reception area. A sullen looking woman, who was sat so low she could just about see over the wooden desk, looked up with a short "yes" followed by a pause no doubt waiting to be filled by Sophie or her mother.

"We're here for the cooking class that starts tonight," Sophie said quietly so none of the other people behind her could hear.

"Which one?" the receptionist, who didn't look much older than Sophie, said with even less interest, "there's about five different ones."

"Oh, sorry I didn't know that. It's the beginners' one, we're here for that one," replied Sophie, who was now feeling a little embarrassed by the rudeness of the receptionist and the fact a small queue was starting to build behind her.

"You need to walk straight out of the doors behind me, take the first set of doors on your left which will take you outside and you need to go into the buildings that say home economics."

"Well, how wonderfully helpful you've been," piped up Beryl. "It's wonderful to receive service with a smile, isn't it darling."

"Come on mum," said Sophie whose cheeks were now burning red at her mother's sarcastic comment.

The classroom was filled with the smells of the day's cooking, a mixture of baked goods and various spices. There were eight cooking stations, each with a pair of hobs, two ovens and enough workspace for a couple to prepare ingredients.

Sophie and Beryl were the first in the room and took a station at the front. Within a few minutes, the room was filled with fourteen other people who had also, it appeared, come in pairs. They were of different ages, sizes and backgrounds. Some looked to be young couples, while others were older and there were also a few pairs of women who looked to be Sophie's age.

"Right class," boomed a voice from the back of the room. "Welcome to cookery for beginners', I'm your tutor Meryl Booker and over the next six weeks of the course we'll be learning how to prepare various simple meals as well as the technical skills you'll need if you're going to make these things at home."

Meryl was a plump lady who looked to be in her mid-fifties. She had a dark blonde short bob that wrapped around her chubby face. Below a harsh straight fringe were a pair of rectangular glasses and her lips were coloured pink. She was wearing chefs' whites and a small light blue neckerchief that was tied around her throat at a jaunty angle.

"Today we're going to be making a lasagne," Meryl, now standing at the front of the class, shouted. "It is one of the easiest pasta dishes to make and will provide you with at least half-a-dozen meals, which can either be served there and then or frozen and kept for another time."

"Sweetie," Beryl whispered to Sophie. "I thought you said this was a beginners' class. I've tried cooking lasagne before, and it turned out to be a complete mess."

"She said at the start it was for beginners," Sophie whispered back.

"Is there something you would like to share with the rest of us, ladies?" Meryl was now looking at Sophie and Beryl. Her face was red with annoyance at having to stop what she was saying, and Sophie could feel the eyes of everyone else in the room on them.

"Nothing exciting, darling. I was just saying to my daughter here that I thought lasagne was more of an expert dish," Beryl answered a now tomato-coloured Meryl.

"Excuse me. You are questioning the dishes I have selected to show this class how to cook," she boomed back, taking a few steps closer to get a better look at the pair. "I suggest you two listen and watch very carefully. You may have paid to be here, but I am your teacher and you will do as you are told in my class."

"Someone's not a happy bunny," Beryl whispered to her daughter, which was met with another warning glance from the hot-headed tutor.

Working in their pairs, the class was given careful instruction on how to make a bechamel sauce by creating a roux with butter and flour before adding warm milk infused with onion, nutmeg and garlic. They then added cheddar cheese to the sauce to make it thick and rich.

Once that was prepared, they were then told to finely dice their sofrito of vegetables. So, with great difficulty, Sophie and her mum each sliced their carrots and celery lengthways before turning them into julienne strips and cutting across to make the tiniest cubes as possible. Or, at least that was the idea.

Beryl's knife didn't seem to be that sharp, so every time she tried to chop a carrot vertically the vegetable would launch across the room. When it landed at Meryl's feet, she huffily scooped it up before coming over to their workstation and chopping it herself, all the while looking straight at Beryl with menacing eyes.

Onions, thought Sophie, were easy to finely dice. She'd seen Nigella on one of her cookery shows do it, although Sophie had never tried it herself until now. She sliced the onion in half from root to tip, cut off the top of each half, peeled them and then cut lengthways four times. It was then a struggle to cut vertically into onion without it falling apart, however, the task was completed near perfectly and Sophie could then dice it up.

"Add your diced onion, carrot, celery and garlic to a pan with a little oil in it and then gently fry your vegetables. This is your sofrito, it is the vegetable base to any savoury Italian dish you make, such as risotto, or in this case a dish inspired by traditional Italian cooking," shouted Meryl over the struggling class.

Sophie turned around and saw fourteen sweaty people, all looking fearfully at the unforgiving tutor who was standing in a dominating position at the front of the class, hands on her hips.

"Darling, we have to get out of here," Sophie's mum said in a voice that was just louder than a whisper. "I'm worried that I'll die in here and she'll get the class to marinade me."

"Shush mum, you're being melodramatic. You're not going to die in here and nobody would cook you, you'd be too gristly," smirked Sophie, who silently agreed Chef Booker was slightly menacing. Yet, despite the constant threat of a tongue lashing from angry Meryl, Sophie felt she was learning.

After sautéing the vegetables until they were soft, the class added minced beef, tinned tomatoes, tomato pureé and whatever herbs and seasoning they wanted to use to give extra flavour. Then they smeared a generous layer of bechamel on the bottom of a baking dish before adding a layer of dried pasta sheets, followed by the mince and tomato sauce, which they repeated until there was no more sauce.

"You can add a layer of your bechamel sauce on the top before sprinkling with cheese," shouted Meryl. "I like to use a mix of mozzarella and cheddar, but it's up to you."

Sophie turned to see a frantic Beryl next to her. There was sauce all over her apron and her blue turban was now covered with white patches of flour and sitting at an awkward angle. Her glasses were steaming up and her face was scrunched with concentration. The lasagne she'd prepared for the oven was a messy concoction. It wasn't layered properly, and sauce was oozing over the edges of the dish.

After cleaning their workstations down under the watchful eye of Meryl, sixteen now cooked lasagnes were presented, with various levels success, at the end of each workstation. Sophie thought hers looked the best of them all, from what she could see of the others in the room.

"Now for the taste test," Meryl shouted and greedily licked her lips. She pulled a fork out of her chefs' jacket pocket and began working her way around the class from the back, making mostly dissatisfied noises. When she reached Sophie's station, she curled her lip at Beryl's lasagne saying: "I'm not even going to risk tasting that".

Sophie thought she saw a smile momentarily break across Meryl's mouth when she looked at her dish. She tasted it and simply said: "Very good, Ms Defoy. We might make a cook out of you yet. Although, I'd be lying if I said your mother here had even an ounce of talent when it comes to food."

Beryl, however, had other ideas. "Excuse me," she said, raising the pitch, tone and volume of her voice all at once to a hysterical level. "This is the best dish in the class, hands down," she shrieked while pointing to the disfigured lasagne at the end of her workstation. "You're clearly a busybody who thinks lasagne is some sort of haute cuisine, but it's not a patch on my Malibu chicken."

The cookery tutor's face had now turned raspberry red, while her eyes and lips began to twitch with anger. Before Sophie could apologise to Meryl, the chef's plump chops, along with the rest of her rotund figure, began to shake as she roared out a myriad of insults that Sophie thought would make even the usually fowl-mouthed drag queens from Sophisticats blush.

171

"Ok, mother. I think we should leave now. Come on, grab your lasagne, we don't want it to go to waste now do we," Sophie said as Meryl took a deep breath in preparation for another onslaught of cursing.

"Don't you ever come back and disgrace my profession again," they heard Meryl's menacing voice boom down the hallway before they were finally safe in Sophie's car, a warm lasagne each on their lap.

"Oh sweetie," said Sophie's mum now studying her lasagne more closely. "I see what she means. Mine does look terrible compared to yours. Well, no harm done. Do you think you'll go back tomorrow night?"

Just look straight ahead and breath, Sophie told herself as she drove the two of them back to their respective homes.

"Mum, it was important for me to do this tonight. It was something I wanted to tick off my list and I can't go back now," Sophie eventually said after several minutes of silence while driving.

"I know. I'm sorry. You'll work something out though," Beryl replied, hoping the drama she'd caused in the class wouldn't result in her daughter reverting back to the old Sophie, who she could sense would still be able to easily scratch her way to the surface.

Chapter Eleven: Restaurant

Learning to cook was still staring at Sophie from the bucket list, mockingly. It was silly, she knew, but the voice at the back of her mind was telling her she couldn't do this. Everything she'd managed to tick off over the past few months was just a fluke. If she couldn't even complete a simple task like learning to cook, then it was inevitable life would return to the monotonous normality of before.

As she struggled to shut down the debate in her mind, willing herself to give it one more go, her mobile phone on the kitchen table vibrated twice before lying dormant again.

It was a beautiful spring morning, dry and fresh. Having breakfast with the door open into the garden on morning's like this were one of Sophie's favourite things. There was little noise other than the birds singing and the occasional light breeze making the roller blind tap gently against the kitchen window frame.

She picked her phone up and saw a text from Paris.

If you haven't already left, don't come into the bar this morning. Pretty please can you pick up a pair of shoes for me in London? Mya was supposed to be getting them, but she flaked out.

Sophie knew Paris wouldn't ask her to do something like this unless he was desperate. Thinking about it, being held up in the club's dark office on such a beautiful day wasn't appealing. A trip out on a mindless errand would be good to clear her head.

Sure thing, she wrote back. *Text me the details and I'll sort it.*

As well as an excuse to do something braindead, it would also be a good opportunity to tackle another point on the list. She pulled the notebook from her handbag on the floor beside the kitchen table and flicked through the tasks. She stopped turning the pages and focused on one that most people would surely find banal and scoff at. 'Eat in a restaurant alone'. How hard could that be?

Two hours later and Sophie was on a train into central London, the first time she'd be visiting the city on her own. This morning the trip seemed so simple. But then the realisation she would be wondering around the bustling city alone was playing on her mind and leading to second thoughts. She looked at the few people who were on the train with her – a mixture of elderly people taking day trips and mothers with young children.

London Victoria Station was busier than Sophie had imagined it would be. The train pulled into platform nineteen and exiting it proved to be difficult as a scrum of agitated commuters, eager to board the train, blocked her way.

"Excuse me," she said pitifully as people started boarding before she could step down onto the platform. "I'm trying to get off."

No one listened and Sophie had to slide her way through tight spaces in the wall of people. Feeling flustered and dishevelled, she finally made it to the ticket gates and tapped her bank card on the barrier to leave.

The station was buzzing with people, who were scattered across the concourse like errant geese. It was everyone for themselves and people were treading quick random paths to avoid colliding into one another.

Sophie's breathing began to quicken. Although the distance between her and the entrance to the tube station was only a couple of hundred meters, it might as well have been miles considering the number of people she'd have to avoid.

Maybe she could just turn around and get back on the train. Stop being an idiot, she told herself. And then after a deep breath made her way calmly to the Victoria line on the Underground and managed the two stops to Oxford Circus, with only a little discontent.

Once she'd surfaced from the dark, people-filled station on Oxford Street, Sophie was once again confronted by a horde of bodies. Instead of walking with purpose as they were in Victoria, now a large proportion of the crowds were idling along. It was a mixture of tourists and workers vying for space on the pavements and attempting to move in one way or another at different speeds.

Sophie stepped into the safety of a quiet shop doorway where she could tuck herself away from the bustle to tap the address of the shoe shop into Google Maps on her phone. It was just a fifteen-minute walk away, and a blue line came up on the screen showing that Sophie would be able to go straight down Oxford Street, before taking one left turn and a right into a narrow lane.

The smell of so many people living and working on top of each other added to the unpleasantness of the walk. She'd seen this street in pictures and thought it looked charming and magical, but in person it was stressful and unpleasant.

After navigating her way through the crowds for a while, Sophie finally reached the right shop which was called Stilts for Queens. It wasn't the glamorous outlet she'd been expecting. It consisted of a small dirty window with peeling paint around the frames and a glass door with a triangular wooden handle on it. No wonder Paris wanted Mya to get the shoes from this dump for her, Sophie thought.

Through the heavy door, however, the interior of the shop couldn't have been more of a contrast to the grimy outside. It was lit by bright white lights making it look as though the tiny grey window onto the street outside could let in more sunlight than possible.

Each of the shop walls were painted with full-length pictures of women in different shapes, sizes and colours. Shelves and units in the centre of the shop housed hundreds of pairs of immaculate shoes that had been carefully displayed to showcase their glittering and shimmering designs.

It was nothing like a typical shoe shop on the high street. Although the heels were clearly designed to be feminine, each pair on display looked to be around a size nine or ten. Some of the styles available also looked like they had been made for what her mother would call 'women of immoral means', Sophie thought to herself as she picked up a pair of thigh-high black patent leather boots.

"Can I help you?" a slender twenty-something wearing blue skinny jeans and a t-shirt cut just above his bellybutton asked with half concern.

"I'm here to pick something up for Ben..." Sophie realised she didn't actually know Paris's full boy name. But before she could even say anything else the assistant butted in.

"We don't have anything on hold for anyone named Ben, you must have the wrong shop."

"Sorry," said Sophie beginning to feel flustered. "I mean Paris Le Grand. She messaged me this morning asking if I would pick up a pair of shoes for her... Mya Ding-a-Ling was supposed to come, but she couldn't. So, do you have them?" she asked again while nervously wringing her hands.

"You know Paris Le Grand and Mya Ding-a-Ling," said the assistant, mouth wide open in awe.

"Errr. Yes, yes I do," Sophie answered, not really knowing why her affiliation with two drag queens was so important.

"I've heard so much about Sophisticats, but I've never been. I don't really leave the city that much, unless I go back home south to Cornwall. Have you been?"

"To, Cornwall? Once on a family day trip," Sophie answered, now confused.

"No, Sophisticats. Have you been to Paris Le Grand's club Sophisticats?"

"Ah, right. That makes more sense," she said, glad that the conversation wasn't taking some sort of awkward turn. "I'm actually the general manager there, Paris hired me a couple of months ago."

"That is amazing, I'd so love to go. Actually, I think I saw you on BBC Breakfast with them a few weeks back, you looked so nervous."

"So, the shoes." Sophie demanded with a little venom in her voice at the mention of her vulnerability on the tele.

"Right. Yes, sorry. It's just so amazing that you know Paris. I'm a drag queen too, but it's more like a hobby at the moment and I'd really love to get into it fulltime, you know, like Paris has. Do you think you could mention me?"

"Mention you?"

"Yeah, you know, tell Paris I'm a drag queen too."

"I'll see what I can do. But only if you get me the shoes, I've got things I need to get on with today."

"Of course. Sorry."

At that, the chipper assistant trotted off to the till at the back of the shop and deposited a box on the top which he'd taken from underneath the multicolour-sequinned desk.

"These are the ones. Came in especially from Italy, cost an absolute fortune – three thousand pounds...

but Paris likes good quality. She's already paid for them, so don't worry," he said in response to Sophie's mouth dropping at the mention of the price.

"Perfect. A bag would be nice too," she prompted as he stared at her, as though waiting for Sophie to say something else.

"I'll give you a bag – and will wave the ten pence price of it – if you promise to get Paris to call me," he stipulated, one hand on his hip and the other on the shoes, ready to stop Sophie from taking them until he got what he wanted.

"Fine. What's your name?"

"Bruce."

"Right, Bruce..."

"But my drag name is Tabatha Black."

"Ok. I promise to get Paris to call you. And I won't tell him you held his shoes as ransom so you could get the call. Now hand them over."

She snatched the shoes up and gave Bruce a death stare she thought Paris would approve of, before turning and leaving.

Once out of the shop, shoes safely by her side in a bag, it was time to find somewhere to eat so Sophie could finally tick something else off her list, not having done so since her night with Josh. Instead of walking back the way she came, she turned left out the shop and found herself on another main road lined with boutiques, cafés and restaurants. It was late afternoon and the sun was still high in the sky making it warm enough for people to eat on little bistro tables outside.

Most of the coffee shops were full of people drinking or enjoying the rest of their lunchtimes with a sandwich. It would have been easy enough to join them as many were sat on their own. It was more acceptable to dine and drink alone in a café, Sophie thought. But she wanted to do this properly. It would have to be no fewer than two courses and a glass of wine, she stipulated to herself.

There were so many unusual places she could choose from: Turkish, Polish, Ethiopian… Sophie had never really given other types of food much thought beyond the usual Chinese or Indian takeaways. But it didn't really matter as most of these restaurants had closed until the evening now the lunchtime rush was over.

On the corner of the street, however, was an Italian restaurant called Arborio. It had blue awnings and a few customer enjoying salads and white wine while sitting at the few tables that hugged its outside wall.

Sophie stood in front of the restaurant for a little while, pretending to read the framed hung on the wall next to the front door. It's just lunch, she told herself.

"Can I help you madam?" said a waiter with what sounded like a genuine Italian accent. He was wearing slim black trousers, a white shirt and a black apron that hung close to his body from his neck to just below the knee.

Sophie looked at the waiter who must have been in his mid-thirties. He had brown eyes and dark thinning hair that was swept backwards. His face was friendly, and he smiled as he asked Sophie: "A table for one, yes?"

Sophie nodded and followed the waiter into the restaurant. It was decorated with images of famous Italian cities. It looked on the verge of tacky. However, the atmosphere was warm and inviting and there weren't too many people eating.

"Will this suit madam?" the waiter asked and gestured to a table for two with a good view of the restaurant.

"Lovely," said Sophie and allowed the waiter to help take off her long grey duster jacket that she'd thrown over the top of her light blue skinny jeans that she wore with a cream fitted long-sleeve blouse and brown suede ankle boots.

"Now, I come back with the menu and some water for the table."

Quite comfortable that no one was watching and judging her, Sophie began to settle into the experience. Why had she made such a fuss about coming to eat out alone, she thought after ordering an insalata caprese to start and a big bowl of penne Luganica as well as a large glass of Grillo, a white wine grape Sophie hadn't heard of before, but had been suggested by the waiter.

Lunch went by without a fuss. She ended up having two glasses of wine and began enjoying herself so much that she reasoned this could be a once a month treat. There were very few times in her life, thought Sophie, when she had been waited on and could relax and read a book while someone else prepared and brought her food.

Bill paid, she thanked the waiter and gave him what she thought was an overgenerous tip of £10 and left.

Although her belly was full, the wine was kicking in and she couldn't remember how to get back to Oxford Circus for the tube to Victoria. The volume of people around her had started to become a struggle. It was quiet on some of the streets, but on others she was surrounded by what felt like thousands of people.

Everyone was in a rush, striding past her, giving Sophie barely enough time or room to manoeuvre out of their way and not crash into them. But even when she did manage to evade someone, she'd be faced with another person determined on getting to where they needed to be, making her change course again to avoid crashing into them.

Feeling flustered, panicked and claustrophobic, Sophie looked for a retreat so she could compose herself and work out where the tube was. She stood still in the middle of the street, meaning people now had to avoid her, which they did in their hundreds, parting like a torrent of water would against a large rock in the middle of a river, loudly tutting as they swerved away from her. She spotted a coffee shop on the other side of the road and headed towards it as quickly as she could.

She was now a refugee in Starbucks, peeping out through the floor to ceiling windows at the hell outside. Christ, why did I think I could do this she asked herself, wishing she'd gone back home straight away after picking Paris's shoes up. Or, better still, telling Paris she had too much on to run an errand for him.

"You can't stand in here without buying something, lovey," a Polish woman who worked in the coffee shop blurted.

"I'm sorry. I was just trying to work out how to get to the underground. It's my first time in London on my own and I thought I'd be fine, but there are just too many people coming at me from all directions, it's making me feel ill."

"Can't hack it, can you not?" the barista replied with a smirk on her face, eyeing the shopping bag Sophie was holding. "You bloody rich yummy mummies with your bags full of designer clothes think you can do anything, but you haven't had to work a day in your life and as soon as you find yourself in a little trouble, you think you can just waltz in somewhere to find a knight in shining armour. Well not in here you can't. 'Op it!'".

The stress of not knowing where she was, the panic of being surrounded by so many people and now having someone yell at her caused hot salty tears to build in Sophie's eyes. She could feel them stinging the brim of her bottom eyelid, but she was determined not to let a single drop fall, and willed herself to stop blinking in case one did.

It was clear the woman in the coffee shop could see just how weak Sophie was. Yes, she was dressed nicely and had looked as though she'd had a nice day out shopping. But really, she was pathetic. She had no right to be on an adventure, however small or mundane it was.

"Come on. I said get out," the worker pushed again, this time with a bigger smirk as she could see Sophie's eyes were about to relieve themselves of the tears still building up.

But then something else washed over Sophie. This woman didn't know who she was, she'd just assumed, because she was dressed nicely, that she was a rich hoity toity type with a husband, a nice home and nothing much to do other than shop or lead a life of leisure. Her tears were no longer being produced by fear or embarrassment, but rage.

"Who the hell do you think you are," she screeched at the top of her voice, stuttering a little in surprise of the volume. She also quelled a sob before continuing the assault, tightly gripping the bag with Paris's shoes in them.

"I'm not some rich wife from the suburbs. Not that I need to explain myself to you, but I've been working fulltime, as a single mum, for over a decade and if I feel a little overwhelmed by an unfamiliar experience, then I'm bloody well entitled to. Now, are you going to point me in the direction of the tube or are you going to continue to be a complete bitch?"

The few people seated at the tables in the coffee shop were now all looking at Sophie, as were the other servers behind the counter. The barista who had given her the hard time was standing, her face turning red with either anger or embarrassment. But, before Sophie could find out whether she was going to have her berating returned, one of the other customers stepped between the two of them.

"Hello," she said in a sickly-sweet voice. "I hear you're lost and need help finding the tube." She was dressed in a pink tea dress with a peach coloured cardigan and white trainers. The wrinkles on her face told Sophie she was probably in her early fifties, but the clothes looked as though they belonged to someone much younger.

"Well, obviously you heard that because I've just shouted it at this complete cow," Sophie blurted, rage still prickling under the surface of her skin.

"There's no need to be quite so rude. I know you're stressed out, but I'm only trying to help you," the woman, who was a foot shorter than Sophie, replied with the same sugary tone as before.

"I'm sorry. I've just had a long day and I'd really like to get home. Please, just point me in the right direction to the tube and I'll be out of here."

"Don't worry petal, I'll take you myself. I'm just off shift, I work over the road, you see. I'm going to Victoria train station myself."

Just like that; from being completely out of sorts, berated by a barista and after screaming at her, someone was being kind.

Sophie didn't feel like talking as the woman led her back to Oxford Circus station, but that didn't seem to matter to her new companion who droned on and on about how nasty some people in the city were. "It never used to be like this, mind," she said while they both stepped out of the path of an angry looking businessman talking on his mobile.

"No. People used to be quite friendly. You could ask anyone for help, and they would do their best. Now no one could give a damn. But, then again, people do have their off days."

"Uh huh," said Sophie, only half listening, her eagerness to get out of the city and back home taking up most of her attention.

"Righto, this is us. I'm going to go and grab a coffee, if you think you can make it from here yourself that is. You need the Victoria line south two stops. Cheerio."

It was a short trip on the tube back to Victoria. Another half-hour train ride and Sophie was at her local station, where she had parked the car earlier that day.

She'd give Paris the shoes in the morning, rather than dropping them at the club that evening. She was tired after the ordeal and didn't fancy speaking to anyone. Right now, Sophie just wanted to get home and bask in the joy of ticking another task off her list.

Chapter Twelve: Mechanical Beast

Mundane to many it might be, but the thrill and liberation Sophie felt after eating at a restaurant in London alone, as well as giving some busybody barista an earful, had given her a buzz. She'd accomplished something all on her own and wanted her next kick, like an addict.

Her hands itched with the need to manufacture another hit as she sat at her laptop in the club's office. It was just before five in the afternoon and Sophie was waiting for Paris to arrive so she could him a handover from the day and leave for home.

"Yoo-hoo," she heard from the door. "Sorry I'm late, I was a little longer at the beauticians, apparently my eyebrows were more unruly than I thought. Anyway, enough about me, I want to plan another midweek event to see if we can get Wednesday's sales up. Any ideas?"

This could be interesting. Sophie began to think about the things she had yet to tick off the list and remembered something about a bucking bronco. "Perfect," she said aloud rather than thinking it.

"Sorry hun, what's perfect, have you thought of anything?"

"Oh, I was just thinking of something I saw in a magazine the other day, it was in one of those event ones Felix signed us up to, or maybe I saw it on the tele..." she gave a little pause to think about how to make the idea strong enough for Paris to want it to happen.

"Well, are you going to push me off this cliff hanger or do I have to jump?" he joked, breaking Sophie's concentration.

"What about something like The Big Gay Hayride?"

"I'm not with you. Is this a night for the club or are you suggesting we go to some dirty farm and ride around on the back of a tractor?"

"Ok, maybe that's not a very good name, but I was thinking about some sort of cowboy and cowgirl night. The girls could dress up in denim hot pants, dresses and other things like that. We can get haybales and theme the drinks, maybe even have one of those mechanical bulls, but see if we can get one that's a little bluer, you know, in a rude shape or something."

Paris looked in silence at his employee for a few minutes, which Sophie had seen him do a few times before deciding on something. An outsider would think he was confused, but Sophie knew is brain was just processing and putting the pieces of something together to see how it would work. Only when he'd built it in his brain would he make up his mind. This one was taking a little longer to click into place though, which could mean he wasn't into it.

Before losing the chance of an easy win, she chipped in again: "And we could even get some muscly topless cowboys to dance, you know, like in that Coyote Ugly film where she dances on the bar."

Sophie thought she could see the attractive muscled cowboys line dancing into Paris's head and just like that, his blank thinking face turned into a smile.

"I think that's a great idea. We can see about getting some hen parties in or something, maybe send out an email and put something on our Facebook page too. Sophie, I think this could be a great night."

Relieved, Sophie just had to wait a little longer now until she could tick the next thing off the list that was tucked away safely in her handbag by her desk.

"Look, I know you're due to finish at five, but do you think you could start looking into the bucking bronco now, I don't know how easy it would be to get one... and don't worry about a dirty one, let's go more traditional – we are a classy establishment after all."

Did she mind? Of course not. She'd quite happily stay glued to her desk for the rest of the night, making phone calls and sending out emails just to make sure she could get her next hit.

"Not at all. I'll search for a few numbers now and that way I'll be ready to start pinning one down first thing in the morning. Should I drop Felix and email about it too, he may have some contacts?"

"Great idea, I keep forgetting we're paying him to do things like this. I think the girls are going to love it, especially Mya, she's always trying to get away with short shorts on stage, but now I guess I'll finally have to give in."

It was as though Paris saying her name was some sort of an official announcement and Mya Ding-a-Ling waltzed into the room, not yet dressed in her drag for the evening ahead. She unslung a large handbag from her shoulder and draped herself onto the leather sofa in the corner of the office. "What's this about short shorts? You know how I feel about tight denim, it leaves little to the imagination. Tell me what you were talking about, don't toy with a poor girl's emotions."

Although she was joking, Mya put on a convincing performance of exasperation. She was the more dramatic of the club's drag queens and had been comfortably part of the House of Paris Le Grand for several years now. She was short and round and, while most of the other girls in the club had to pad their bras to give them a cleavage, Mya had enough of her own to make a convincing pair of boobs.

Sophie ignored the commotion of more drag queens in the background as they came in to see her and Paris before getting ready for their shows. She wanted to make sure this next task could be ticked off as successfully as the previous one had, so she blocked out all the noise and set about searching for bucking broncos available for hire in the area.

There were hundreds of strange offers online, and she came across several types of what her mother would call 'adult' variations of the mechanical bull, but as Paris said, it should be in keeping with the theme. One of the websites for a local company offering various styles of what she wanted was still open, so she called the number at the bottom of the page and, just like that, got what she needed. Everything was booked in for the coming Wednesday, which meant they had five days to get other things sorted.

After several early starts and an equal number of late finishes and some favours called in from their events consultant Felix, Sophie and the girls had pulled together something that resembled a bar that would fit comfortably in America's Wild West.

Great big panels of clinker board had been brought in to make the walls of the bar look like a saloon from an old cowboy film. Sophie had ordered a wagonload of haybales which had been dotted around long tables in place of their usual café-style seating and the acts were all dressed as cowgirls, apart from Paris who had been inspired by a madam from a Wild West brothel and wore a revealing dress with cowboy boots.

The final touch was yet to arrive, but would be coming in a matter of minutes. It needed to be installed quickly, thought Sophie, because Sophisticats would be opening soon and the bar had been fully booked out by parties. As soon as they had sent out the first email and posted about the event on Facebook, the bookings came in thick and fast. Hen parties, football teams and groups of people who just wanted to let their hair down on a Wednesday had all reserved spaces at the long tables or bought tickets. It was sold out, which Paris was exceptionally happy about.

The bucking bronco was a pull to the event, but the main attraction, Paris told the girls, was them and their performances. They had worked hard creating a set together to fit with the evening's theme, with most of them coming in earlier for rehearsals before they had to get ready and perform their usual acts that evening.

And of course, as requested by Paris, the muscular half-clothed cowboys they'd hired from an agency had to be incorporated into every routine. Inevitably, this involved the girls straddling the poor boys and riding them like horses across the stage while miming to songs by artists like Shania Twain, Dolly Parton and Patsy Cline. But the half-clad men took it in good humour and Sophie made sure they were comfortable before the choreography was agreed.

A loud buzzing made Sophie jump while she was arranging metal lanterns across the bar, it was the backdoor. The cowboy boots she'd bought to wear that evening, with a pair of skinny dark denim jeans and a pink and white gingham blouse, were already hurting her feet. Despite the pain, she ran excitedly to the greet the delivery, which was being pulled in on a dolly behind three burly men with beer guts, who huffed and puffed until it was in position in the centre of the club.

To Sophie it was a glorious site. She'd never though a hulking great big shiny mechanical bull with its brown plastic covering and furry head with big plastic eyes would ever incite any form of excitement. But the thought of ticking another item from her list was wildly bubbling around her brain.

She watched as the delivery men set it up and plugged it in to ensure all the controls worked. She waited eagerly as they methodically carried out their tests. Then she quietly studied the technique of the one who rode it to make sure everything worked properly. An enclosure of padded walls and thick plastic-covered foam mats were also placed around the bull, so when people did fall off, they wouldn't hurt themselves.

"Is it you who needs to sign for this?" one of the delivery men said from behind Sophie, who jumped from her absorption in what was happening in the middle of the club.

With a nod, she took the clipboard from him and signed on the line where he'd pointed. She then tried to listen to the instructions he was giving her about any damage, the health and safety precautions and that the right insurance policy had to be in place because the hiring company couldn't be held responsible for any injuries or accidents.

"And Alan here will be staying to look after the controls. Do you have any other questions?" he asked at the end of his long list of dos and don'ts.

"Yes, of course. How fast does it go and what's the best way to stay on? I don't want to make a fool of myself when I have a go."

"Well, that's an industry secret, I'm afraid, I can't really tell you," he winked, which gained him a blank response from Sophie. "There's no method, really," he said shortly after, realising his joke hadn't landed. "Just hold on tight and try to move with the beast, but I've yet to see anyone stay on for a long while."

"Can I have a go now?" she asked, like a child wanting to pet a stranger's puppy.

"Sure, climb up and sit with your legs either side as far forward as possible and hold tightly on to this strap."

With a boost from the delivery man, she sat up on the mechanical beast, and like in the movies, held her left hand up high to signal her readiness while her right hand gripped the leather strap at the bull's neck as tightly as she could.

"Fire her up, Alan... hold on tight!"

The bull juddered into life and twitched forwards a little as though slowly waking up from a long sleep. But the small jerks steadily increased into stronger lurches as it moved backwards, forwards and to its side before completing a full turn, allowing Sophie to take in the entire bar.

As the bull spun back to its starting position, Paris and the other girls appeared from the stage door, curious to see the hubbub.

"You go girl! Ride that bull!" Mya shouted between letting out long whistles by using her fingers in her mouth.

"Oh my god hun, what on earth..." Paris began, but then her shocked face cracked into one of hysterics. "Make it go faster, she can handle it!"

"No, this is fast enough for me, thank you," Sophie shouted at Alan, who pushed one thumb into the air and then said: "Alright, go faster then. You got it."

A violent lurch from the beast almost unseated Sophie who had so far managed to remain relatively still. The thing swung round faster, spinning and tilting at odd angles. Oh god, I'm going to pee myself.

"I said that was fast enough, slow it down."

Alan cupped his hand around one ear and gave another thumbs up. "If you're sure. We don't normally do this for first timers... but you're the boss. Faster it is."

Sophie let out a scream as the bull, with her still holding on for dear life, twisted sideways and leaned so far from one side to the other that her head and body almost touched the mats. With each angry flick and gyration, Sophie felt the beast trying to dislodge her, but she held on firmly as the room spun faster around her, bringing Paris and the girls into shot, out of shot, into shot. Faster and faster she spun, leaned, rose and fell, making it feel as though the organs inside her were churning around inside her, stopped only by bone and skin.

She let out a shriek as the grip of her legs around the beast and her hand on the leather strap began to weaken. "I'm gunna fall!" she screamed to the girls who were now bent double with laughter as their friend's flailing body finally released itself from the bull and flew to the outer edge of the ring, slamming into one of the padded walls with a thud.

Slightly dazed, she opened her eyes and first saw the bull's operator Alan and one of the delivery men standing over her. Oh god, I hope I haven't peed myself, she thought and moved her hips a little to see if she could feel anything without having to use her hand.

"Oh Christ, what happened?" she asked, the room spinning a little and her vision still not fully focused as a blurred Paris in full drag hovered over her.

"Well, hun, you were riding the thing like a pro – pretty impressive, actually – and then you flew through the air. Not very gracefully either, I might add. I'd liken the whole thing to a drunk pigeon attempting to stay aloft in hurricane winds. Quite sad in the end, really."

"Charming," Sophie replied, her pride bruised.

"Are you hurt though? You landed with such a thud, must have hurt. What were you thinking, telling him to go faster?" Paris said, thrusting her pointed finger towards Alan who was back behind the control booth, unbothered about the commotion and now fascinated with something on his phone.

"I don't think I'm hurt, maybe a little bruised. And what do you mean? I wasn't asking him to go faster at all. When you told him to turn it up I said it was fast enough and then I asked him to slow it down!"

"Oh, well that makes sense now. The look on your face each time he knocked the power up didn't really say you were loving it. I just thought you were being brave." Paris found it funny and wasn't helping Sophie to feel less self-conscious about the antics and started cracking up. "You should have seen your face towards the end, I can't even describe it. And then when you flew off, I swear you were air born for a good ten seconds before hitting the ground."

"I'm glad I've brightened your day, now help me up and make sure that stupid man behind the controls doesn't ramp the damn bull up so high tonight, he'll end up breaking someone's neck."

With a hand from Paris and the still concerned delivery man, Sophie was hoisted up on to her feet and escorted to the office where she sat for a little while. What on earth was I thinking? She questioned herself. You're a forty-four-year-old woman. Riding a mechanical bull in a drag club is not what you're supposed to be doing at your age.

But then she stopped chastising herself, looked around and pulled the notebook with the scrawlings of her bucket list from her handbag and placed a neat tick next to it, smiling with a little pride when she closed it.

The question now, was what to do next? Each of the things she'd ticked off so far seemed easy once completed, but the remaining tasks were looking more difficult, and some impossible.

Getting a mechanical bull into the bar had been easy to manufacture, but how on earth was she going to make something like a whirlwind romance happen? She couldn't exactly order a man online to come and wine and dine her, could she? It would be handy, but a little desperate, she thought.

Although, after another look at the list, she quickly settled on the next task.

Chapter Thirteen: Thomas

Thomas was in his bedroom at his mum's house. It felt unfamiliar as he'd been there so little over the past few months, which made it feel unfamiliar. It was the Easter Holidays and his dad had suggested he spend some time with Sophie, rather than dossing around at his place.

It was Friday and his mum was at work. She'd left the house every day that week before Thomas had woken up and came back home late, making her youngest son feel avoided. Tonight, though, Sophie had promised to be home earlier. They could have a takeaway and watch something good on the tele together, she told him.

But it was now almost seven in the evening and Thomas hadn't heard from her. While he was annoyed and a little hurt by what he thought was a snub, it didn't surprise him. Sophie hadn't been a constant presence throughout Thomas's and Ralph's lives, and waiting for her now brought back memories of his childhood.

Sophie never had what anyone would consider a highflying career. Every job she'd done was somewhere near the bottom rung of the hierarchy. Despite this, she was rarely at home. When Thomas and Ralph got up for school, their mum would still be in bed. Their dad would take a coffee in for her and maybe her sons would go in to say goodbye before Carl walked them both to school in time for the bell to ring at ten-to-nine.

At the end of the day, Thomas and Ralph would be brought back to the house by a friend's parent and their dad would have dinner on the table while Sophie was still at work. She wouldn't be home for bedtime either, and so during the week they saw their mum for no more than half-an-hour.

Things differed little on the weekends and holidays. Sophie would often isolate herself from the family. She would either clean the house from top to bottom, scolding her sons if they played in their rooms and "made a mess" after they'd been tidied.

She would sit on the sofa and read or watch tele while Ralph, Thomas and Carl made their own fun. On summer days, especially over the school holidays, Carl would take his sons to the local woods. It was a twenty-minute walk up a steep main road, down a farm track and up a grassy hill, which usually held livestock.

Thomas would carry an old clear plastic bowl that once housed a beloved pet goldfish named Spooky. Ralph would usually be in charge of the fishing nets and their dad would smoke a thin cigar, which all three of them knew was taboo and so it should therefore not be mentioned to Sophie.

Once they'd navigated the cow-filled hill, they'd take it in turns to step over the stile, which stopped the livestock from getting into the woods. On the other side was what felt like a magical place. Thomas knew he was surrounded by all kinds of adventure and possible mystery. There were at least three ponds in the woods, but the third was the one they all wanted to get to. It was the furthest away – at least an hour's walk for their little legs – and was filled with newts and frogs, which they'd come to catch and look at, before being told by their dad to return them.

The three of them would stare into the water and dip in their nets, hoping to scoop out a creature to look at. Their dad was the best at it though, with Ralph and Thomas rarely catching anything. But they would try for hours.

After their fill of hunting little creatures, they would then clamber over fallen trees and walk so far up the surrounding hills that they would be able to see right across their hometown. This is when Carl would point to different parts and explain their significance, but it meant nothing to his two sons who, at the time, were no older than five or six.

But then the night would draw in and the warmth of the sun would fade, signalling the need to return before it got too dark to see their way back out. Thomas would be the one who'd panic about walking in the woods at night. Even though he knew nothing bad would happen, he would frequently ask his dad if they were lost.

Yet, with each step he took closer to home Thomas would feel the enchantment of their adventure fade. There were no more newts or frogs to catch and no fallen trees to climb. They would be going back to the house where the atmosphere was far from fun and magical.

After such an outing, they would usually return to their mother who would be sitting on the sofa, legs curled up and engrossed in a soap on the tele. She wouldn't ask how their trip was, what they got up to or why they had taken Spooky's old fishbowl with them. The only thing she would notice, if they hadn't been careful enough, was if they had stained their clothes or not.

Although their childhood had been darkened by Sophie's peculiar approach to motherhood, she did show love in her own way. Their home was always spotless; she would always kiss her boys before they left for school or went to bed; and Sophie would always tell Thomas and Ralph she loved them.

Yes, his mother had been late home this evening and had spent little time with Thomas while he was staying with her this week, but he had noticed a difference in her. She was no longer shuffling around in baggy jeans and jumpers and there was the extraordinary regular occurrence of a smile – something she'd worn so infrequently when her sons were younger.

His mum had changed and because Thomas's visits with her were uncommon these days, it was a shock for him to see this new mum. The mother he knew as a child wasn't the one around now. This person was who he wanted as a kid. She was happy, laughy and engaging. So, for all he felt Sophie had neglected him this week, Thomas had less resentment for her now compared with the mum from his childhood.

These thoughts had crossed Thomas's mind every day of the Easter holidays while he was staying in his old bedroom. He was due to return to his dad's on Sunday morning, so had decided to make dinner for Sophie as a special treat. He knew not to start it for the time she had said she'd be home and waited an hour longer instead.

It was now approaching half-seven and he heard his mum's car pull up on the driveway before the keys in the door signalled her return.

"Tom, I'm so sorry I'm late. We were one person down tonight and I had to find cover before I left. Oh, you've started dinner," she said putting her keys and bag on the table in the hallway. "I am so sorry, I was going to get us a takeaway."

"It's ok. I thought I'd cook something a bit nicer and healthier than a Chinese anyway. It's only pasta, but I've made it before. It tastes nice."

So, the pair sat down in front of the tele and ate their pasta without a word to one another. Thomas knew his mum needed half-an-hour or so to relax before she would acclimatise to being at home and in someone else's company.

"That was wonderful, son," she said to him with a wide-eyed smile as she took his empty bowl and used fork. "I'll sort the dishes out. Should I bring in some chocolate for dessert?"

Thomas nodded his appreciation at the prospect of chocolate and waited for his mum to come back into the room with a small bar of Dairy Milk each.

"I'm sorry I haven't been around much this week. I thought I'd be able to take a day or two off so we could spend some time together, but things at the club have been busier than we thought they would be."

"It's ok. I know you're busy."

"Well, perhaps we can go into town tomorrow and I'll buy you something nice. Do you need anything for college – clothes, books, anything?"

"I wouldn't mind a new pair of shoes," Thomas answered, perking up at the thought of some Vans. "And maybe we could go somewhere nice for lunch? I'll be going back to dad's on Sunday morning, so tomorrow will be our last full day together."

"I know, it's a shame we've hardly seen each other. But let's do that tomorrow. I'll treat you and then take us both somewhere nice for food."

Some idle chitchat followed, with Thomas asking how his mother's day was and Sophie returned the query, learning that her son was studying hard for his A levels. He wanted to go to Manchester University like his older brother, but fancied studying English or journalism.

Usually Sophie would try to push Thomas into a subject that he'd be certain to get a decent job with after graduation, like science or maths. But she had realised in recent months how important it was to do something that made you happy. However, she did give her opinion on the matter, saying she'd heard journalism was a tough industry to get a decent job in and that the salaries were notoriously low. She also pointed out that, while English was a great subject and could offer many more opportunities than journalism, Thomas should consider what he could do with such a degree outside of teaching.

"Mum?"

"Yes Tom."

"Why are you so much happier now? You weren't like this when we were kids. You're smiling a lot more and you don't wear your baggy jeans and scraggy jumpers anymore."

Sophie thought on the question or a little. She hadn't been the type of mother Beryl had been to, nor had she been the sort you'd see in films or on television shows. Her style was more about making sure there was enough money coming into the house; that their home was clean and tidy; and that the family always looked loved. This strategy had given her something to focus on other than the black hole that had hounded her entire life. The focus had helped her get through one day at a time and pretend that she was completely happy achieving what she thought she was supposed to.

But looking back it was clearly the wrong thing to do. She had never really been happy and that had clearly impacted Thomas. He didn't come around that often and their relationship, although completely amicable, wasn't the one he had with his father.

"Well," she started. "I've decided to do things a bit differently. All those things I did when you and your brother were younger were because that's what I

211

thought I had to do to make myself and other people happy. But I know now that wasn't right and I'm trying to do it another way. I hope you'll be able to see and feel that things are better for me now."

Chapter Fourteen: Kilt

Speaking to Thomas about their relationship and hearing him say how much she'd changed made Sophie ever more determined to keep cracking on with the list. Because of that, and after embarrassing herself in front of the girls in the club on the bucking bronco, she'd decided to take on something she deemed to be a little safer in the sense that the likelihood of her being flung across the room by something was slim.

Rarely had she travelled outside of the town where she'd grown up. Despite her mother's adventurous past and the fact her doctor father had been well off, the family hadn't ventured much further than seaside breaks in the likes of Brighton. As a grown up, she'd never been on holiday abroad and had never taken up offers of girls' trips away to Benidorm or other monstrous destinations.

When she'd married Carl, he'd suggested taking the boys away somewhere abroad, but Sophie, rightly in her mind, pointed out that they shouldn't be spending money on vacations. Mostly this was because she didn't want to leave the safety of her routines, and quite early on into their marriage she'd realised being with Carl was a mistake, so the thought of creating happy memories with him seemed unfair.

But now, this powerful little list gave her a reason to do something daring and adventurous. It wasn't really a feeling of having permission, but more of a drive to follow a new path that she'd just discovered and now felt the need to continue down, with each step she'd so far taken showing her something new.

She had an idea. Technically it wasn't going abroad, but she'd have to get on a plane, which Sophie had never done before, and Scotland was another country, so it would be reasonable to say it was going abroad. The itching sensation she got when on the verge of planning to tick something from her list began to take over her fingers as she picked up her phone from the kitchen table where she was sat having breakfast.

Edinburgh had been somewhere she was interested in after watching a documentary about the city on the tele a few years ago. The idea that it had transformed itself hundreds of years ago from slum-like dwellings into a vibrant and thriving metropolis stuck with Sophie. It was almost as if it had two personalities – the old and the new.

Thinking about the programme, she remembered how the lively, young historian presenting it had explored the underbelly of a city, where death, plagues and poverty had led to the need for the city's rebirth.

While it was going to be an adventure, it wasn't one she could do alone, there was no question about that. Exploring Manchester with Paris had been fun, until she'd had a minor meltdown about Ralph potentially being gay. She'd just ask Paris, surely there's be something for him to do there; some drag clubs where he could seek out new acts perhaps. It wouldn't hurt to ask.

Hey, thinking of going to Edinburgh for a midweek break, fancy coming along? Could maybe find some acts for the club?

She text, the phone still in her hand while scrolling through her search results of what to do in the city.

Sophie washed her breakfast dishes in the sink, dried and put them away before she left to go to work. The phone, still on the table, buzzed into life. The name on the screen said Paris was calling.

"Hello, I take it you read my message?"

"You want to go to Edinburgh?"

"Yeah, I think it could be fun. I've always wanted to visit."

"You've never flown", he said plainly.

"No."

"And you want me to come with you, to look at drag acts for the club?"

"Yes."

"You don't have any sons at Edinburgh University who you may discover are leading a secret life, do you?"

"Oh, ha ha. Very funny. Do you want to come with me or not?"

"Well, I've never been to Scotland, but I've heard lots of good things about the nightlife in Edinburgh. Maybe we could go next week?"

That was easy, Sophie thought with relief, as she went into a little more detail on the phone about what they could do together on the trip. As she started to talk about where they could stay and how long they might like to spend up there, the house phone rang.

"What's that noise?" Paris asked as the shrill sounded from the hallway.

"It's the landline, I need to go and get it. It's probably my mother."

"I haven't heard anyone say that in forever. It's like being in the olden days isn't it? I didn't know people still used them."

"Oh, you are very funny today aren't you. I need to go. I'll see you at work later, maybe you could come in on time so we can book our trip."

"Now who's funny? See you later hun."

The offensive ringing of the white plastic phone got louder as she walked into the hallway while speaking to Paris. Beryl wouldn't ring off until Sophie picked up the receiver, she knew her daughter didn't leave the house until eight. So, Sophie took her time to gather her coat and bags, ready to leave when done speaking with her mother.

Finally, the vile noise ended as she lifted the receiver to her ear. "Sweetie, darling. I thought you were dead, why did you let it ring for so long? It could have been an emergency you know."

"Sorry mum. I'm just about to leave for work, can you make this a quick one?"

"Darling, we hardly ever speak, and you'd like to rush one of our very rare conversations?"

"Sorry mum, but you know you can call me on my mobile anytime... we could have more frequent and longer chats if you did that."

"I don't like the things. Always glued to people's hands. They're turning the youth into zombies. And some of the elderly too. Betty at the Stich n Bitch is always scrolling through her faces and twits, she showed me this video of a cat being scared by a cucumber once and..."

"Mum, I've really got to go to work before I'm late and I'll need to stay back a bit tonight too," Sophie butted in before Beryl could go into one of her diatribes.

"Oh, sorry sweetie. I forgot. What do you need to stay back for?"

With a sigh she told her mother about the plans to go to Edinburgh in a few days' time, but immediately regretted it as excited stories about her mother's time in the city as a young woman were recounted.

"Daaarling, I had so much fun in Edinburgh and I haven't been back for years and years. I was there long before I met your father. Oh, it would be wonderful to go back again, but I've never really had the opportunity or anyone to go with. All of my old biddy friends aren't much up to adventures these days."

Sophie said nothing and listened as the telephone line buzzed gently, filling the silence while she thought of how to dissuade her waiting mother from wanting to join them on the trip, but brain freeze got the better of her.

"Well, we would have to leave incredibly early."

"That's fine by me, sweetie, us oldies are usually up at the crack of dawn."

"There'll be lots of late nights."

"I just won't take my sleeping pills."

"We'll probably be moving at a quick pace."

"I'm as spritely as you or Paris, sweetie."

"We'll be visiting lots of gay bars."

"I love the gays! Did I ever tell you about the time I met Elton John? I think he's a Dame or a Sir now, well..."

"Fine, mum, you can come with us," Sophie butted in before another story was reeled out. "I'll call you tonight to let you know what the plans are."

"I could just meet you and Paris at work to arrange it there?"

"No," Sophie said forcefully, before checking her tone and repeating it more neutrally. "No, it's fine. I'll just sort everything out, Paris will probably want to put us up in a suite and put it down for work so it will be cheaper."

***

Gatwick Airport was noisy and busy. It was a blustery day and Paris's distaste for early mornings was showing. He was wrapped in a big puffy parker jacket, wearing jogging bottoms and Ugg Boots. Not his usual glam self. But Sophie didn't dare point this out in case he gave her an ear bashing.

They'd all stayed at Sophie's the night before to travel the half-hour to the airport silently in a taxi together. Beryl, on the suggestion of Sophie, as she knew Paris was likely to throttle her chatty mother at this time of the morning, was sat in the front of the car making animated chitchat with the driver. At first, he didn't seem keen on being a pensioner's distraction, but he soon warmed up to her, answering questions and listening to her stories with a polite interest.

Security, although quiet, was a nightmare thanks to Beryl, who insisted on being frisked by a male guard, despite there being no need for it.

"Make an old lady's day," she pleaded with the staff at the scanners, much to Paris's amusement and Sophie's mortification.

"That will be me one day," said Paris, nudging Sophie with his elbow as they collected their bags and put their coats back on.

"I just hope it's not genetic. I'd like to say it's her age, but she's always been like this," Sophie muttered while gathering no fewer than fifteen pieces of her mother's jewellery from one of the grey trays that has slid down the metal rollers, fresh from the security scanner.

"I hope you two are talking about a Champagne breakfast, come on, my treat," Beryl shouted from the security desk, where she'd just finished being patted down. "I was hoping there'd be a strip search," she said with genuine disappointment and sauntered over to Paris and Sophie.

"Come on mother, put your things back on. I told you not to wear so much jewellery."

"Darling, a woman should always look her best before having so much contact with a gentleman."

"Poor man didn't know what to do with himself," Paris chuckled, nodding towards the young member of security staff who looked flushed in the face having drawn the short straw.

"It would do you the world of good to be patted down by a young man, Sophie. Very invigorating," said Beryl as she put her arms through the long purple felt coat Sophie was helping her back into, before securing an emerald green turban on her head.

"Right, I said Champagne breakfast. Come on then, keep up. We've only got an hour before the flight and I'd like at least two glasses to see me through."

Struggling to keep pace with the spritely pensioner, Paris and Sophie followed in Beryl's wake as she meandered through the shoppers in duty free, who moved quickly out of her way as she loudly announced, "elderly lady coming through, watch out, come on young man, move out of my way!".

Eventually they were all seated at a long bar in the centre of the departure area, with Beryl eagerly people watching, commenting on who was likely to be doing what and where they were probably off to.

She tapped her hand loudly on the bar, telling the server they wanted a bottle of fizz and a breakfast menu and that Paris and Sophie could choose anything they wanted to eat. "My treat!"

Sophie nursed a glass of Champagne while they waited for their gate to appear on the screen was fixed to a tall column close to where they were sitting. Paris had now warmed up to a near human state and was happily chatting to Beryl, laughing at her jokes as she told him stories about Sophie's childhood.

"Once she came home from school and announced she'd made a best friend," Beryl said between sips of Champagne and mouthfuls of smoked salmon. "Her father and I were amazed and thrilled. She was a quiet child, never made any friends and always quite gloomy. So we asked who this new friend was and when we could meet them. 'Now, he's here with me now', she said with one of her rare smiles. So, Bernard and I looked around the room, in the hallway and out the front door. We couldn't see anyone. 'Where's your new friend, dear?' we asked. Well, she pulled out a jaggered piece of rock from her pocket, looked us firmly in the eyes and said, 'this is Borsi, my new best friend'."

Paris had unfortunately taken a sip of his drink at the punchline and sprayed it with a loud cackle over the bar and onto the server standing behind, drenching her clothes with the expensive liquid. Most people would be apologetic, but Paris and Beryl laughed harder. While Sophie tried to be the more mature of the group, the scenario was infectious and she too began to laugh at what had happened.

"I'm so, so sorry," said Paris eventually to the woman behind the bar, offering a napkin. "I really couldn't control myself. Really, I am very sorry." But she just scowled and thundered off to the other side of the bar.

After another embarrassing story from Sophie's childhood, Beryl paid the bill and Paris, now feeling guilty, left a hefty tip for the still drenched server. Their departure gate was showing on the large screen at the centre of the terminal's main waiting area and they all shuffled tipsily to where they needed to be, wheeling their suitcases behind them.

**

The eight o'clock flight landed in Edinburgh before half-past nine. The trio hadn't drunk anything more on the plane and slept off what they'd shared at the Champagne bar so deeply that morning they had to be nudged awake by a flight attendant who told them they were now in Edinburgh.

It was a short walk through Edinburgh's small airport to the outside world. It was chilly and dry, the perfect weather to explore a new place, thought Sophie. They each struggled with the ticket machine so they could get a tram into the centre of the city to find their hotel, where Paris had paid for an early check-in so they could freshen up before adventuring.

Still feeling a little groggy from their boozy nap though, there was little conversation on the tram journey. While Paris flicked through emails and social media on his phone and Beryl snoozed again, Sophie looked out of the window.

The tram whirred gracefully along its tracks, gliding almost silently by green fields, modern office blocks and Murrayfield Stadium.

The scenery was pleasant, even when the tram moved into the more built up areas. Apart from the odd block of old-fashioned concrete flats and the occasional scrapyard, it was a lovely journey. But in no time, they were finally trundling through the more built up areas of grand old buildings with their grand sandstone blocks that gleamed golden in the morning sunshine. Long rows of the buildings looked out on to green parks or more rows of handsome terraces that housed shops, restaurants and people's homes.

As they rounded another corner, Edinburgh Castle came into view causing Sophie to gasp. She'd never seen a castle as close as she was to this one. It looked strong and fierce stood on a what she knew to be an extinct volcano.

Outside, the streets were getting busier with people as the tram continued to move further into the city. Locals, businesspeople and tourists were all striding up and down the strong grey stone paths on their way to work or elsewhere. Along the way a pre-recorded female Scottish voice announced which stations they were approaching and what was local to each of them. After around half-an-hour, they reached the final stop, which was theirs.

York Place was in Edinburgh's New Town and consisted of buildings just as grand as the others Sophie had seen on the tram journey so far. She tapped her mother awake and nudged Paris to distract him from his phone. "We're here, you said the hotel was in York Place, right?"

"Huh, oh that was quick," mumbled Paris, putting the phone back into his pocket and looking around to see that the landscape had somehow miraculously changed from the modern one at the airport to a more elegant, historic setting. "It's supposed to be a minute's walk from this stop," he said, questioningly while getting his phone out again to check the map.

"Well, I think we should get off now otherwise we'll end up back where we started," Sophie said, grabbing her case and her mother's. "Come on, we can work out where we are from the platform."

Just as Paris had thought, the hotel was very close to the tram stop. Sophie was thrilled to see it was a sandstone building like the others on the road and not a modern metal and glass one. It rose tall into the sky, at least five or six floors, she thought, and had a grand set of steps to the entrance with a gold and blue checkerboard tile platform at the top.

Inside, they were faced with a handsome mahogany staircase with a navy-blue tartan carpet runner that stretched all the way to the top of the building and across every landing. On their right was the hotel bar and restaurant, which was decked out in furniture sympathetic to the building's age and to their left was the check-in desk.

Paris gave their details to the receptionist, who snapped his fingers for two people to come and help with the bags. They then followed their bags into a lift, which clicked and clacked up to the top floor of the hotel. When the lift doors opened, they found themselves in a small entrance hall with a set of mahogany double doors at the end.

"This is the penthouse," said one of the young Scottish men carrying their bags. "We'll let you in and show you around so you can all get settled."

The suite took up the entire floor and was bigger than Sophie's house. It had four bedrooms – each with its own bathroom – a living room, kitchen, dining room and study. Beryl was the first to voice her approval, saying how they would all be living like royalty for the next few days.

"Balloch, your butler, will be through in a second to make sure you're all settled, he's on hand to fetch anything you might need, as well as to make theatre and restaurant reservations, but you might like to dine in your suite this evening so you can all be well rested for whatever adventure awaits in the morning," the bellboy said and closed the doors behind him as he left.

"Paris, this is way too much for us. Please let us pay our share, it was my idea to come to Edinburgh and this must be costing you an absolute fortune," Sophie asked, knowing he would refuse to take any money from her and Beryl, which he'd made clear when booking the hotel.

"Nonsense, I know a few people here, so I've been given a very good rate. Anyway, it's midweek and not prime tourist season, so it's likely to have been sat empty if we weren't here. Now, which room should I take?"

Paris turned on his heel and inspected each of the bedrooms, the doors to which were just of the lounge and wide open. They were identical in size but had been decorated differently. One was dark and relaxing, with deep green walls, gold accents and wood furniture. "Well, this just screams you," said Paris, picking up Beryl's bag and placing it in the room.

The next was grey and pale yellow, with meadow flower decorations and pictures. "I don't think this one is for me. Sophie, it could be yours, what do you think?"

Not really having a nose for design, Sophie shrugged her shoulders, her home was basic and functional and this was glamourous. She had no need for ornaments or knickknacks, they were a waste of space and were just another thing to dust and clean.

"I suppose, if you don't want it then I'll sleep in here. I'm not fussed either way," she told Paris, who pointed to the next room, peeped in and disappeared with the closing of the door.

"Well, I guess he's having that room," Sophie said as she brought her bag in and closed her own door too.

It had been agreed they'd have a quick freshen up in their rooms before going out for an explore. Paris was the first ready and could be heard talking to a man with a thick Scottish accent in the living room. Sophie pressed her ear to the door and could hear her friend laughing and flirting, a skill of his she'd grown to envy, which he was very good at.

Although she'd only known Paris for a few months, Sophie soon found out he could get whatever he wanted. She'd watch in awe as her friend would give a compliment to someone, before brushing their arm lightly with his hand and then laughing at something they'd said – even if it wasn't worthy of a chuckle. This method would usually take a matter of minutes for Paris to get what he sought, be it free alcohol for the club, discount on some clothes or another man's number.

Sophie pushed open the door from her bedroom and saw who Paris was speaking to. The man was tall and broad, not fat, but muscular. He was wearing a dark blue tartan kilt and black a dress jacket that cut just above his waist. As Sophie entered the room he turned, giving her a full view of his face and dark red hair which was parted down the centre of his head and long enough to cover his ears. If she was to imagine what a Scotsman looked like, this is who would come to mind.

"Hullo, you must be Sophie. My name is Balloch, I'm pleased to be of assistance to you on your stay in our fine city."

Sophie had never heard a Scotch accent in real life before. She'd heard plenty of actors give a bad impression of one on the tele and so hadn't expected the real one to be so rich, deep and warm. She gave a loud involuntary swoon and felt she needed to sit down to catch her breath for a second, but quickly told herself to get a grip as Paris and Balloch gave her a curious look.

229

"Sorry, I must still be a little tired from the early start. Yes, that's me, very pleased to meet you. What would you suggest we do this afternoon before we come back here for dinner?"

Straight away Paris clocked her blush of attraction towards the butler and shot what he intended to be a warning glance towards Sophie, which she mistook for something else.

"Paris, are you feeling ok? You look a little flushed, is that salmon repeating on you? I remember you saying oily fish didn't really agree with you."

"No, I'm fine thank you dear," he replied through gritted teeth. "I must be getting a little hungry, as soon as your mother's ready, we'll head out."

Like a perfectly timed stage entrance, Beryl's door swung open, allowing an invisible mist of her perfume to engulf the room and gag its inhabitants before she waltzed in and clocked the company.

"Paris, darling, who is this handsome man and why have I not yet been introduced to him?" Her eyes widened behind the lenses of her thick black-rimmed glasses as she made her way towards the small group standing in the centre of the lounge.

Beryl's shawls and scarves billowed behind her as Paris, Sophie and Balloch all watched her glide to the middle of the group, where she faced the new person in the room and took her time inspecting him.

"And who might you be?"

"Balloch, ma'am. You must be Sophie here's sister, aye?" he said winking as Beryl threw her head back with an appreciative laugh. "I bet you say that to all of the old ladies. Well, I may not be a young woman anymore, but Balloch, darling, I am still very much in my prime."

"Mum! Stop it, you're making a fool of yourself,"

"Sweetie, he knows I'm only playing. He wouldn't be able to handle a woman like me anyway."

"Oh for goodness sake mother..."

"Maybe we should head out now for a bite to eat," Paris cut in, annoyed the attention had moved quickly from him and onto Sophie and Beryl. He'd just started to work his magic on the handsome Scot before their family drama had begun.

They took some suggestions of what to eat from Balloch, who then called the lift for them to get downstairs. He spoke to a waiting taxi driver and saw them on their way to a gastropub owned by a famous Michelin-starred chef, which was a short drive away.

Sophie hadn't expected the pub's food to be as fancy as it was. Instead of burgers, fish and chips and lasagne she had the choice of deconstructed this and gel that, which was all served with a jus of some sort. So much choice and the number of unfamiliar dishes made it difficult to choose.

Unlike Paris and her mum, who were in awe of the menu, fancy food was wasted on Sophie. She cooked nutritious meals for her sons when they were younger, but since they'd both grown up and been able to fend for themselves, she'd just lived of microwave food and sandwiches. But, she was determined to give the fancy stuff a whirl and pretend to enjoy it, even though it was too much and made her stomach churn.

After deciding on a slow-cooked feather blade of beef served in its juices along with wholegrain mustard and truffle mash with seasonal vegetables, she decided that although the description was far removed from the one on her supermarket ready meal, it was just meat and two veg and therefor a safe bet.

Once they'd munched their way through appetisers, a main course and dessert, as well as a bottle of wine, the trio decided lunch was a tasty success and that the restaurant owned by the chef on the other side of the city would be worth a visit before leaving.

Much of the afternoon had passed while they ate and drank. Once they'd had their fill, Sophie and Paris had got their phones out to search for things to do that evening and settled on visiting a few of the gay bars in the city, which Beryl thought was a good idea too. Sophie had tried to convince her otherwise, but her determined mother had said staying in the hotel would be an incredible bore and a waste while the whole of Edinburgh was out there to see.

Paris had suggested they walk back to the hotel and have a look in a few of the shops on their way. They would save the main shopping strips for another day and were quite happy pottering around some of the smaller boutiques and independent outlets that were dotted around the streets en route to the hotel, where they would have dinner and change ready for an evening out.

Balloch greeted them as they entered the tall building where they were staying. He requested the lift and said he'd left some gin and tonic in the suite for them to enjoy while deciding what they'd eat for dinner, which he'd call down to the kitchen and order once they were ready.

The curtains in their suite had been drawn, candles lit and some soft piano music from hidden speakers was playing in the communal areas. It was relaxing and as soon as Sophie sat on one of the plush sofas with a gin and tonic, she could feel her eyelids slowly closing.

Sometime later, she was woken by the noise of ice cubes being tipped into a glass. She looked around and was alone apart from Balloch who, still in his kilt, was preparing three more drinks, which he made by pouring a golden liquid into a cocktail shaker, followed by what Sophie thought was coffee and then some coffee liqueur.

"Hullo, sorry to wake you, but ah thought ah'd make you three some Scotch espresso martinis to get you all in the mood for a night on the tiles. Paris has ordered food for you, said pizza would be a good stomach liner. It must be a big one ye'v got planned then?"

She hadn't fully woken up and was conscious of being alone with such a good-looking man after just waking up. There had definitely been some dribbling, she could feel it had dried into a thin line of crust down her cheek, which she tried to rub away before Balloch noticed it.

"Ach, don't worry, ye looked so relaxed and peaceful while ye slept there, I'm sorry to have woken ye, but your pal said he wanted cocktails before dinner."

The music had switched from relaxing piano pieces to some lively pop songs, and sounded very similar to what Paris played in his car and in the office of the club, so Sophie guessed he'd had it changed. "What time is it? I feel like I've been asleep for hours."

"It's seven, this will perk ye up though, there's nay need to worry about tha."

Sophie stood up and looked at herself in the mirror that hung above the gas fire opposite the sofa she had been slouched asleep on. Her hair was flat on one side and as she'd expected, there were deposits of crusty sleep under her eyelids and dribble down her right cheek.

She rubbed the offending patches off with her fingers and tried to smooth down her hair to match on both sides. With some success, she then turned again and took one of the drinks from Balloch. It was cold, sweet and had a nutty depth from the coffee. She could taste the whisky, which gave it a warm caramel flavour.

"This is wonderful, what is it again?" she asked, wiping some of the drinks froth from her upper lip.

"It's an Espresso Martini with Scotch, much better than tha usual vodka ones."

"Did someone say cocktail?" Paris walked into the room and straight to the tray of cocktails that had been placed on a sideboard in the living room. He was wearing skin-tight black jeans that hugged his sparrow-like legs all the way down to a pair of black stiletto boots. On top he had thin, floaty black shirt with a white print that cut just above his knees.

"Yah, look smashin," Balloch chimed, which made Paris spin in place. "Yeh'll fit right in on the scene tonight. Av ne'er been, but ah heard it's a great night out. Ah'll be back in a wee bit with your dinner."

"He is delicious, isn't he," Paris said to himself, staring at the door Balloch left through like a wild cat hungrily sizing up its prey. "I wonder what his story is, who he's interested in."

"I suppose he's attractive, I haven't really given it much thought. Anyway, I'm not wanting a repeat of the Josh incident, especially with my mother so close."

"Even if you were interested, I doubt you'd get anywhere dressed like you are now. What on earth is going on with your hair?"

"I fell asleep and woke up like this, I'll quickly get changed. I was thinking black pencil skirt, black heels and that silver top?"

"Sounds wonderful, but hurry up. I want to go as soon as we've eaten."

Several cocktails later and slightly squiffy from the drinks earlier, the trio found themselves in a VIP booth in one of Edinburgh's most notorious drag bars. Eileen's was packed full of excited people who were lined up three or four deep at the bar waiting to be served. It was after ten at night and Sophie, Beryl and Paris were waiting for the show to start.

Beryl was clearly the oldest in the room and her quirky clothes were drawing lots of attention from the drag queens working the club and serving their booth. "This is marvellous, sweetie, I don't think I've had this much attention since I was a performer myself," she shouted above the loud hum of conversation and music.

"You were a performer?" Paris asked, eyebrows raised.

"Darling, people would travel from miles around to see my acrobatics when I was in my youth."

"You were an acrobat?"

"Only the best in the country. I was a trapeze artist in the circus long before Sophie was even thought of and I toured the UK and the world doing it."

Paris cocked his head to the side and squinted with one eye at Sophie, looking for confirmation that it was true.

She nodded. "It's true, my mother led quite an interesting life before she decided to settle down..."

"Shush, sweetie, it's about to start."

The chatter in the room dulled as the music simmered into silence and the lights shrank bringing the club to near darkness. A loud voice commanded the attention of the guests, telling them to be upstanding for Lady Meringue's entrance.

Paris sunk in his seat next to Sophie when a glamourous, tall and slender drag queen strutted onto the stage miming to a Britney Spear's song.

"What are you doing, what's wrong?" Sophie said into his ear.

"I know her."

"Well that's good if you know her."

"No, it's not. We don't really see eye to eye, and we haven't really seen or spoken to each other in more than five years."

The music switched from one upbeat number to another while Lady Meringue strutted and twirled from one end of the stage to the other, moving her lips in perfect sync to the words of the songs.

Much of the room remained dark with only the dim lighting in their booth giving Sophie an idea of

Paris's expression. Sunk so low in his seat, he looked like a petulant child at the dinner table being told by his parents to sit up and eat his vegetables. Harsh lights from the stage occasionally swung round to cast bright colourful lines across his face, making him look sinister each time they danced in their direction.

"Sit up, for goodness sake," Sophie eventually hissed. "It's not like she's going to be able to see you in a packed room like this."

"I can't, she'll spot me a mile off and then there'll be..."

The music shifted to a slower, more sensual tempo and Lady Meringue picked up a microphone from the side of the stage. Now the spotlights were still and white. Sophie could see the drag queen's face was made up to look like a burlesque dancer's. Her long, red sequin dress covered a voluptuous bosom, before cutting in at her waist and fitting tightly over big round hips that gave her a perfect hourglass figure.

"This one's for all the straight men in the house tonight," a deep slow voice sounded from the speakers around the club, which was returned with laughs, applause and wolf whistles.

"Oh god, oh god!"

"What is wrong with you? You're behaving like a little girl," Sophie said, nudging Paris with her elbow.

"Are you quite alright sweetie?" Beryl asked, having been focused on the stage, but now noticing Paris's odd behaviour.

"She's coming into the audience," fretted Paris.

"No she's not, you're just being silly and even if she does. Oh…"

Just as Paris had feared, the glamourous drag queen was guided down from the stage by two topless, muscular men. Once her eyes had become used to the duller lighting, she looked straight over to where they were seated.

"It's your bloody turban, she's spotted your bloody turban," Paris hissed at Beryl and shifted even further down so he was now almost sitting on the floor.

Beryl's silver lamé turban was like a shiny beacon in the darkness of the club and so the first thing to grab the searching drag queen's attention.

"And who do we have here? You must be the most glamourous lady I've ever met, simply fabulous. Well, not as fabulous as me." said a chocolatey voice, which was returned with more wolf whistles from the audience.

As she covered the short distance between the stage and the VIP booth they were seated at, Sophie could still hear Paris cursing while he scrabbled around the floor on his hands and knees, failing to find somewhere safe to escape.

"Hello, my name is Beryl and I'm from Surrey," she said, reaching out to take the microphone from Meringue. "And this is my daughter Sophie and this young man on the floor here is Ben, but he goes by Paris because he's a drag queen too. Aren't you Paris? Oh where have you gone, silly?"

Over the soft music and the dull chatter of the punters in the club who weren't listening fully to what was going on, Sophie heard Paris groan loudly under the table.

"Well, I haven't heard those two names together in a very long time. I believe I'm already familiar with Ben the drag queen who goes by the name of Paris. What are you doing down there, you little minx?"

Knocking his head on the underside of the table as he gracelessly emerged from the hiding place, Paris gave a grimace in place of the smile he no doubt intended to forge for Meringue.

"I just dropped... erm. I just dropped this here," he said thrusting a paper straw into the air as though it was a prize he'd won.

"How wonderful, we have so few of those at Eileen's, thank you for finding that. Now, ladies and gentlemen, we are in the presence of one of the most cowardly drag queens in the industry. I believe she now goes by the, in my opinion, misleading name of Paris Le Grand."

More groans from Paris, who sat back down and squirmed in his seat, ready to take a verbal bashing.

"Yes, this dried up fruit here was my best friend since the age of sixteen and, I'm sorry to overshare, my lover later in life. We were inseparable for years and then do you know what she did to me?" the pitch and volume of her voice raised as she asked the question. The audience shouted back: "No, what did she do to you Meringue?"

"She went out to the hairdressers one afternoon and never came back." Gasps in the audience turned to loud boos. Sophie could see, even in the dark, that her friend's face had turned beet red and any attempt to compose himself failed.

"Yes, the little trout had been slowly moving her things out of our flat without me knowing and didn't come back. No note, no phone call, not even a text or a tweet. I was heartbroken, thought my life was over. But do you know what?"

"What Meringue?" the room erupted louder this time.

242

"I said to myself, good people: I. Will. Survive."

As she slowly said those words, leaving a second's pause between each one, the room erupted once again with loud whoops and cheers as the Gloria Gaynor song fired up over the speakers. Meringue touched Paris's face softly and then gave it a playful slap before she turned and got back on the stage to perform the song.

"What the hell was that? What did you do to that poor person?" Sophie whispered to Paris, who was now staring down at the table.

"Your friend seems very nice, sweetie. Did you know she was going to be here?" Beryl asked, oblivious to what had just happened.

"It's a long story and one that I don't want to get into right now," Paris eventually said in response to Sophie, ignoring Beryl, who was again engrossed in the performance.

They sat and watched the rest of the set, trying to work out how and when they could get away without being noticed by the audience and Paris's old flame. When she left the stage, the lights went out again and the regular thumping music rose, giving everyone in the room permission to go to the bar or the toilet.

"Right, let's get out of here now," Paris commanded and stood, looking around to make sure they hadn't left anything on the table or seats.

Before they could get away, though, one of the topless men who'd helped Meringue down from the stage appeared next to Paris, who, even in his stressed state of mind, couldn't help to turn on the charm.

"Hello, handsome. How can I help you?"

"Lady Meringue would like to see you in her dressing room."

"Oh, how fabulous darling. I'd very much like to meet her."

"She only wants to see this one here," the half-naked man addressed Paris, pointing his finger at him to confirm the invite's exclusivity.

"That sounds like a lovely invitation, but unfortunately my friends and I have plans to go for some more drinks and a little food."

"Sweetie, don't let us get in your way of visiting with your friend. She did say it had been a long time after all. And anyway, we've had about enough to drink and we ate before coming out. Don't you remember, dear?"

Paris's eyes rolled almost to the back of his head, Beryl had made it impossible to say no. Sophie was useless in these situations and offered no help. But, if he didn't go back and see Meringue, she'd know he'd snubbed her. After all, he did at least owe her an explanation.

"Fine. I'll go back and see her. You two go to the hotel and I'll see you there," he added before slumping off behind the man, no doubt looking at his bottom, Sophie thought.

"Well, that was a wonderful show, wasn't it, sweetie? I am very tired now though, perhaps we could go back to our rooms and have a little nightcap before bed. I think Paris might be some time catching up with his friend in there."

It was Sophie's turn to roll her eyes now. She wondered what Paris had done to this poor Meringue all those years ago. She knew little about his past, other than he hadn't gotten along with his parents and had managed to make a comfortable life for himself, despite all of the odds being against him.

"Come on then, mother. Let's get a taxi back and I'll wait up for Paris once you've gone to bed."

Hours later, back at the hotel, Sophie heard a kerfuffle outside the door of their suite. Someone was repeatedly dropping keys and swearing loudly. Then there was a bang against the door before a loud groan and then silence.

She opened the door and saw Paris laid in an untidy heap on the hallway floor, rubbing his head with one hand and fumbling for the dropped keys with the other, sighing loudly as his hand kept grasping at thin air every time he reached out to grab them.

"Paris. Paris," she hissed in case the commotion woke her mother.

"Huh?" He looked up, almost cross eyed and squinting at the bright light from the doorway behind Sophie.

"Paris, what are you doing on the floor – are you drunk?"

"I hit my face on the door when I tried to get the keys into the little hole," he slurred back.

"Paris," Sophie said firmly, "you're drunk. Why are you drunk? We left you hours ago, you're going to wake the whole hotel up at this rate."

"I'm not drunk, just a little giggly. Meringuey got a bottle of that clear stuff," he paused while searching for his next words. If he was mechanical, the cogs turning in his head would be clunking loudly right now.

"You know? It looks like water, but burns. Especially that cheap stuff she always drinks."

"You mean vodka?"

"That's the one. You're so clebber, Sophie. Did I ever tell you that I love you? Well, I do. You're like the person I never met until I met you."

"Wow, high praise indeed from Mrs No Feelings."

"What did you call me?"

"I said you should get up off the floor, it's not so clean."

Paris giggled and squinted again as Sophie squatted down to the same level ready to hoist the drunken mess up off the floor and into his room.

"You so funny sometimes."

"Your breath reeks of booze. Are you sure it was just the one bottle you shared?"

"Beryl! Berrrrryl!"

"Shush, you'll wake her up."

"Beryl, Sophie said I smell."

"Paris, you're being silly. Now come on, help me get you in here."

With a mixture of persuasion and sheer force, Sophie managed to get Paris into the suite and onto the sofa under her own strength, pushing his head and torso on first and then picking up his legs and twisting them so his whole body was eventually nestled there. She took off his shoes and tried her best to tilt his head to the side in case he needed to be sick.

Throughout the rigmarole, Paris did and said nothing. His eyes were shut and Sophie thought he was sleeping. She left a glass of water on the coffee table next to him and put the empty ice bucket Balloch had used when he'd made cocktails earlier in the crook of her drunken friend's arm.

"You're quite sweet when you're sleeping. Not so ferocious, really."

"Sophie. I did the worst thing to my friend."

"You don't need to talk about this now, Paris. Wait until you're sober in the morning."

"No!" he said loudly, sitting up straight, eyes wide and determined. "I need to tell you, so you know that I'm a bad person. I'm not always the kind and generous lady you see before you right now."

"Now who's funny," she scoffed.

"I bailed on Gareth..."

"Gareth?"

"Lady Meringue, that's her boy name. Gareth, it's pretty, don't you think?"

"Just lovely. Now what do you want to tell me? I need to get some sleep if I'm going to have to look after hungover you tomorrow."

"I left her. We had a life together and money. Lots of money that we'd made working our own drag nights and I just upped and left with most of it."

"Why did you do that?"

"I wasn't happy," he said with a mouth full of saliva and a runny nose, making him seem almost childlike and far from his usual strong assured self. "I'd made most of the money and Gareth was abusing me, mentally. He used to say the most awful things to me, that I was nothing without him and I'd never find anyone or anything else."

"Paris, did he..."

"No, he didn't hit me. But in a way I wish he had sometimes, at least I would have been able to see the damage sooner. Maybe I would have left earlier, made the decision to leave if my nose or ribs were broken."

"But you went back there tonight, what did he say to you?"

"He apologised. Said that he knew why I'd left and that he'd worked hard on becoming a better person. Built his life up after getting help."

"And that's what he wanted to tell you, that he was a better person?"

"He sees what I've made, and he wants us to get back together. He wants to be part of the House of Paris Le Grand again."

"Paris, no. He may have changed, but you've done this all yourself and you don't know whether he has changed, not really. Paris don't."

"No. I said no. I stood up to him and then he said drink with me. So, we did. I thought I'd toast myself saying no to his ugly little face. We toasted again and again to me being successful and me getting away from him. And that's when, well I guess you could say he seduced me."

His face cracked and snot mixed with streams of tears that flowed out freely one after the other. Sophie, who wasn't capable or comfortable dealing with even small displays of emotion, patted his back gently as it lurched up and down like he had a bad case of the hiccups.

"Oh, Paris, did he..."

"No, he wouldn't have dared do anything like that. It was, what do the kids these days say? It was consensual. Don't worry about that. It just brought back so many painful memories. I don't want to go back to that place again, to risk everything."

"Try to get some sleep and then we can talk about it more in the morning if you like," Sophie said, trying to pose her face with an understanding expression. She went into his room and brought out the duvet and laid it over Paris, who fell asleep as soon as it touched him. She turned off the light and went to sleep in her room.

The next morning at breakfast, Paris said nothing about the previous night. Perhaps he couldn't remember what had happened or maybe he was embarrassed, either way, Sophie had decided not to bring it up either. Hungover, Paris allowed himself to be guided into a taxi to the airport before the three of them returned home to the south a day earlier at Paris's request.

Chapter Fifteen: Hens

Edinburgh eventually felt like a distant memory, although not too distant as it had only been a matter of weeks since Sophie had learnt about one of Paris's darker moments in life.

Things had been a little awkward between the two of them at work the day after they'd flown back. But they soon got into the swing of a familiar routine again and Sophie thought it had brought them a little closer together.

Paris had arranged to go on a two-week holiday abroad and left Sophie in charge of the club, which he'd never done before. Perhaps the stress of encountering an old flame had taken its toll on him. Either way, the responsibility was a thrill for her at first, although a little daunting as she'd never been trusted with anything like this before.

Rather than working the shifts Paris did – starting in the early evening and working until late – as he had suggested, Sophie thought it best to continue working her usual shift and then Paris's.

She started at nine o'clock, went home before five for a couple of hours' rest and then returned to Sophisticats in the evening. Although this routine made her tired, knowing everything was getting done properly made it feel worth it. Her boss would be so pleased things were running smoothly and the tills were ringing as they normally would.

One morning at her computer in the club's office an email with a special request came through. It was a woman asking on behalf of her friend to arrange a hen party. This wasn't out of the ordinary, Sophisticats was a popular destination for soon-to-be brides, however, the woman had asked whether it would be possible to arrange a cocktail making class for a party of no fewer than sixteen women.

Sophisticats wasn't necessarily that sort of a bar, although it did serve several of what Paris called disco cocktails. "Something fun and not to serious," he said about the offer when introducing it to new bar staff. But then most of their bartenders were capable of making the classics, so surely there'd be no harm bringing in a bit of extra money and trying out something new, she thought.

Her mobile was on the desk next to her. It had been near silent over the past few weeks, especially in the days after Paris had flown out to San Francisco on his holiday. She tapped the home button to see if there were any messages or missed calls, but nothing was there, not even a text from one of her sons or a missed call from her mother who would occasionally ring it from her landline. She continued to look at it, wondering whether she should give

Paris a text or even call him to get a second opinion about putting on a cocktail making night.

"Nah, I'm in charge. He trusts me," she whispered to herself, deleting the start of the message and then putting the phone in her bag.

Instead, she got to work looking online at what a cocktail masterclass for a hen party might look like. Pictures of penis-shaped straws and other rude things came up, which she thought could be fun. But the woman's email had also wanted assurance that there would be no male strippers or anything unsavoury. Surely, they would expect this sort of thing on a hen party in a gay bar, why not just order a few and see how things go?

After hours of searching the internet for hen party paraphernalia, Sophie had eventually spent over three hundred pounds on all kinds of, mostly willy-shaped, things that she thought a hen party might laugh at.

Quite proud with herself, and double checking that everything would be delivered in time for the shenanigans that weekend, she confirmed in an email to the woman's enquiry that they could put on a masterclass and they would see them at six on Saturday evening. Before sending it, she added that they would appreciate a deposit ahead of the party.

Nice touch, Paris would be proud, she thought while clicking on send.

In the few days leading up to what she thought was going to be a successful evening, Sophie had briefed some of the girls to come in early, dressed in drag of course, to help out at the masterclass and had agreed to pay some of the bartenders a few hours' of overtime if they led the class.

She went over the cocktails they were going to make, some of which she'd found on the internet and others that were already favourites in the club and had everything set up for the arrival of the hens. One of the bar staff had also told her they'd taken a deposit from a woman for the party while Sophie was at home between shifts.

 "Ok, this is going to be a fun night and I think it's something Paris is going to want to do again in the future if we can show how successful it can be," she told the two bar staff, Mya Ding-a-Ling and another queen called Fischer a few hours before the party was due in.

"I know this isn't our usual set up, but the boss is always saying we need new ways to make money, so let's get this right." Very nice, she thought, giving herself a mental pat on the back for such a good team pep talk.

"Just one question, Sophie dear," asked Mya, who was wearing a black catsuit that clung closely to her voluptuous figure. "You do realise this party is for a group of born-again Christians?"

"Heh?" a sort of choking squeak came from Sophie's mouth. "What do you mean, born again Christian?" she asked, searching Mya's face for a sign of a joke. Surely, she was joking, that's what she did. She was the funny one.

"Well, honey," the answer came out in the high-pitched tone Mya liked to use when stating the obvious. "They are church goers. They like God. Love him in fact. I heard the woman who came in with the deposit say she was going to church for the bride's and groom's blessing and that they'd all been there most of the day. In fact, it was some of the younger ones in the group who'd encouraged the bride to say yes to tonight as she's not really one for this sort of thing."

Sophie looked around the room, heart pounding in disbelief of how she'd missed the subtle hints that were so blatant now.

Willies were everywhere, following the crazy online shopping spree she'd had in a bid to make things festive. This was what she thought all hen parties wanted, not that she'd had any experience herself, since there was no such event before her wedding and she'd never had an invite to one either. This was all based on what she'd gleaned from trashy television programmes.

"Oh god!"

"Yes, dear. I think that's the problem."

"It's almost six, they'll be here any minute now. Help me hide of all these penises, Mya."

"I'm very good at that, don't you worry dear. We'll get rid of them all before they turn up. And are you still happy with the bartenders being topless?"

"Christ on a bike!"

"Maybe keep the blasphemy to a minimum too, yes?"

"I don't know anything. Paris will have an absolute hissy fit if he finds out how much I've screwed things up while he was away," Sophie shouted from the other side of the club where she was now trying to remove a rude version of pin the tail on the donkey.

"That cow won't know anything's happened petal, don't worry," piped up Fischer, who was shoving willy confetti that had been sprinkled on the bar into her handbag.

As they dashed around the room trying to hide the unsavoury evidence of what they all agreed would have been acceptable for any other hen party, a quiet chatter from the entrance of the club stopped them in their tracks.

"They're here, I'll stall them while you get the rest of it away. And for goodness sake, Bryce, put your shirt on," Sophie said to the still half-naked bartender before turning on her heel to greet the party.

She walked quickly out of the main bar area and into the lobby. There was a group of well-dressed, reserved-looking women standing in a group speaking in hushed voices to one another. They were all staring, concerned, at the space above the double doors that led into the main part of the club. Sophie turned and felt the colour drain from her face as she spotted a giant inflatable pink penis with the words 'Happy Hen Party Maria" printed on it.

"Welcome to Sophisticats, we have a wonderful few hours organised for you, Maria," she shakily said, turning around again to face the group and jerking her head in the direction of the offending object with a whispered apology.

"Now, where is Maria? Oh, there you are. Come on, come this way, don't be shy we've got everything set up for you."

Maria was pushed forward from the group and stumbled a little. She was older than Sophie had expected, closer to her age, perhaps. She looked like a terrified cat nervous about a visit to the vets.

"Come on, I promise we'll take good care of you in here. We've got two of our best bartenders to lead the class and two of my favourite girls are here to get the party started."

This *was* like leading a frightened animal to the vet's table, perhaps if she put a little trail of cheese on the ground into the bar they would follow.

Eventually, after explaining the inflatable object was a mistake and left there from another woman's hen party the night before – "I know, two brides called Maria in one weekend, what are the odds of that?" she stuttered.

Sophie eventually coaxed the group to where she wanted them and seated them at the bar ready for the masterclass.

Things were going well, the women – sixteen in total – slowly began to make their way behind the bar two at a time to make the drinks they'd chosen from the lists Sophie had printed out earlier that day. Fischer and Mya were on top form, at first gaining titters from the group before their hard work was eventually rewarded with giggles and

Sophie thought she'd once seen one of the women's eyes water with laughter.

The cocktail making was done and the group was now ready to enjoy what Sophie had called an exclusive show, which would be performed by the two girls. She'd arranged a comfortable seating area with sofas and tables in front of the stage and had all of the women in the group seated with their cocktails and the promise of more throughout the show.

Mya was the first to take to the stage, she started with a few jokes, her comedy makeup and tight catsuit being the brunt of most of them, which the women seemed to enjoy. Then it was Fischer's turn.

She pranced around the stage in her leotard, high heeled boots and was swinging her purse while dancing and miming to pop songs that the group had chosen from the 90s. She dropped into the splits causing the women to gasp and clap in amazement and then got back up and pirouetted in place.

The final song marked the end of an hour-long private show. As Whitney Houston's I'm Every Woman blared loudly from the club's sound system, and Fischer began to thrust her arms out pointing to the small audience as if empowering them. The handbag she'd been carrying around with her all evening was swinging up and down her arm. She stopped it at her wrist as it spun down from her shoulder and began to twirl it around as though she were getting ready to lasso a cow.

Her movements were getting grander and more powerful as the song built. The women on the hen party mesmerised, as though they'd witnessed Whitney Houston's spirit materialise on the stage. The strap on Fischer's bag was frayed, and it soon snapped, launching the bag into air at a rapid speed right over the women's heads where it dumped a glut of confetti over them.

At first, since the song was over, they thought it was part of the act and let out dignified cheers and applause for Fischer, but then Sophie heard gasps. A few of them were shouting in disgust as they stood up from the sofas and began vigorously brushing themselves and each other down, picking bits of confetti out of their hair and clothes.

"This is disgusting," the woman who had organised the party shouted while marching over to Sophie who was watching at the bar, unsure of why a bit of confetti was so upsetting. "You said that thing above the door earlier was from some other hen party."

The woman was holding out a hand of small, colourful paper penises that had been released from Fischer's bag as it launched from her arm and ended up stuck somewhere in light rigging on the ceiling.

"I am so sorry, I don't know how that got there. I promise you, it wasn't part of the act or the plans for this evening. You wanted something tame and that's what we delivered."

But the woman stood, hands on hips and her mouth pursed tight like a cat's bottom, looking at Sophie as though she was a naughty child who'd pulled a prank on a teacher.

Just as Sophie was about to give the woman a mouthful back about how it was a silly accident, Mya shouted that something was going to fall and release the balloons.

What balloons, Sophie thought and then realised she'd had a net secured to the rigging ready to drop a load of rude balloons onto the hen party below at the end of the show. When they were tidying all the other things away earlier, Sophie thought it best to leave the balloons unseen where they were.

"Stop them!" she shouted back to Mya and Fischer.

"Too late," Mya said half to herself as the handbag plummeted to the floor, bringing the net down with it and a bombardment of giant inflated penises that, according to the website she'd bought them from, were anatomically accurate.

Dozens of willies cascaded from the ceiling in one big, slow movement which Sophie thought would never end. The women were screaming now and calling Sophisticats the Devil's house.

"This is a cesspit of immoral filth; you've ruined my friend's hen party and you're going to pay for it. Mark my words," the woman said with a hard, pointed jab from her finger to Sophie's shoulder. "We thought we'd escape this sort of thing by coming to a place like this where we wouldn't be bothered by sinful men and women looking to sleep with each other."

She looked ferocious, like she was capable of releasing a biblical wrath of unforgiving punishment on Sophie for raining down penis balloons on her and her friends.

"But this is a gay bar, surely that is sinful. Why would you come to a drag club if you're so easily offended..." Sophie started but stopped as the woman's face turned a darker red and the skin on her forehead creased into deep crevasses of hatful anger.

"This is a what?" the woman muttered through her puckered lips; teeth clenched so close together it was hard for the words to escape. "This is a hive of sodomy! Those women are men," she questioned to herself with what sounded like the last of the air in her lungs.

"We can fix it. You've had such a lovely evening so far and this was all just a mistake, please stay and enjoy some complimentary drinks," Sophie stuttered back.

"No. We're leaving. Come on Maria. Girls, get your things we're going. This is a house of horror; I knew there was something manly about those two on the stage."

"Oi! There's nothing manly about me, luv," Mya shouted to the backs of the group who were now speedily walking to the door. "It's all tucked in!"

"Shush, you're going to make it worse," Sophie fretted and trotted off after them to the front door, but they had already left and were halfway down the road by the time she'd made it outside.

What was the worst that could happen, really, she thought? It's not like they could pray for a plague to hit the club. What was it, frogs and locusts? She doubted they'd hear anything else from them again. But it was a good job she'd taken the deposit, which paid for all the decorations and the staff's time.

No, nothing would come of the blunder, Sophie assured herself before going to bed that night.

***

Sophie hadn't given the previous day's mishap a second thought. She, Mya and Fischer had all been all in agreement that the women would soon calm down and might even see the funny side one day. So instead of dwelling on it, they got on setting up the club for its regular opening that evening.

It was mid-morning on Sunday and Sophie had just woken up and made her way downstairs to have coffee and breakfast. She was sat at the kitchen table with a magazine and was slowly flicking through the pages, not reading anything but looking at the pictures, when her phone started to vibrate.

She didn't know the number, but the area code was local, so she answered it thinking one of the girls from the club was calling her.

"Hello?"

"Good morning, I'm sorry to disturb you on a Sunday, could you tell me if I'm speaking to a Sophie Defoy?"

"Yes, this is her, I mean me. Who's that?"

"Ahh, good morning Ms Defoy, or may I call you Sophie?" a man's voice asked.

"Sophie's fine," she said, wondering what they wanted and how long it would take for her to get back to the lazy morning she had planned.

"I'm a local freelance journalist working for the *Daily* Times. I'm calling to follow up on a story I've spotted on the *Surry Sun's* website about you and wondered if I could get some quotes."

"A story? I'm sorry, I don't understand. What do you mean there's a story about me?"

"Apologies, I'd assumed you'd have seen it as it's been getting a lot of reaction on Facebook and I wondered if you'd give me the national exclusive on it. It's about the Christian woman's hen party last night. You know, the penis balloons and such?"

Sophie wanted to ask more questions, but her mouth was dry, and her throat began to itch. She took a sip of her coffee and again tried to say something but she couldn't speak. This must be a prank, Mya or Fischer must have put one of their friends up to it.

"Hello?" The man on the other end of the phone prompted after seconds of silence, kick-starting Sophie's brain back into the moment.

"Can you put Mya or Fischer on, please? I know this is prank and it's not funny."

"I don't quite understand what you're saying, these are the names of the drag queens who were there last night. Ms Defoy, sorry, Sophie, I'm going to be publishing the story online today and there's a good chance it will make it into the newspaper tomorrow too, I couldn't get hold of the proprietor, but the voicemail on his mobile gave me your number as a contact. I'll need some quotes for the story."

"This isn't a prank?"

"No."

"You're not one of Mya's or Fischer's friends?"

"I'd never heard of them until I saw the story on the *Surry Sun's* website today."

"And you want a quote from me about penis balloons and confetti?"

"Yes, and about one balloon with the Christian bride-to-be's name on it too."

"And this is for a national newspaper."

"Erm, yes. Now I don't have much time, so please could you answer a few of my questions and I'll let you get back to enjoying your Sunday morning."

"I'm sorry, but I can't comment on behalf of the business," she said and hung up.

A quick search on Google revealed a story about Sophisticats with a picture of a miserable looking Maria and her friends all gathered around a large dining table and holding bibles. The headline on the story read: 'Disgusted Christian bride's hen party rained off by shower of penis balloons.'

Sophie almost choked on her coffee when she read it. She scrolled through the story and read how the women had been mistreated and were forced to watch gay men dressed as women gyrate on stage before being bombarded with rude objects.

"We thought it was a nice, quiet and sophisticated cocktail bar as the name suggested. We don't have a problem with gay men, but it's an environment we would prefer not to be in and it feels like we have been misled," a quote from the angry woman who'd prodded Sophie read.

There was no two ways about it, Paris was going to hit the roof. He'd left Sophie in charge of keeping things running, which she'd so far been doing a good job of. But now she'd managed to get the club into the national press for the wrong reasons, annoyed an entire faith and apparently misled some innocent women.

As she continued looking at the story, cringing each time she reread it, her phone vibrated. This time it was Paris. Maybe she could get away with not answering, just ignore him. Perhaps she could convince him it was fake news, written by a journalist who'd gotten the wrong end of the stick. Whatever she did, it would probably end with Sophie losing her job, so maybe it was best to just pick up and resign there and then.

"Hello, Paris, how's America treating you? I hope the weather is nicer than it is here…"

"Don't start drivelling on about the weather, Sophie, you know why I'm calling."

"What do you mean? I didn't think I'd hear from you at all until you were on your way back."

"Sophie!" Paris rarely shouted and this, she knew, meant he had been told about everything that had happened. "I've had every national newspaper in England calling me this morning about a load of Christians being bombarded with willies and God-knows what else. Now tell me what's going on so I can fix it.

"If you could give the *Daily Times* the exclusive on it then the very nice reporter who called me would probably be appreciative," she replied, trying to lighten the mood.

Paris sighed and Sophie decided that she should probably just answer his questions before she got herself into more trouble. So, over the next half-hour or so, she talked Paris through everything that had happened, including how Fischer's handbag had cannoned penis-shaped confetti over the hen party and then caused the balloon drop from hell.

"Right. I appreciate you listening to me and trying to think of new ways to make money, and I understand that this catastrophe could have happened if I was there too, but this could be quite bad for us, so I need you to listen very carefully."

For another half-an-hour Sophie jotted down Paris's instructions and promised to carry them out to the letter and call him if anything else cropped up. She was to start with a phone call to Felix to find out if he knew anyone in crisis management PR who could help them. He did and quickly got a woman called Emily from an agency he'd worked with in the past to get in touch with her minutes later.

The PR had told Sophie to meet her at the club where they would set up their crisis headquarters and get the whole thing sorted. Under no circumstances, was Sophie to speak to a reporter or anyone about what had happened until she'd been briefed by her.

In what felt like minutes, Sophie had showered, dressed and driven to the club and met a dark-haired slim woman who looked to be in her mid-thirties. They went up to the office and talked through the few strategies for dealing with the press. They then called Paris and agreed that they would kick things off by issuing a statement to the press about the club and how the whole thing was a misunderstanding and that they were extremely sorry about it. They would donate a substantial amount of money to the church the women belonged to and pay for the bridal party to go to a spa the night before the wedding as an apology for causing so much stress. It was also decided they wouldn't open the club that night so they could properly deal with the fallout of the incident.

After hours of phone calls to reporters and interviews with the local media, Sophie was feeling and looking tired, she'd been shut in the dark office with Emily since the early afternoon and it was now gone nine in the evening. She'd spoken to nearly all the national newspapers who'd also requested pictures of her and the club to publish in the next day's newspapers, while many of them had published stories about the hen party online that day.

The last telephone interview was coming to an end and Emily was about to pack away her things and leave Sophie to lock the club up when they heard a loud crash coming from downstairs. They both jumped out of their chairs and quickly walked from the office and down the stairs into the main part of the club.

Thousands of razor-sharp shards of glass were peppered across the floor and twinkling like evil diamonds in the moonlight that was now able to shine through the glassless window frame. The broken glass crunched under Sophie's shoes as she carefully walked around, open-mouthed at the damage and wondering whether it had been an accident or if someone had tried to break in. She walked slowly to the bare window frame and peered through it to find the street outside was quiet apart from the occasional car going past.

"What do you think caused this?" she turned around and asked Emily.

"I don't know, there's no one outside?"

"No one's around, but if someone did smash it then they'd be long gone now."

"I really don't know, I can't see anything on the floor other than. Oh wait, what's this..."

Emily bent down and picked up what looked like a large piece of paper and walked over to Sophie to show her it.

"Is that? No, I didn't think people actually did that other than in films," Sophie, who was in shock, whispered.

The object wasn't a ball of paper, but a heavy round stone that had been wrapped in a note and secured by an elastic band. Sophie took it from Emily and unwrapped it, placing the rock on the bar so she could read what the note said.

"Turn the light on over there, I can hardly see," she said to Emily, pointing at the switches behind the bar.

"What does it say? We should call the police."

Sophie studied the crumpled piece of paper in silence for a few moments, reading it repeatedly in her mind before finally telling Emily.

"Queers get out. We don't want your sort in our town get out before we burn your place to the ground," she said slowly, making sure she read out every word carefully to see if Emily got the same cold chill she did.

"I'm going to call the police, come on. It's not safe in here if they're close by and threating to burn the place down," said Emily before running upstairs to get their things.

She was back a moment later with Sophie's coat over her arm as well as both of their bags. Sophie was still standing next to the bar with the note in her hand, reading it.

"Come on Sophie, let's get out and call the police."

Sophie couldn't move though. She was scared that she'd ruined everything with one stupid hen party. It had all felt under control just minutes ago with the newspaper journalists, getting their side of the story and publishing comments about apologies, donations and free spa breaks. But now Paris's little empire was under threat. Her little sanctuary.

She heard Emily calling the police and telling them what had happened and then felt herself being led outside and guided into the back seat of Emily's black four-by-four. Her hands were shaking, the note still in them, and she couldn't say anything when Emily asked if she was ok.

They sat silently in the car for a few minutes until it was broken by sirens and the flashing blue lights of two police cars coming their way. Emily got out and waved the cars down outside the club and started talking to the three police officers who'd driven there. She pointed to her car and walked towards it with a female officer.

"Sophie, this police officer would like to talk to you. Are you ok to get out of the car?"

"I, err. Yes, sorry, I think I'm just in a little bit of shock, nothing like this has ever happened to me before. I'm ok now though, sorry."

She took Emily's hand and got out of the car to talk to the police office, who asked for the note and to tell her where the stone was. The note wasn't handwritten but had been printed out in big black letters, so the typed words filled most of the piece of paper.

The police spent an hour looking around and waited with Sophie until the window had been boarded up. Emily had to get home and left shortly after giving a statement about what had happened. The police had said they would investigate what had happened, but it was unlikely they'd be able to find the person as there were no security cameras nearby. It would be a surprise if they actually followed through on the threat anyway, said the female officer.

"Probably just a kneejerk reaction to all the press coverage you told us about, I wouldn't worry about it. Do you have anyone at home or someone who can stay with you tonight," she asked.

"Erm, I live alone, but my mother could come round or I could ask my son to come over," she said, thinking about the dark empty house that was waiting for her. She didn't want to go there alone, but felt silly because the person who'd smashed the window was unlikely to know where she lived, but still she couldn't shake the feeling of worry that had gripped hold of her.

When she arrived home, having been followed by the female officer in her police car, Sophie saw that the lights were on. Probably her mother, which was confirmed when she walked through the door and was greeted by an excited Beryl.

"My superstar daughter has returned. You're famous, darling" she shrieked and clung onto her daughter in the hallway.

"Malcom from next door came around this morning with his tablet thingy and showed me all of the stories about you. It's marvellous how you've helped those frigid women get to like drag queens."

"That's not quite what happened mum but thank you. It's been a long day though, I need a drink. Can I get you one too?"

"Sweetie, I have a bottle of fizz in the fridge for us to celebrate with. I'll get it now."

"I think I'll need something stronger after the day I've had. Get the gin."

"What's happened, dear? You look white as a sheet."

Sophie didn't feel like enduring the dramas of her mother, so decided to give a potted account of what happened and omitted the fact the club and the people who worked there had been threatened by a vile note strapped to a rock.

"Darling, that does sound terrible," her mother said, comforting her by placing a hand on Sophie's at the kitchen table where they were sitting together. "I'm sure Paris will be very forgiving of you, it sounds like everything is under control now. Here, let me get you another drink and you just sit there while I make some dinner, yes?"

After eating yet another wild concoction of Beryl's (rehydrated flavoured noodles from a packet served in two slices of buttered bread), Sophie felt comforted and in her exhausted state took her mother's suggestion and went straight up to bed.

Following a surprisingly good night's sleep, one from which Sophie didn't stir until the alarm on her phone woke her at seven, the previous day's events didn't seem too bad. Perhaps the police officer was right, the threatening note was just a heat of the moment kind of thing. The club had been there for years with Paris running it and everyone in the town knew what went on there.

She went downstairs to have breakfast with her mother, but she'd left a note saying her Monday morning yoga class had been moved to an earlier time, so had to leave. There was some coffee in the percolator which she poured into a mug and helped herself to some of the fruit and yogurt Beryl had left in the fridge for Sophie's breakfast.

Once she'd had a quick shower and threw on some clothes, Sophie drove into town to start her day at the club. Paris would be back tomorrow, so she wanted to get the window fixed properly and make sure everything was spick and span for his return. She may have marred Sophisticats' reputation in the national press and incited homophobic hate, but there was no need for her boss to come back to a dump.

She opened the front doors of the club and noticed things had been moved and the lights were on. None of the other girls had keys for the venue and the bar manager wouldn't have come in early without messaging Sophie. Her heart made loud hard thuds against her chest as she considered whether the author of the stone note had come to follow through on their threat and burn the place down.

Sophie moved slowly and quietly through the club, sniffing the air in short sharp bursts for the smell of a flammable liquid. There was nothing out of the ordinary and the bar smelled as it always did in the mornings – cleaning fluids, a touch of stale alcohol and sweat.

"I thought I heard someone down here. You're in earlier than usual."

"Jesus Christ! You almost scared me to death, Paris."

Out of all the scenarios that were going through her mind, Paris was not the one who she thought would be in the club.

"What are you doing here, I thought you weren't getting back until tomorrow?"

"Well, I actually flew back yesterday and was going to take today off to get rid of my jetlag. But Emily called last night when I landed to give me an update on the press interviews and she told me what had happened with the stone, so I decided to give jetlag the finger and come see how you were. I would have called sooner, but I passed out as soon as I got home. How are you?"

"As soon as my heart stops trying to burst out of my chest, I'm sure I'll be fine. Paris, I'm so sorry about all this mess – the newspapers and the note. You must think I'm useless."

"Hun, if only you knew how badly I've screwed up over the years. In fact, what you've done doesn't even come close to my lesser mess-ups. You're ok and you don't need to worry. And this note, the police have still got it?"

"Yes. They said they'd take it for evidence, but they didn't sound hopeful about finding the culprit."

"I wouldn't worry, we've had a few similar threats in the past. No one's ever done anything though."

"Really?"

"Oh yes, one time someone smashed my back doors in and then graffitied something horrible across one of the walls. It happens every now and then. It's not good, but we just get on with it. Obviously, these people have nothing better to do with their time."

"Well, what can I say? I'm thrilled that homophobic abuse and threats to your business are a regular occurrence, you don't know how worried I was thinking I'd encouraged some nutter to come and torch the place," she said relieved, a huge weight lift from her.

"Are you ok though, Emily said you were a bit shaken by the whole thing. Do you need to be here today?"

"Oh, I'm fine. I was just worried about what you would think about it all. If I'm honest, it's just a relief that you're not going to fire me."

"Now, I didn't say that did I?" Paris said with a wink and turned around to go back upstairs to the office. Although Sophie knew he was joking, she couldn't shake the thought at the back of her mind that he was serious.

Chapter Sixteen: Christmas Tree

Paris had returned from his holiday in America over a month ago. An unseasonably early heat had wrapped itself around the UK making the air everywhere suffocating and sticky and the drama from Sophie's big cocktail masterclass idea had all been forgotten.

It was approaching the end of May and the whole country had been subjected to almost two weeks of the sickly weather where not even a breath of cool air had been felt. Even at night, the air remained hot and heavy, causing the bedsheets to stick to Sophie's skin as she tossed and turned night after night too uncomfortable to sleep.

That morning, Sophie was looking forward to getting into work earlier than usual so she could crank up the air conditioning in Sophisticats while she got on with things. She wasn't the only one either, as almost every member of staff coming to the club at least an hour early for their shift every day of the heatwave.

Business had also improved during the warmer weather, with revellers flocking to the club to escape to the artificial coolness it provided. Paris, on the advice of Felix who was still working with them, suggested they put on themed nights for the duration of the heatwave. By far the biggest success had been their *Cuba Meets the North Pole Ball* where the whole room was dressed as an ice palace and the cooling crushed ice drinks like mojitos flowed from the bar all night.

For these nights, Sophie had to make sure the club's ice supplies were double the usual order and that the ice machines, which were proving incapable of dealing with such high demand, were working. Ordering done, she shut the computer down and went into the bar to make sure the events team had begun redecorating for the club's first Christmas in June event that evening.

"Hun. Hun where are you? I need you to see if this looks a mess or not," Sophie heard Paris shout out from the other side of the room.

When she got to where the voice had come from, she couldn't see her drag queen boss.

"What are you doing just standing there like a lemon," he shouted from inside a cluster of thick fake Christmas trees that had been decorated with white twinkly lights and brightly coloured baubles. "I need you to tell me if they all look good where they are, because if I ever manage to get out from behind all these, I won't be bloody getting back in."

"They look very, er, gay, but not as gay as the fairy in the middle," she replied before a bauble was flung at her from inside the mass of trees.

"Very funny. Now help me out. I feel like I'm tapped in frigging Narnia."

Causing as little destruction as possible, Sophie managed to pull Paris from the trees and playfully brushed him down.

"It all looks about ready," she said while turning in a full circle on the spot to see the club decked out in tacky Christmas decorations.

Not one part of the venue had been untouched by Christmas. The bar been turned into a snowy tundra by a group of scenic artists who had also erected a Santa's grotto in the middle of seating area as a special VIP booth that had already been hired, despite the high price.

Hundreds of meters of fairy lights had also been wrapped around the club's supporting columns and strung across the ceiling, which had also been studded with giant gold and silver paper stars. Finishing the look was Paris's snowy forest which consisted of a dozen trees all decorated in garish colours.

"You don't think it's too much then? I would have just stuck a Christmas tree up on the bar and brought in a Santa for people to sit on. That Felix has got us doing things I never thought we would."

"If it wasn't you and Sophisticats, I'd probably say it was a bit much, but I think it's just the right amount of over the top."

"Great, we're just waiting on one more thing to be delivered from Felix's company and then we'll be done. This must be it now, actually," said Paris as the club's doorbell rang. "Wait there, I'll go let them in."

Sophie tinkered with a few of the decorations while she waited for her boss to come back. As she'd finished moving some of the baubles on the tree a familiar voice from behind made her freeze.

"It's bad luck not to kiss while standing under the mistletoe."

Her cheeks filled with colour as she realised whose voice it was. She hadn't heard it since she'd begged him to leave her house, mortified, that her mother had walked in on them after he'd stayed the night following too much drink.

"I think it's only a rule at Christmas," she said, still facing away. Her stomach began to twist and feel fuzzy. Josh had popped into her mind a few times over the months, but she'd never considered calling him or even thought she might see him again, despite the fact he worked for his brother Felix.

"It feels like Christmas in here to me."

"Well, it's not and the mistletoe isn't even real, so I'm sure that's a deal breaker too." Sophie still didn't turn around. She didn't want him to see her flustered and embarrassed.

"You didn't call or text me. I thought you would have once you'd calmed down. I've asked Paris how you were a few times, but he said you'd call me in your own time if you wanted to."

Damn, Paris must have known Josh was going to be coming here to drop something off, Sophie thought, making a mental note to get him back for it.

Cheeks now feeling cooler, Sophie turned around as casually as she could and reached out behind her to feel for the back of a chair to lean against. Even though she'd just been facing that way, she'd forgotten they'd moved the furniture around to make room for Paris's festive forest.

It was too late to try and keep her balance and any shred of dignity as she fell back. Her eyes, wide with shock and embarrassment, saw Josh's jaw drop as the top half of Sophie disappeared into the middle of the trees. The only thing he could see were Sophie's legs sticking out from a messy pile of fake pine and dislodged plastic baubles, which were now bouncing across the club's floor like ping pong balls.

Sophie just laid there, hoping that, if she closed her eyes, it would all go away. But no, of course that's not how it was going to work. She could feel the weight of the trees on her reduce little by little as Josh lifted them and stood them up again, causing more plastic baubles to fall, hitting her as they tumbled to the floor where they made hollow tapping noises as they bounced and rolled around the room.

"Well, that was quite the reintroduction," said Josh as he finally found Sophie crumpled and mortified at the bottom of the pile. "Some might say you're trying to avoid me, and I'd say you're doing a poor job of being subtle about it."

"Of course I'm not trying to avoid you. Surely what happened between us was just a one-night thing. Paris has told me all about you, it's what you do."

Josh had helped Sophie up from the floor where she gained some composure and tried to project some sort of dignity.

"I wasn't aware Paris had psychic abilities. I shall have to remember his talents extend that far next time I put the lottery on. Yes, I've got a bit of a history when it comes to women, but do not believe you were just another of them. I haven't stopped thinking about you. Did Paris tell you that?"

Sophie didn't know what to say. She had thought about him several times since the night they'd met, but hadn't allowed herself to dwell on what could have been. It was just what it was. Afterall, since divorcing Carl, there had been no space for a man in her life. Even when she was with Carl, there wasn't really space for one.

Then again, she'd never made such a fool of herself in front of Carl or any other man for that matter. Josh made her stomach lurch with excitement. It was unfamiliar. How was it that a stranger could walk into where she worked and make her think differently about everything?

"Well, are you going to let me take you out one night? I never did get to show you that I can be the perfect gentleman. I promise, this time no cocktails and no vodka."

The last time Sophie had been asked out ended up with her being married, having two children and then a divorce, followed by a decade of singledom. Josh was a good few years younger than her, didn't have any kids to speak of and, as far as Paris had fathomed, hadn't ever had a serious relationship. Why would he want to pursue a forty-four-year-old woman who had two grown children and worked in a drag club?

"I don't understand. You really don't want to get involved with me, I'm not that exciting, and I don't have a lot to offer. I'm doing you a massive favour

288

turning you down and telling you to find someone younger and with less baggage."

"Well, when you put it like that," Josh began, feeling a little downbeat, "you've made me even more intrigued than I was at first," he finished with a smile. He was determined to get what he wanted, to pursue this woman who clearly didn't see in herself what he did.

"I'm not really up for an argument." Sophie was now trying to fight a smile back as her stomach started to buzz. This beautiful man wanted to take her on a date. "But I did try to warn you about my uncanny ability to disappoint people."

"Ok, let the record show I was warned about this woman's power to disappoint," he said, throwing his arms out and making a statement to the empty room. "Let it also show that I do not believe her and consider our two brief encounters some of the most intriguing I've had."

Sophie tried to pinpoint what it was he wanted. It seemed impossible to her that someone like Josh would even look twice at a woman such as Sophie.

There wasn't anything particularly special about her. Although she now dressed better, she still had the body of a woman who'd given birth to two children and hadn't been to the gym a day in her life. She was also in her forties and while her face and skin hadn't been haggard by years of drinking or smoking, she pretty much looked her age, or at a push, a few years younger.

It was obvious, she considered, Josh must have thought she was a woman of means. Afterall, when he met her mother, she was dressed like a flamboyant aristocratic widow. Sophie owned her own home on a single income and could afford nice things. Whatever it was, she'd suss it out on a date with him and then set him straight.

"I have next Friday night free. I don't want to travel too far, and I certainly don't want to be out in London all night."

"Ahh, she has rules. I shan't disappoint. Now, may I have your phone number so I can keep you updated as the plans unfold," Josh said with cheeky smile while handing over his phone for Sophie to key in her own number. "This way I won't have to wait for you to call me." And then he pecked her on the cheek and walked off.

Sophie sat down and mulled over what had just happened. She'd made a complete fool out of herself in front of someone she'd had a one-night stand with, an occasion where she'd also made a fool of herself.

"What the bloody hell has gone on in here?!" shrieked Paris, who looked at the mess with his mouth wide open. "I've been in the office for twenty minutes and I come back down to a frigging bombsite. Sophie, I spent hours getting those trees up and decorated."

It took Sophie almost half-an-hour to tell Paris what had gone on. It would have been a ten-minute job if she didn't have to wait for him to stop laughing every five minutes at the thought of her lying under a pile of trees. Apparently Paris didn't realise it was Josh who was delivering the giant inflatable snow globes. He didn't have chance to look at the delivery man as he could hear the phone ringing in the office.

Sophie's embarrassment and the prospect of a date were payment enough for Paris to forget that she had felled his forest. They both agreed it had looked too perfect anyway and so just threw everything back together as quickly as they could, leaving some of the baubles on the floor under the trees.

"It's not like people will be going in there anyway," he reasoned. "It's just for show. But, tell me more about this date Josh is taking you on. It's been so long since a nice rich handsome man has asked me out. I'm beginning to worry I'll be an old maid living on my own."

"There's nothing really to tell. He came in, dropped off the delivery and made me so nervous that I fell over. Then he asked me on a date. That's everything. He said he'd be in touch soon," she repeated to Paris, hoping he would now drop the topic as talking about it made her nervous.

"You deserve a little bit of excitement, girl," he added and walked off to the dressing rooms to get ready for the evening.

Chapter Seventeen: Date

Clothes were piled on to Sophie's bed, every item from her wardrobes and draws had been pulled out and were now laying limp and crumpled with shoes, belts and handbags dotted on top.

Paris had suggested he go up first to prepare a few outfit choices for her date with Josh that evening. A few days had passed before Sophie got the text from him, simply saying: *'Dress glam, I'm taking you out on Friday. Be ready for seven in the evening.'*

Her skin had prickled with nerves ever since the text came through. Josh's words, too, hadn't left her mind since their second meeting at Sophisticats the week before. Any ability to dress herself in her new clothes had strangely disappeared, so whenever she tried on an outfit and looked in the mirror she either looked fat, overdressed or like her clothes were wearing her.

"Right hun, get your butt up here and come and see what I've put together for you," her boss shouted down the stairs.

Doing as she was told and eager to discover what Paris had been doing for the past hour, she ran up the stairs two steps at a time. Her face was green from the mask Paris had told her to smother across her face and her hair was oily from a treatment he'd given her.

"He's a lucky man, I'll give him that," Paris said with a smirk as Sophie walked in.

"Did you really have to get everything out and throw it all over the room?" she said looking around at her usually organised belongings that had been flung carelessly in all directions. "I hope you're going to tidy this up before you go."

"Fashion genius, daaarling, materialises in the ugliest of ways. Now I've put these three outfits together for us to choose from. Pop them on and let's have a look."

"You want me to put them on here, in front of you?"

"Hun, you haven't got anything I want, don't worry. It's just us girls."

Sophie couldn't remember ever getting changed in front of another person. Even as a child when it was time for PE at school she'd run off to a corner somewhere so no one would see her. Carl hadn't seen her undress either – she'd always do it in the dark. Josh didn't count as they were both too drunk to even know what was going on.

The first of the three outfits that was hung on the back of her door was a figure-hugging black shift dress that cinched in at her waste before tapering into a loose pencil-style down to just below her knees. She put it on and Paris handed her a jade green belt and threw a pair of black stilettoes at her.

"This is super-glam, fun and sophisticated. It says, 'I'm a powerful, sexy businesswoman who knows what she wants, but my green belt here says I also know how to have fun'," said Paris while making Sophie trot up and down the bedroom. "Thoughts?"

"Hmmm. It's nice, but I'm not sure."

Her next outfit was a pair of black skinny jeans, a purple printed silk top and yellow patent leather pointed heels.

"I don't think this one's for a first date, these jeans make me look too fat around my waist. I wouldn't feel comfortable," Sophie said without even trying on the choice, throwing the clothes back.

"Well, you're not fat and you have a beautiful figure. But I'm listening and willing to move on to the third and final option."

This choice, which was also on the door, had been hidden by a blanket that Paris had hung over it keeping it out of sight. He pulled the cover from the outfit in one smooth tug as though he was unveiling a piece of expensive art.

"Why's this one covered up? Oh, Paris, it's beautiful, but I don't wear..."

"Consider it a bonus for all of your hard work lately. And I'll have none of this 'I don't wear bright colours, I only wear black and dark things.' Hun, you need to experiment, and this will make you stand out for all the right reasons."

The dress was made from silk and was buttermilk yellow. It was printed with what looked like a cross between black feathers and sweeps from a paintbrush. Once it was on, she tied the thick black belt that Paris handed to her around her waist and looked in the mirror.

Her dark hair and eyes popped against the bright colour. The long sleeves finished in a subtle bell shape at her wrists and the bottom of the A-line dress finished at midcalf.

"It's beautiful, but I don't have any shoes to go with it."

"Oh hun, you clearly don't think much of me," he said before kicking a box out from under her bed and sliding it across to her with his foot.

Inside was a pair of black leather cowboy-style Chelsea boots with a heel and silver accents on the tips. Once on, the top of the shoes ended just above her ankles.

"Paris, I don't know what to say," she told him while staring at herself in the mirror. "You're so kind to me and I don't know what I've done to deserve it."

"There's nothing in the law saying I can't treat my friend to something nice for her first real date."

No one had called Sophie their friend before. She'd never really thought about hers and Paris's relationship being anything other than employer and employee. But considering everything he'd done for her and how much time they spent together away from Sophisticats, she had to admit it was closer to friendship than anything else.

A wide smile sprang across her mouth as she turned to look at Paris who was sitting on her bed with one long slim leg crossed over the other. He was wearing skintight black jeans and a black floaty shirt that almost touched his knees.

"Then I'm very lucky to have a friend like you."

"Yoo-hoo. Sweetie, darling," they both heard from downstairs. "Where are you Sophie?"

"We're up here mum. I didn't know you were coming over today."

"You know I like to surprise you, sweetie," replied Beryl as she walked into Sophie's bedroom, out of breath from coming up the stairs too quickly.

She scanned the room, noticing the disarray of clothes and shoes and then made her way to Paris, greeting him with two flamboyant air kisses and a "darling, you look fabulous", before sitting down.

"Sweetie, I must say it is quite the state in here. I don't think you've ever had such a messy bedroom before. It's quite refreshing. But, oh, don't you look gorgeous. Is this for your date? Darling, if your father was here to see you now, he'd be bursting with pride."

"Mum don't start blubbering," she warned as Beryl pulled out a purple silk handkerchief with bright yellow daffodils printed on it.

"I just can't help myself, sweetie," she said through teary eyes. "I don't think I've ever seen you look this beautiful before."

"Well, thank you. I guess," her daughter replied sarcastically, taking the comment in good humour as she too knew it was the truth.

"No, no. Of course, I think you're always beautiful, but what I mean is you look so different and... Well, I'm just so happy to see you go on a real date. I worry that you'll be lonely for the rest of your life. You're not in your thirties anymore and I know I never moved on after your father, but he meant so much to me."

Sophie rolled her eyes at Paris. Her mum was of course being overdramatic, but there was some truth in it. She'd always told herself that living alone for the rest of her life was fine, she didn't need another man. But that was a cover, the fact was Sophie had been afraid to try and meet someone else.

"It's just a date, mother. It's hardly marriage and I'm not even sure if it will go anywhere. He's not exactly my type."

"Hun, if rich young, charming and gorgeous isn't your type, then you don't deserve that dress," Paris butted in. "Anyway, I've got one more surprise for you, wait there."

Beryl's and Sophie's eyes followed Paris as he left the bedroom and they both sat in silence listening to him pad down the stairs and into the kitchen.

"I do love him, sweetie," Beryl said, breaking the short comfortable silence with an approving whisper about Paris.

Sophie was looking at herself in the mirror again, swishing her dress and making the material flutter over her legs. "He's a very special person."

"He's very attractive, you may want to think about pursuing a relationship with him, although he might be a little to..."

"Gay for me?"

"He's gay, sweetie? I didn't realise. He buys you nice things and looks after you, I thought he was trying to woo you darling."

Reading a person had never been one of Beryl's strongest qualities; there had been many times where she'd opened her mouth and said something that wasn't quite right. Obliviously causing lots of embarrassment for everyone in the room.

"Mother, he's a drag queen at Sophisticats. He owns the club and he's not even thirty yet. If those two reasons aren't enough to stop us from having a romantic relationship, then I'm not sure what would."

"Some men are just a little flamboyant, sweetie, especially these days. Look at that man on the baking show, the one with the long dark hair, apparently, he has a wife, but he swishes around like something else. Paris, on the other hand, isn't effeminate at all,"

Beryl's straight face told Sophie her mother was being serious about her perception of Paris, which she found endearing.

"I suppose he's not really one for swishing around, but he does dress up as a woman for a living – and a convincing one at that. When you see him as the real Paris Le Grand and not his boy self, we can talk about this again."

"I hope you're both talking about me," Paris sang while bounding into the room with an ice bucket, Champagne and three coupette glasses. "I'd hate to think I wasn't worth talking about after vacating a space."

"Don't worry, we were... oh, Champagne. You're too much Paris, are you trying to sabotage my date before I even go on it?"

"Hun, this evening should start the way it is set to continue, with a pop and a fizz. Now, you ladies drink up, I ordered a case of this for the bar a while back and no one has bought a bottle of the overpriced stuff."

The popping of the cork was met with the obligatory cheers and claps opening a bottle of Champagne incites, before Paris raised a glass to toast Sophie.

An hour later, she was sitting on the edge of the sofa in the living room with another small glass of Champagne. Paris had offered to take her mother home before he went to the club for a show and Beryl had taken him up on the offer, "it will give us chance to get to know one another", she'd said.

Sophie's stomach was skipping as she waited for seven o'clock to come. Waiting was her least favourite thing to do, it made her anxious and the thought of having to do something at some point later in the day always prevented Sophie from doing anything else while waiting for the time of whatever it was to come.

She checked her phone to see if Josh had messaged her, it was just after seven. Obviously, he's not going to come, she thought. He's probably found someone younger or more attractive or both.

There were no texts or missed calls on her phone though and, while she did believe Josh could have had a better offer from another woman, she knew, even after only meeting him twice, that he wasn't the sort of person to bail without notice.

She put her phone in a little black clutch bag Paris had chosen from her wardrobe and heard a car pull up outside. It was easy to see out of the window without getting up or moving much and parked in front of her house was a big swanky car in gun metal grey.

Sophie shuffled closer to end of her seat on the sofa to get a better look. A man in a suit got out, walked to the rear passenger door and opened it, following which Josh got out.

"Wow," Sophie said in disbelief.

A knock on the door stirred Sophie who was still looking open-mouthed at the chauffeur-driven Rolls Royce outside her house. Legs shaking and now more nervous than she'd ever been, she gulped the rest of her Champagne down and walked to the front door to open it.

Standing a few steps back from the entrance, so she could take him all in, Josh was holding a small bunch of cream-coloured roses and beamed at the astounded woman in front of him.

"It's not too much is it? I borrowed it from Felix. My brother may be over the top at times, but he has good taste and is very generous."

Sophie didn't speak for a few moments, but craned her neck to look past Josh, whose white shirt was unbuttoned enough for her to see a small amount of hair from the top of his muscly chest. He was wearing dark blue slim leg jeans and camel desert boots.

"Is it too much?" Sophie whispered, convinced now more than ever that Josh had made a mistake in pursuing her. "I, err. I don't know. It doesn't seem real."

"Well, it's not my car," he said taking a step closer as the look on his face shifted to one of anxiety. "I have an old Land Rover, and I didn't think picking you up in that would set the tone I wanted to."

"You've certainly set the tone," she replied bluntly.

"Look, I can take this back and come and get you in a taxi if that would be better?"

"No, it's a really nice that you want to make tonight special. I'm sorry, it's me being silly. It's just the sort of thing you'd see on the tele or in one of those chick flick films, that's all. I'm over the shock now. Promise."

"Well come on then," he said, smile now reinstated. "We've got to get going if we're going to make it on time."

Her recently wobbly legs were now something close to firm again, Sophie took the flowers and put them in some water in the kitchen sink before grabbing her coat and bag and locking up. Josh linked her arm and waited until she was in the car and then got in the other side himself.

"You look wonderful tonight, you really do."

"Oh, it's really nothing. Thank you," her face prickled and began to turn red. She still didn't know how to react to compliments and instead looked away out of the window, giving herself some time to try and think of something interesting to say. But it was as though she'd lost her grasp of the English language. Even in her mind she couldn't form a suitable sentence.

"I know you said you didn't want to go into London, but there's somewhere I've been keen to try. It's just a forty-five-minute drive and the roads will be quiet later this evening, so we'll be back in good time."

"The water in London has been through the kidneys of around seven other people before the eighth person drinks it, you know!" she suddenly blurted.

"That's, errr. Well, that's a fun fact. Maybe we'll stick to bottled water tonight," was Josh's reply to her clumsy attempt at what she thought was interesting small talk. Although Sophie was now dying inside and chiding herself for what just came from her mouth, Josh thought her nerves were sweet.

"I'm nervous too," he added after a short silence. "If I'm being honest, this is the first time that I've done something like this. I don't tend to date. If you like, we can just go somewhere a little more casual."

"No, you've planned a special evening out for the two of us and we'll do it. We both just need to get over our nerves a bit. If you think about it, this is technically our second date."

"What do you mean?"

"Well," continued Sophie, "We had drinks together the night we met at Sophisticats and if we just pretend that we didn't get so drunk and that it didn't turn into something else, then we're on our second date."

"That makes sense," Josh agreed and, like Sophie, began to relax enough to make sensible small talk.

Their journey ended up taking almost an hour. Although Sophie didn't want to travel that far for a first date, she didn't mind now she was in the car and talking to Josh. He pulled out a small bottle of Champagne and she began to get to know him while taking sips of the bubbly he'd poured into flutes for them.

He and Felix were born into a wealthy family, but they'd both been taught to make their own way in life. The only financial support their parents had given their sons was paying for their educations. Both had gone to private schools from the moment they could walk and then on to Cambridge.

Felix was a year younger than Josh but had always achieved more and made is parents the proudest. Josh, on the other hand, found it harder to be the sort of person his parents wanted him to be. He was intelligent and graduated with a First-class Honour's Degree in Philosophy, Politics and Economics. However, he didn't know what to do with it.

Others in his class had gone into things like banking, journalism or politics, but that wasn't what Josh had in mind for himself. Although, if he was honest, he didn't exactly know what he wanted to do anyway. Instead of progressing into something his parents would approve of, he ended up working behind bars at pubs and nightclubs, reaching management and head office positions with good salaries.

However, when one of the companies he was working for was bought out, he lost his job and at that point his brother Felix's events and promotions business was turning over significant amounts of money and so it made sense to go into that.

"I appreciate it all sounds very much like first world problems," Josh said as he finished answering Sophie's questions. "But even well off and well brought up rich people can be unhappy. I just couldn't be the sort of person my parents wanted me to be."

"Perhaps I can't understand everything you just said, but I do relate to many parts."

"Oh, you do?" Josh answered, now even more curious to understand Sophie. He'd seldom opened up to anyone, but whenever he had told women a little about his background, they were either more interested in how wealthy his family was – wanting to know whether Josh would inherit the whole fortune as the older brother – or if he could get them a job working with Felix, who was well known and paid his staff a good salary.

Those sorts of questions were heartless and shallow, but what irked Josh more was people telling him to get over himself. Yes, he'd come from a very privileged background, but he'd learnt the hard way that the cliché 'money doesn't make you happy' was a fact.

"Most girls just want to know how rich I am when I tell them about my background and who my brother is."

"I don't really care about money. I've always worked, and I've been lucky enough to save enough money to help my sons out whenever they needed. But I've never been materialistic and have always lived well within my means."

Although Sophie didn't know it, a woman had never said anything like this to Josh and he was beginning to fall for her, despite the fact it was only the third time they'd met.

As the car drove on, the streets around them became busier and more built up. It was getting later, but the sky was still bright, and people were milling around on their way to dinner or coming home from work.

Conversation hadn't dried up at all on the journey as both Josh and Sophie asked one another all kinds of questions two people on a first date ought to. Finding out more about Josh was so enjoyable that Sophie had forgotten they were heading to dinner on a date until the car stopped and the driver opened the back door to let her out.

She stepped onto the street, running he hands over her dress to make sure Paris's work still looked in pristine condition. Looking up, Sophie was met with a breath-taking view. In front of her stood a silver-brick Victorian building covered in wisteria. Its purple blooms billowed across almost all the walls from a thick gnarled trunk and its branches wound the width and breadth of the building, leaving space only for the sash windows and a big black door that sat in the centre.

"This is supposed to be the best place to eat in Kensington and all of London, for that matter... or so I'm told," Josh said as he approached Sophie from the other side of the car.

"I've never seen anything like it. I didn't think there was anything like this in London, it's beautiful."

"I suppose it is quite the sight. We're lucky, actually, wisteria only blooms in May and June, but I think I heard on the radio the other day that it was late in London this year for some reason. But we didn't come here to stare at the flowers, let's go and eat, I'm starving."

Josh offered Sophie his arm to link and they climbed the steps outside the restaurant together before being greeted by a polite French maître d' who welcomed them to restaurant Ligne Ondulée.

Although she'd never been anywhere like this before, Sophie had seen similar restaurants on the tele and had always wondered what it would be like to eat somewhere so opulent.

The walls were covered in rich duck egg blue silk papers with silver foil details. Paintings of people, animals and plants hung in clusters on the walls and above their heads was a big glittering chandelier. This was all just in the entrance to the restaurant and Sophie wondered what waited on the other side of the dark wood double doors in front of them.

When the doors slowly swung open, it was like being granted entry into a palace. Soft, plush furnishings dotted a large dining room whose floors were covered in a rich red carpet, soft under Sophie's feet. Tables with seating for no more than four people each were set so far apart from each other there was no chance of overhearing or being overheard by the other diners.

Ligne Ondulée's maître d' had followed Sophie and Josh through into the dimly lit room and showed them to a table in the corner which had been set for two. "I ope zis will be satisfactory, monsieur Geller?" he said while pulling a chair out for Sophie and draping a napkin across her lap.

"I will leave you with complimentary Champagne before ze head waiter comes and sees to your every need." And with that, he sloped off back through the double doors in silence.

"Wow. I've never been anywhere like this before in my life," Sophie said, bewilderment in her wide eyes as she turned to look at every part of the restaurant.

"Me either. Felix has been doing some consultancy work with them on experience and making every part of the diner's time here feel special. He's got his annoying quirks, but I have to hand it to him, he's bloody good at what he does."

Conversation at dinner was flowing, along with the wine and Champagne. They followed the wine waiter's suggestion of having a flight of wine with the tasting menu they'd both ordered, which meant a glass of specially chosen vino came with each course.

But then the conversation turned towards Sophie and her background. The questions Josh began asking, although inane to most people, were uncomfortable for Sophie. Ignoring them would only work for so long, especially as Josh had answered all of those asked of him in the car and so far at the table. She continued brushing them off and steering the conversation in different directions, but Josh was cottoning on to her evasive manoeuvres.

"Why won't you tell me anything about yourself?" he asked bluntly, which dimmed the comfortable atmosphere they'd both built. Sophie could feel her cheeks flushing red and anxiety prickled over her body as she stumbled for words.

Simply saying this is the single most exciting night of my life and anything before the past few months was a grey sludge of boring wouldn't do.

"There's not much to tell. I've not lived a life worth talking about like you have. There are no funny anecdotes or points of interest," she said to her now silent dinner partner.

Josh looked at her, trying to calculate why Sophie was so closed when he'd opened up to her. No one, not his brother or parents, he felt right now, had learnt so much about him as Sophie had this evening and he felt bruised. For the past few hours he'd described every element of his life that had been asked for, but it was so far a one-way transaction.

"Look, I've been very honest with you this evening. I thought we were connecting, that this could be something special. When I say I've never done this before," he said thrusting his arms wide open as if to present the room and the situation. "I'm not saying this lightly, there is no one on the planet right now, other than me and now you, who knows more about my life and thoughts and yet I know nothing about you. You won't tell me, or you don't trust me."

Sophie looked down at the white tablecloth that was freckled with a few faint splashes of red wine and peppered with some crumbs the waiter hadn't managed to brush away between courses. Josh wasn't being indignant or rude in pressing Sophie, but she could see hurt in his eyes. Simply, there was no way of sharing anything of herself with him. Not because she didn't feel anything for him, but it felt unnatural. The idle chitchat had been ok, but anything deeper was too much.

The walls that she'd been built up around her were now so thick and high she wouldn't know where to start even if she wanted to scale them or smash them down. This had all been a big mistake. Allowing herself to be driven so far away from home with a strange man who she'd only met three times. What was she thinking?

Anxiety turned to panic without hesitation or warning. Her legs and back began to itch as though big welts were crawling across her skin as Josh continued to look at her, eagerly awaiting for his date to spill even the smallest morsel of information about herself.

"I'm sorry," she whispered, struggling to catch her breath. "I don't know what to say. It's difficult for me. Please. Could we go?"

Josh nodded at the waiter who brought the bill over. He paid and messaged the driver to bring the car round, which he knew would be there as soon as they left the door of the restaurant. As a young man, such a snub would have angered him, but his experience had taught him to think better. He wasn't violent or resentful these days and took everything in his stride.

However, what he considered a rejection made him numb. Or maybe it was the wine they'd had with each course. Either way, he felt as though the world was spinning, not around him like would happen after too much to drink, but as though he was turning with the earth.

The journey home was quiet and a stark contrast to the one on the way into London. But it was late and the roads were clear of other cars, so it flashed by in a shorter amount of time.

When Sophie thanked Josh for a lovely evening, he gave her a weak smile and turned his cheek as she leaned in to peck him on it.

Although the night hadn't gone to plan and it ended rather gloomily compared to its start, he found himself with a greater need to find out who Sophie was.

Chapter Eighteen: Losing It

It had been a few days since the damp ending to Sophie's and Josh's first date and she hadn't heard from him. But she hadn't tried to get in touch either. Even though she knew it was her job to text or call him after making things so awkward, Sophie couldn't emerge from the mortification of how she'd allowed their last meeting to end so uncomfortably.

Instead, work at Sophisticats was used as a distraction and any questions about the date from her mum, Paris or the other girls at the club were brushed away and closed down with a simple: "I don't think he likes me".

She knew this wasn't true. The truth was she didn't think he would like the person who emerged from the questions he had wanted answered. It was just easier this way. It was pure fantasy to think someone like Josh would have a relationship with Sophie, and allowing her hopes to rise was silly.

With difficultly, Sophie tried to think on the bright side. At least she would be able to tick *Go on a date* off the list. Once again, however, she began to question her need to complete the silly tasks that had been desperately scrawled on a piece of paper over a decade ago. Other than leading her to a job that she now loved, the list was becoming difficult and putting her in uncomfortable situations.

There was now a nice balance with what she and her mum were calling the 'Old Sophie' and who she'd become. Having a list of things to do that most people did without a thought was ridiculous. Forget about it, she told herself. Things were as good as they had ever been, and it was impossible for them to change much more. With that, she took the notebook from her bedside table and put it in a drawer. It was pushed from her mind and now she could return to some sort of routine again.

***

A week had passed and the Sophie who had emerged only months ago had almost disappeared. She no longer took time and effort to make herself look even halfway presentable. Although the jumpers and jeans hadn't returned, from head to toe, Sophie was dulling, just like a flower at the end of summer. Laughter and smiles disappeared once again and like in the past, tasks and her work were carried out dispassionately and through necessity rather than joy.

It didn't take Paris long to clock the difference in Sophie, he'd spotted it a few days following the disastrous date, but whenever he broached the subject of Sophie's mood, she'd become defensive before a thick and hostile silence enveloped her and the space in the vicinity.

"Sophie, I think we need to talk," Paris said one morning in the office, which provoked a grunt in response from the dowdily dressed woman who was working hunched over a desk at the back of the small room above the bar. "Look, I know you don't want to discuss this," he continued, hesitating at the prospect of another rebuke from Sophie. "To be quite honest, I don't care if you never speak to me again because I've dared to mention the fact that you're in a very different place to the one you were in only last week."

"Sophie are you listening to me!" he snapped.

His target stopped tapping at her keyboard and slowly turned to reveal a worn-out face with bags under eyes that sat small below a mass of hair that looked as though it had never in its life been tamed. Her mouth was dry, and her voice hadn't been used all that much over the past twenty-four hours, so Sophie had to swipe her tongue between her lips and teeth before saying anything.

"I've told you, there's nothing wrong with my mood. I'm behaving as I always have done, but constantly being told you're in a bad mood and asked if you are ok is of course to going to warrant some sort of hostility."

The tone she used had an edge to it that Paris had never heard Sophie use before, which settled in his mind what he had to do next. It wasn't an easy decision, but to watch this happen to her was more difficult.

"I have to disagree," he started, making sure each word he used was chosen carefully so she couldn't read anything into what he was saying, other than the facts.

"If you want to believe that how you're behaving now is normal, then that's fine. But let me point out to you why you're wrong and how it comes across to everyone else. You are so different to the person I met earlier this year and more so than who you were just last week, and I don't understand why you're choosing to not see that. You don't even dress how you used to and that tells me how you're feeling too."

In seconds Sophie's face turned from the pale white to fiery red, her eyes were wide and filling with tears of rage, but before she could blurt her rebuttal to Paris's accusations, he held up a hand silencing her so he could continue.

"I'm not saying this as your boss. This is your friend, Paris speaking. I want you to take some time away from the business. To think about what has happened and to work out for yourself what is going on. I have the number of a psychiatrist who I'd also like you to consider seeing. Sophie, I don't know a lot about you, but believe me this is for the best."

"What do you mean take some time away from the business, are you firing me?" she asked, with both anger and fear. "Is this you telling me that you don't want me anymore, that because I'm not behaving in a way that fits with the House of Paris Le Grand you want rid of me?"

"That's not what I'm…"

"No, now it's my time to speak to you!" she shouted before Paris could begin to defend himself.

Each question she asked Paris was empty, Sophie knew it wasn't what he was saying. But she couldn't help it, her fury had blinkered any perspective and there wasn't an ounce of care in her words as she slammed shut her laptop before shoving it into the handbag at the side of the desk.

Turning to Paris, staring him straight in the eye, she said: "I don't want to be part of the House of bloody Paris Le Grand. You can shove the job and your friendship in the same place."

With that Sophie stormed down the stairs into the main bar, let herself out of the club without locking up behind her and drove home with bitter tears streaming down her face. The tears didn't stop flowing when she got home and curled up on the sofa where she fell asleep.

Sunlight coming through the living room window woke Sophie early the next morning , her eyes soar and itchy from crying and her and back stiff and tender from sleeping uncomfortably on the sofa where she'd tossed and turned all night, too stubborn and fragile to go upstairs to her own comfortable bed.

Yesterday's argument replayed in her mind and the more thought it was given, the more determined she was that Paris had used it as an excuse to get rid of her from Sophisticats. But that was going to happen anyway, she thought.

From the first shift, she'd told herself that Paris and the other girls would eventually find her out to be who she really was. No amount of makeup, pretty clothes or job promotions would be able to hide the strange person who'd been unwillingly built over the past forty-four years.

In the same thought, Sophie recalled how things had been almost magical for her the past few months. She'd experienced a life that she thought would never exist for her.

The list, she thought. Only a few things had been ticked off, but there had been an effort to do more with varying levels of success. This was the first time she'd thought about it since throwing it into her bedside table drawer.

After giving the list a moment more thinking time, it was once again shoved to the back of her mind. An experiment had been tried and clearly it hadn't worked. There were moments when it all seemed to be coming together until it just didn't work anymore, especially when Josh proved that she hadn't changed all that much, at least not deep down. Superficially this new Sophie had looked nothing like the old one, but when push came to shove, the old Sophie won outright.

Now Paris didn't want her, perhaps she could look for another job in a call centre. She'd never be able to go back to the energy company where her old boss Maurice would just love to see her crawling back for her job. After the way she'd caused a scene in front of him and Lynda from Human Resources, he'd love to see Sophie beg him for forgiveness.

There was enough money in the bank to sustain her meagre lifestyle for months, and maybe she'd wait a while and see if anything came up before admitting defeat and approaching Maurice. Afterall, it's not as if she considered herself a proud woman, she didn't mind saying what people wanted to hear, as long as they left her alone, she'd just get on with it.

Sophie's tummy started to rumble. She hadn't eaten anything since breakfast the day before and now decided a few slices of toast with butter would be good. She sat up on the sofa and saw her bag on the coffee table next to the sofa. Unzipping it, she reached in for her phone, just to see if she'd missed any calls from Ralph or Thomas.

There were fifty-two unanswered phone calls from almost everyone in her contacts, which wasn't really that many people. Paris, her mum, the boys and a few girls from the bar had all left her voicemails and text messages. She didn't listen to the voicemails, but scrolled through a few of the texts, which basically asked her to call or reply when she'd received them. She guessed the voicemails would say the same thing.

Deciding to ignore the phone, she threw it back into her bag which caused it to fall on its side, following which a piece of scrunched up paper rolled out and onto the floor. It was the number of the psychiatrist Paris had handed her yesterday. She remembered snatching it from him, crumpling it up and shoving it into her bag before storming out. Why did she take it? Surely, objecting as she did to Paris's suggestion of a shrink would have caused her to just throw it onto the floor or back at him. Without another thought, Sophie shoved it under the coffee table with her foot and went into the kitchen to make breakfast and coffee. She really needed coffee.

"Hello, sweetie. I didn't hear you were up and about."

Chapter Nineteen: Lost

Sophie was surprised to see her mother sitting at the table, the fingers of her hands interlocking so she could rest her chin on them. A magazine was open in front of her with a pen next to it. It looked as though she'd been doing a spot-the-difference in one of the women's magazines she'd subscribed to for years.

"Mother, how long have you been here?" she asked, still shocked that Beryl had been in the house without her knowing.

"I got here last night and came in to find you sleeping on the sofa, it looked as though you'd been crying. Is there something wrong?"

Beryl's eyes, magnified through her large black-rimmed glasses, were studying Sophie's face before they slowly and carefully moved down, as if reading every part of her daughter. This was a familiar experience for Sophie. It was as if Beryl could absorb the truth from another person by scanning them with her eyes. She knew full well something was wrong and Sophie didn't need to answer her mother, and slumped down onto a chair opposite her.

"I've messed everything up, mum," said Sophie with a deep, pitiful sob that allowed more burning hot tears to escape her tired eyes, which stung as each drop fell. "Paris has fired me. He hates me. I don't have a job. I don't have friends. What I was doing with that stupid list has made me feel emptier than ever. There was a short moment when I thought I was happy, but like everything else in my life it's disappeared and now I feel more desperate than ever."

Puffy red eyes, a bird's nest of hair and shaking with a desolate sadness. This was not an unfamiliar sight for Beryl where her daughter was concerned. She couldn't count the times she and Sophie had been in this exact situation. That said, if she had to describe her daughter's disposition for someone today, it would be one of despair. Dark, grisly and lonely. A black cloud had descended over Sophie, so thick and dense she could hardly be seen or see out herself.

"Sweetie," she started before placing one of her warm hands across the table to lay over an icy one of her daughter's. "Darling, you've been doing so well. What happened? I received a call from Paris yesterday saying you'd stormed out of work in a terrible state. He was worried about you, said he'd wanted you to take some time away from the business, not fire you. He wanted me to tell you that he hasn't fired you. He wouldn't think of such a thing. I know how important your friendship is to him and he wouldn't do that to you. I know he wouldn't, and I think you know that too."

The sobbing began to subside, just a little, but Sophie's head was still resting in the crook of her crossed arms which were laying on the table, meaning Beryl was now talking to a matt of hair that move slightly with each of her daughter's little whimpers.

"We haven't been here, in this position for a long time, Sophie darling. What's happened? You were getting out there, meeting new people and starting to have some sort of a life." A long pause from Beryl did not give way to an explanation from Sophie, so she pressed further. "Your pills, have you still been taking your pills?"

The sobbing stopped. Sophie raised her head, allowing her eyes enough space to peek through the space between her fringe and arms.
Antidepressants had been part of her daily routine for as long as she could remember. Little happy pills were something she'd taken in various types and doses since her father noticed his daughter was different to the other children her age. She couldn't remember at what age they crept into her life. But the memory of visiting the family GP with her mother and father where the diagnosis of depression was made had stuck with her. She remembered her mother crying. It wasn't normal

for a child to take antidepressants. 'She's just a child,' her mother had cried into a handkerchief while in the doctor's office.

But Sophie had stopped taking them some months ago. She knew this wasn't the right thing to do, but life had become so good. She was happy. There had never been a time – both on and off the pills – that she'd ever experienced such joy. The thrill of getting up and doing something; having a purpose and somewhere to go where someone needed you, like at Sophisticats. The list, that was just Sophie's, it had allowed her to plan and work towards something.

Taking the pills wasn't necessary if she had all these things to help her now, so she just stopped one day. She couldn't specifically remember when she'd made the decision to do it, but tipping them all into the toilet, hearing them plop into the water one at a time, felt like freedom and just added to the bliss and contentment that was pulsing through her at the time.

Of course, being on the medication for the time Sophie had, she knew going cold turkey was the wrong thing to do. Dangerous, in fact. But she did it anyway. Nothing could take away the happiness that had infected her at that point.

"Mum, I haven't been taking my pills. I don't know how long for now, but I was feeling so much better when I stopped. Not taking them every day made me feel so free, as though I wasn't relying on something artificial to get me through. Taking them had always felt like cheating. It was as though I needed them just to survive, just to get out of bed and through the day. My whole life, that's what it's been like. I had the freedom to stop. To experience things in full colour for the first time."

There was as short pause and Beryl's lips pursed ready to speak again, but Sophie opened her mouth again. "I'm not going back on them."

Her eyes were no longer flooded with tears but were fiery with firmness, again an attribute Beryl had never seen in Sophie. While her daughter had, in some way, relapsed towards her old ways, something else in her had sparked into life. Determination had never been one of Sophie's traits.

"Ok, Sweetie," she said and stood up to walk to where Sophie sat, hands firmly gripping the top of the top of the table while still fixing Beryl with a solid stare. "Why don't you go and have a bath. I'll give down here a once over with the hoover. Tidy up a bit. Yes," she instructed rather than asked.

While Sophie went upstairs to the bathroom, Beryl did as she had said, but also began looking for any sign of the pills her daughter had stopped taking. As she moved the vacuum cleaner back and forth, trying to reach as far as possible beneath the coffee table in the living room, it made an odd sucking noise and blocked the thing. She switched it off and turned it onto its side to look at the obstruction.

Tutting, she removed a ball of paper. On one of the sheet's curls she could see what looked like writing. Unravelled and smoothed out, the name of *Doctor Jane Benson, psychiatrist*, along with a phone number and email address, was written on it. This was the answer, surely. Someone like this could help Sophie fix what was wrong in her mind. Beryl folded the scrap of paper over and put it in her pocket and finished the cleaning.

Upstairs, Sophie was in the bath. She'd filled the hot water right to the brim so the foam from the sea moss scented bubble bath she'd added to the running water almost slid over the edge when she got in. Other than the dull sounds of the vacuum cleaner being pushed around by her mother downstairs and the odd bit of banging, it was peaceful with the door closed and the natural light from the window streaming through.

Before she laid back to let the water soak over her hair and face, the door swung open. "Mother! I'm in the bath, what are you doing?"

Beryl didn't say anything, but waited until her self-conscious daughter moved a little lower in the water and carefully placed bubbles across her chest so the only thing visible was a neck, face and hair, which had already been dipped in the water and had stuck together in several brown sections.

"Sorry, sweetie, I thought you might be about done now."

Sophie rolled her eyes. She'd been upstairs for less than half an hour, waiting for the bath to fill up, and had only been in it for five minutes.

"You told me to have a nice relaxing bath and then you barge in when I've barely had time to lay back. What is it that can't wait until I'm back downstairs?"

This had to be handled delicately. Beryl had Sophie as a captive audience right now, there was no way she would get up and out of the bath while someone else was stood there, not at the risk of exposing her unclad body. But if she blurted any old thing out about going to talk to someone professionally, then she risked upsetting her daughter again.

"You don't want to go back on those pills?"

"No. But why…"

"Shush. I don't want you to back on the pills either. I remember the day you went on them. I've seen how they've helped, but I agree with you that it's not right to have been on them for so long that they've become a normal part of your life."

"Ok, but…"

"Shush, sweetie. I'm speaking. While I'd rather you weren't on pills like that, I understand and agree with the doctors. You wouldn't have been on them if you didn't need to be and you certainly shouldn't have come off them without speaking to your doctor either. That was very silly darling."

"Yes, but…"

"Quiet now, I'm trying to tell you something."

The bubbles were thinning and Sophie started to feel more uncomfortable about having someone, even though it was her mother, in a room while she was naked. She shuffled down a little further to try and prevent more skin from showing.

"Mother, I really think this should wait until I've finished have my *relaxing* bath. Could you please just leave and we can talk downstairs."

"No, sweetie, this has to be now," she said and sat down on the lid of the toilet seat between the bath

and the sink. "Now, we both want the same thing –
for you to not be on those pills again. But you see
what coming off them without the doctor's advice
has done to you?"

Sophie took in a breath to answer, but Beryl began
to talk again before she could get a word out.

"That's right, they've done quite the opposite. Now,
what I suggest is you go to the doctor's tomorrow
and explain what has happened. I also found this…"
she pulled out the now folded piece of paper from
her pocket … "in the living room while I was
cleaning. I don't know where it came from, but I
think it is something you should seriously consider.
I'm happy to talk to this doctor before you if you
like. I'll even come to your appointments. Either
way, I think it is extremely important that you look
at this properly, because it might be the only way
for you to be free, as you say, of those pills."

Sophie thought for a while. She just wanted her
mother to leave her alone in the bath, but this
wasn't going to happen until the answer she
wanted – a yes – was spoken.

"Ok. I'll go. Now please, let me finish in here and we
can talk about it downstairs."

"Good girl, sweetie. I think you've made the right
decision. Let's hash out the finer details in a more
appropriate setting, yes?"

Chapter Twenty: Shrunk

Just a day had gone by since Beryl cornered Sophie in the bathroom and she now found herself alone in the wood panelled waiting room of Doctor Jane Benson. A dark blue had been painted above the mahogany wood that stretched halfway up the walls of the small square room.

Sophie was sat on a small brown leather sofa in front of a coffee table with a potted plant and some tissues, but no magazines or books to flick through while waiting.

Around the corner and down a very short hallway she was first greeted by a young, demure receptionist with dark blond hair who asked only for a name and appointment time, before giving directions towards the waiting room. Sophie considered the way she was greeted by the receptionist, it wasn't unwelcoming, but there was something cold about it, maybe just professionalism, thought Sophie.

Wishing she'd brought something along to read, Sophie began crossing and uncrossing her legs while she waited. She studied the images on the wall carefully seeing several paintings of the night sky, peaceful looking forests and gold sandy beaches with the clearest water all dotted around, perhaps to make people feel relaxed, she mused.

The rattle of the door handle on the other side of the seating area roused Sophie from her study of the artwork. A young man with long greasy hair, not much older than her eldest son Ralph, came out. His eyes were sunk into his face with large dark circles around them. She wondered what he'd been in to see the doctor about and turned away before he caught her staring.

A few more minutes past. Sophie's nerves were beginning to rise again. She knew it was her turn next and this wasn't exactly her favourite thing to be doing. It was much worse opening up to a complete stranger than someone like Josh. But this had to be done. She'd had a long talk with Beryl and promised this was going to happen. A psychologist was one of the few things she hadn't tried, writing them off as a waste of time and money.

She stared at the door, her mind on the fence of whether to will it to open or remain closed. It was decided before she could make her mind up, however, when the handle rattled once again revealing, as it slowly swung open, an older lady with short brown curly hair.

"Sophie Defoy?" It was more of a question than a statement, delivered in the soothing voice one would expect in a shrink's office. After a moment's hesitation, Sophie stood in acknowledgement of the call and walked into the office.

"If you just shut the door behind you," said the woman with her back turned to her newest patient. She was ruffling some papers on a large desk at the far end of the room. Sophie looked around, expecting to see a continuation of the dark wood and muted tones from the reception area. But this room was bright and airy, with three large windows that looked out from their third-floor position over the town.

It was the opposite of what Sophie had expected to see in a psychologist's office. Instead of a chaise lounge there were two comfortable grey settees facing each other, with a large metal and glass coffee table in between and a navy-blue armchair at the head of the setup.

"Sorry about that Ms Defoy, I was just double checking I had all of your information and I do, but there's very little of it. You don't like to give much away, do you? Anyway, that's what we're here to find out. My name is doctor Jane Benson, but please call me Jane. It's very informal in here."

Sophie agreed it was not formal. Compared with the rest of the office, this room and the doctor were quite casual.

Jane was a short woman, barely coming up to Sophie's shoulder. She could have been in her early sixties and was wearing a loose emerald green cardigan over a tight white tee-shirt below which were a pair of black bootcut trousers and a pair of running shoes on her feet. The thought of watching Paris pointing out these fashion faux pas brought a little smile to Sophie's lips, which disappeared after remembering they hadn't spoken since she'd walked out of the club.

"Please sit on one of the sofas, or you can lay down if you prefer, it's up to you." Sophie was still standing next to the door while Jane pointed to the big settees as if they were easy to miss, even though they dominated the middle of the large office.

"Why don't you start by telling me a little bit about yourself," Jane said after mirroring Sophie by sitting in the armchair. "We can start with as little or as much as you like. Perhaps tell me what you want to get out of these sessions, or we can talk about something that's been bothering you?"

Then followed a long silence. Not an uncomfortable one, but a space that allowed Sophie time to think and gather her thoughts. She didn't really know where to start or even if she wanted to. The first thing that came to her mind didn't stay there for long and rushed past her lips before she'd even considered whether or not to say it.

In one quick burst with barely a breath between a word came: "My mother and my friend sent me here because they think I'm insane I came off my antidepressants when I was happy ticking things off a bucket list but not an exciting bucket list just one with plain old boring things on it like have a makeover then I went on a date and I wouldn't tell him about myself and he got offended and then we didn't speak to each other again so I stopped doing the list and got really sad again even though I thought I wouldn't and I really miss Josh and I think I've lost the only friend in the world I've ever had because I'm a psycho."

She stopped and took a deep breath. That felt good.

Jane's mouth opened slightly, as though trying to catch all the details from her new patient's long and unbroken sentence. She blinked before scribbling on a notepad on her lap. That took a second and she looked up again, but still said nothing.

Sophie cleared her throat a little as they both stared at each other, but still no word from Jane.

"Have, have I said something wrong?" she finally muttered, thinking the doctor was about to write her up as insane and call the men with white coats.

"How could you have done something wrong, Sophie? There's no right or wrong in this room. I want you to know that everything you say to me is in confidence and won't go any further. You can tell me anything, we can discuss it and hopefully we'll be able to come to some sort of solution to your problems or find a way of working on them."

This is odd, Sophie thought. I can say anything to this person and, if she's being honest about what she said, I won't be judged. It was an unusual feeling for her, she'd never been able to open up.

Other than answering her mother's questions when she was younger, there had never been an occasion where she'd felt she could do this. Even her ex-husband Carl got a rough, pottered answer about how she was feeling; usually one word or the well-trodden brush off 'I'm fine, I've just had a busy day'.

Was she, though, able to tell this stranger all about her life, her anxieties and worries? No one knew the truth about what happened with Josh. Perhaps she could have this Jane woman analyse her parenting skills too – there was still that nagging feeling at the back of her mind about Ralph. He was yet to say if he was gay or not. Also, what Thomas said to her about not being around when they were younger. Yes, there was a level of understanding on his part, but the fact he had to say it to Sophie left her feeling guilty. And what about that other nagging feeling she'd always had in the back of her mind. What was that, where had it come from and how was she to get rid of it? And the list. Everything seemed to be so much brighter when she was ticking things off that stupid list, but then it had many complications too. Josh, for one and the cookery class – they both went far from plan.

There was so much more to her problems than what Sophie had just rambled off to the shrink. And as she thought about it more and more, sat on the sofa with Jane staring at her, trying to see what was going on in that dark, twisted mind of hers, Sophie's chest tightened, and her breathing became quicker. A weight, like a car or an elephant was now pressing down on her and she could hardly breath.

"Sophie, are you ok? You haven't said anything in a while, and you've gone white."

"I think I'm having a heart attack," Sophie panted one word at a time. "I can hardly catch my breath, I'm dizzy and it feels like there's a huge weight on my chest."

Reaching over, Jane took Sophie's hands in hers, looked her in the eye and started to breath slowly. "Sophie, I want you to look at me and take big deep breathes in and out, just like I am. Follow what I'm doing. I think you're having a panic attack."

Oh god, it's not enough to be a complete and utter nut job in the head, I've now got to start having panic attacks. But after several minutes doing exactly what Jane was telling her to do, Sophie began to calm down.

"What on earth was that?" she asked, eyes wide with worry. "That's never happened before."

"Well, what was it that you were thinking about? Panic attacks are more common than you might think, you may have even had one before and just not realised. The important thing to is to try and calm yourself down, otherwise you can work yourself into a bigger frenzy. Now, what do you think caused it?"

Sophie told her what she was thinking about and Jane listened carefully, writing the odd sentence in her notebook as Sophie delved deeper into her life over the two-hour session. At the end, the doctor said it would be good for them to continue meeting every day for the next week, as they'd made such good progress. Sophie wasn't sure she wanted to delve into the dark again so soon, or this frequently. But Jane assured her that once the week was up, they'd switch to shorter sessions on a weekly basis.

She walked out of Jane's office and past the receptionist, who ignored Sophie's "goodbye", and back down the street to head home. Her car was parked a short way from Doctor Jane's office, it was early afternoon and the town was bustling with workers making b-lines towards coffee and sandwich shops for lunch. Shoppers were milling around the high street, their arms laden with bags.

Sophie would have to go past Sophisticats to get to her car. Her heart pounded a little harder at the thought of walking by the club where her friends would have been hard at work last night. She'd missed being there to make sure things were in order. Paris, she knew, would have easily stepped in to take over her bookkeeping and stock ordering. But that wasn't the point, it was her job, something Sophie had achieved herself and now she was back in limbo, no direction or purpose.

The club, as she'd known, was shut up and quiet when she walked by it. The girls didn't get in until the early evening and Paris was probably working from home that morning. It was tempting to use her keys to get in and take a little look, but that would just be silly. It had been made perfectly clear that Paris didn't want Sophie there. It was probably for the best.

Shrugging, as though still trying to get rid of the temptation to go into Sophisticats, she continued walking to the car, which was now just around the corner, parked in one of those big temporary tarmacked lots which had once been a building and now just waiting for the council to decide what to do with it.

She unlocked it with her key fob but noticed a leaflet on the front windscreen which someone had put there to advertise something. Reaching over the bonnet to take it off, she could see pictures of dogs; it was a local animal shelter letting people know it had too many animals in need of homes. She studied the faces of the lost and unloved dogs, some were cute, others had missing eyes or limbs.

Sophie had never been an animal lover. She despised cats and small creatures like hamsters and rats, remembering once when her mother had bought Ralph and Thomas a little rodent of some sort as a pet when they were younger. That didn't last long, they soon lost interest in little Joey or whatever it was called and Sophie had to rehome the thing.

But there was some sort of connection between her and the little faces of the pooches on the leaflet. As a child, a dog was something she'd wanted at some point, her boys too had asked for one many times when they were younger but the argument of who would walk it and what would it do when no one was in the house always won.

There was no harm in going to see them now. It's not like she'd fall in love with one of them and must have it. Besotted wasn't something Sophie had been with anything, animal, human or otherwise. But she had nothing to do for the rest of the day and her week now consisted of several more two-hour sessions in the shrink's office. It was only a ten-minute drive to the shelter, just a quick look wouldn't hurt.

Chapter Twenty-One: Hound of Love

Boshambles Kennels were on the outskirts of town, just off a narrow leafy country lane. Sophie could hear the yapping and howling of its inhabitants before she'd even opened the car door. Signposts directed her to reception advising she'd have to sign in before being able to look at the creatures.

A young man was sat at the reception desk typing something into a computer. Once she was in front of him, he looked up and smiled. "Good morn… oh it's afternoon now," he said followed by a little laugh and a light slap to his forehead. "I'm always doing that, I don't know where I am. How can I help?"

"I had a leaflet on my car," Sophie said showing the receptionist as though he needed some sort of proof. "I'd like to take a little look around, but I'm not sure I'm really able to take a dog on."

"That's fine, they like to see new faces and you never know who you might fall in love with. Just sign in here and the kennels are in two blocks. If you walk through the door to the right there," he said pointing behind himself, "and then follow the path it will take you in a big circle to see them all. If you want to take anyone for a walk, just come back here and we'll make it happen."

Sophie followed the instructions and left the reception area after leaving her name and telephone number in a book on the desk. When she opened the door, a strange smell hit her nostrils. It wasn't unpleasant, but a mix of dog food, disinfectant and animal.

The noise of the chatty mutts grew louder too, they must have heard the door close behind her and she could hear their nails scratching on the painted concrete floors as they ran to the gates at the front of their kennels, waiting to see who their visitor was.

Reaching the first pen, a black Labrador with a grey muzzle pounced up and rested her paws on the gate. She looked straight at Sophie, her joy of having a visitor to see visible as her tail wagged side to side at such a speed it was almost a blur.

Sophie put a finger through one of the door's metal squares to scratch the dog's nose. She was called Trixie, the note on the side of the pen read. Trixie was twelve and her owner had become too sick to care for her and she'd been at Boshambles for six months now.

"Hello," Sophie said, tickling the dog's smooth muzzle. "You're a friendly girl, aren't you?"

The dog stared while being petted, but soon stepped back down on all fours and padded back to a bed at the other end of her kennel and went to sleep. I don't think we're right for each other, Sophie thought.

The next few kennels contained puppies and pairs of dogs that had either been found or dropped off by their owners who didn't want them anymore. Sophie made her way around all the animals, spending a little time at each pen before moving on.

It was upsetting to see so many different personalities trapped, unloved or unwanted, in their concrete and metal kennels. How long had they been here for and how many more days, weeks, months or even years would some have to wait before finding new homes?

Sophie had heard people on the tele say things like "oh, I could just take them all home". At the time, she didn't understand why someone would want to take home broken or unwanted dogs. Surely, they were in here for a reason.

They were cast outs, not wanted by normal people because they had an inability to adapt and become what they were expected to be. But reading the profiles of each dog, although some had personality or medical issues, they were all the same – in need of a little love and affection.

By the time she'd come to the last pen, Sophie wanted to wash her hands, although there wasn't enough space to fit a full hand through the gates to stroke the dogs, she'd petted at least twenty with her fingers. It looked like the final dog wasn't there, but she called the name written on the clipboard that hung on a hook.

"Gracie," she said in that way people talk to dogs before making a kissy noise with pursed lips. "Come on Gracie, let's have a look at you. All of your other friends have had a little attention today, you shouldn't miss out."

A bundle of blankets at the back of the kennel began to move and a little white head with golden patches peered out from underneath. Her eyes were brown, and the jowls of her long muzzle were creased and stuck to her teeth where she'd been lying asleep.

"Well, don't you look a treat when you first wake up," Sophie said with a laugh and bent down so the dog could see her better. "Come on then, let's have a look at you."

Gracie pushed her front legs from the pile of blankets out first, stretching them in front of her as she raised her bottom in the air and yawned. "I think my mother said that's a downward dog, you'd like her if you're into yoga."

The dog slowly trotted to the gate and sat down, looking at Sophie. She was no higher than two foot, with a mix of smooth and wiry white fir. The golden patches on her face were repeated a few times down her body and on her paws.

"Look at your beautiful, long eyelashes, I think Paris would say you'd make a stunning drag queen."

Gracie then stood, wagged her short tail and made a little croaky noise, somewhere between a yap and a bark. It was evident she'd just woken from a long sleep. "I don't sound too good when I've just woken up either. But I think you're beautiful."

Now she'd got her bearings, Gracie came closer to the gate to sniff her visitor, allowing Sophie to stroke her nose, before moving into different positions so other parts of her body could be scratched. "Making the most of it, I see. Well, you're a clever little thing."

"Would you like to walk her, she's the last one to go out today."

Sophie almost lost her balance where she was crouching on the balls of her feet. She hadn't realised someone was behind her now. It was a woman dressed in blue overalls and holding a lead.

"Well, I was just having a look. I've been speaking to them all today. I don't know if I should take her for a walk. I've never walked a dog."

The woman took a step back to give Sophie some room to stand. "It's not hard, I'll clip this lead on to her and we've got a special enclosure behind the kennels where you can let her off, she's a good dog and there's no chance of her escaping, even though she'd probably like to. She's been here for a year."

"I don't know, she might not like me."

"You'd be doing me a massive favour, I really need to get the food out before we have a riot on our hands."

Nothing else needed to be done today and she'd already spent the best part of an hour looking around, so after a few moments, Sophie hesitantly agreed to taking Gracie for a little walk.

"Ok, I'll do it. Would you like that, Gracie?" she said looking at the dog which was now walking excitedly in little circles.

"Great, just step back and I'll pop a lead on," the worker said to Sophie.

Gracie sat patiently while the handler slipped a collar around her slim neck and then followed her out towards Sophie.

"Just take her round that corner and you'll see the enclosure. Here's a bag in case she does anything, just pop it in one of the bins. Take as long as you like."

Sophie took the lead and did as she was told, walking Gracie out into a field with a fenced off area. She pushed open the gate and decided to keep the dog on her lead for a little while as they walked around.

Once they'd done a lap of the enclosure, which was about the size of a football pitch and had trees and areas with long grass and climbing frames for the dogs, Sophie decided to sit on a bench and let Gracie off, looking back at the gate to make sure it was closed.

The dog pelted off at great speed, leaping over the long grass, circling the trees and scrabbling up and down the wooden climbing frames. While Gracie was having fun, Sophie pulled out her phone, there were no messages or missed calls. None from Paris, her mum, the boys or even Carl. But then no one other than Paris and Beryl knew something was wrong.

A squelching noise and a foul stench distracted Sophie from the phone. What on earth was that, she thought looking down beside her. "Oh god! That's vile, you must be ill or something," she shouted at Gracie while trying to use her jacket to stop the stench from going in into her mouth and nose.

Baulking, Sophie pulled out the poo bag she'd been given by the worker and tried to work out whether the gooey brown mess on the ground next to the bench could be picked up. Poor Gracie, if dogs could be embarrassed, then she would be right now, thought Sophie, returning the little dog's stare as it watched her attempt to scoop the runny mess into the small black bag.

"That will have to do, little lady," she said and walked over to a bin near the gate. "Are you feeling a little sicky today? I don't know why I'm talking to you; we've only just met. Hell, you're a dog, you don't know what I'm saying anyway, never mind how long I've known you. Come on, let's get you back."

Sophie clipped the little dog's lead back onto her collar and led the creature, who walked obediently at her side, back to the kennels. The same woman who had convinced Sophie to take the dog for a walk was there, freshening up Gracie's bedding and filling up the food bowl.

"So, what do you think of her?" she shouted before Sophie and her new friend had reached the block. "She's a little character, isn't she? Calm, but she's also got a lot of spirit."

"I think she has an upset stomach; she made a mess in the park and it wasn't the sort of thing you could bag and bin, at least not all of it anyway," Sophie replied, handing over the dog's lead.

"Ahh, that happens to the little ones sometimes, there's nothing wrong with her. She's in fine health, these little crossbreeds are notoriously hardy. Do you think you'd like to take her home with you? She seems to have grown attached and by the way you're looking at her, I think the feeling's mutual."

It would be nice to have some company in the house, especially from someone who wouldn't judge her. I could walk out of here with a little dog, a little life I'd have to worry about, Sophie thought.

"I'm not sure. I didn't really come to take one home, just to see what it was like here, really. I don't know if I'm the right person to look after a dog, I can hardly take care of myself."

"Ahh, well that's why you should get a dog — someone else to worry about. It could make you think differently about yourself. You could take her home for a few days and see how you get on, there's no harm in that, is there? If things don't work out, then you can just bring her back in."

It would be heart breaking to even think of taking her out of the kennels and bring her back. She'd already been in there for a year, surely it would be torture to show her a loving home and then take it away again.

"Fine. I'll have her. But I won't be bringing her back. I've always wanted a dog, having one was even on a list that I used to have."

The woman's face lit up with the biggest smile Sophie had ever seen which then gave way to a whoop of "marvellous! You won't regret it". And before Sophie knew it, the woman had taken her into a tight embrace and was leading her and Gracie to the main reception area.

"What, I'm to take her now? I don't have anything, I'm not prepared to bring her home right now," she stuttered as they walked up to the young man who'd greeted Sophie earlier.

"Dan, this lady here would like to give our Gracie a new home. Could you make sure you go through the checks with her, and she might need a little bit of advice too," the lady said, leaving Gracie's lead in Sophie's hand as she walked back out to the kennels.

"Right," started Dan in an accent that Sophie thought had a slight Somerset twang, "let's go through everything and then we can get you and this little one on your way home. Isn't this exciting, Gracie," he cooed at the little dog who was standing by Sophie, taking everything in with a little wag of her tail. "You're going to your new home."

Half-an-hour of paperwork later, Sophie was driving away from Boshambles with a small dog and a boot full of her food, a new bed and some toys that probably cost more than they ought to.

Gracie sat quietly on the front passenger seat of the car. Sophie had half considered putting the seatbelt around the dog, wondering if it was legal to drive with an unbuckled animal in the front of the car. However, she didn't see how it work logistically so decided to give it a miss and take the risk.

But the journey home was uneventful, and they soon pulled up outside Sophie's house. "Right, little one, this is where you live now. I hope you'll like it."

***

A few days had passed, Gracie had settled into the house and the pair had begun to work out a little routine. They would wake at around seven each day, go for a short walk through the local park, have breakfast and then visit Sophie's psychiatrist together.

Doctor Jane didn't mind the dog coming to the sessions and would give her a little scratch before allowing her to jump up on the settee next to Sophie. But this was now the penultimate daily visit to the shrink. Sophie didn't feel any different, even though they had talked a lot about her past and got all the way up to the present day, in a potted sort of way.

"I think we've made excellent progress this week, Sophie. After tomorrow, we'll be seeing each other on a weekly basis for one hour only."

Sophie agreed that she'd come back the next day for her final two-hour session, but wasn't expecting doctor Jane to give her homework, which was to be completed before her return. She was to get her list out of the drawer again, look at it and think about why she felt so good when things went well and why she'd been defeated and ready to give up when something had a negative outcome.

Pulling the list from the safety of its drawer, where she had left it, forgetting about it, wasn't really something Sophie wanted to do. But she told herself that there was nothing to lose, at this point, she'd managed to bugger up the only close friendship she'd ever had, killed off a potential love life and she wasn't going to get started on what potential mental damage her mothering style had caused her children.

She thanked the doctor and left the office to see the receptionist so the next day's appointment could be booked. "Just do what the doctor says, she knows

357

best," Sophie said quietly while waiting for Trish, which she'd found out was the name of the receptionist, to confirm the appointment for three the next afternoon.

"Huh?" she said, confused.

"Oh, sorry, just talking to myself. But then you probably get a lot of that in a place like this, don't you?" Sophie said, smiling at her own joke. However, the girl didn't seem to find it funny and shoved an envelope into Sophie's hand.

"This is the bill. People tend to speak to themselves when they see this... usually they shout: 'HOW MUCH!'."

Sophie left, her mind whirring with everything the doctor had said to her that week and especially about her last words. The bucket list, she'd decided, was staying hidden in her drawer. There was no way she was bringing it back out, yes it had given her a few good times, but ultimately it had ended like every other of her tries to claw together a life that would seem at least normal to most humans.

"Come on, Gracie, let's get home." The dog followed obediently but stared at Sophie from the front seat of the car all the way home.

Chapter Twenty-Two: Bucket List

Once through the front door, Gracie ran upstairs, instead of the living room where she'd usually go to lie on the couch. Thinking it best to follow and see what the little dog was up too, Sophie found her standing on the bed, sniffing at the bedside table.

"What are you doing up here, silly? Come on, it's time for lunch. And you know better than to be on the bed. Come on." But the dog wasn't moving and began to growl at Sophie every time she tried to shoo her down from the bed, baring her teeth and snapping.

"Now come on!" she said in a firmer voice, but the dog laid down and growled a low warning. "Fine, bloody stay up here then. But you won't be getting any food if you behave like this."

Gracie didn't move for the rest of the day and into the evening. Sophie had to sleep in the spare room because the dog even refused to let her get into bed that night. "This is bloody ridiculous!" she snapped, leaving the door open a little so Gracie could go downstairs for a drink or some food – which Sophie had put out despite her earlier warning.

Sophie woke early in the morning, worried that her little companion would now need to go outside to use the toilet. The dog obediently came downstairs when she was called and ran outside to pee and then came back in, ate the food in the bowl on the kitchen floor and then started scratching at the kitchen door to be let back upstairs.

"No, not this time, missy. We need to go out for a walk before we go to see Jane later this afternoon. Come here so I can put your lead on."

The lead went on easily enough, but Gracie refused to walk and just laid down so Sophie had to pull her along the floor from the kitchen and into the hall. "Come on, Gracie, you've got to go for your walk."

No luck. The dog wasn't moving, and Sophie didn't want to lift her up in case she snapped and growled at her again. Anyway, even if she did lift the silly dog outside, what would she do, drag her around the park?

"Oh, this is just stupid Gracie. What's wrong? Why won't you come for a walk? And why am I talking to a bloody dog? Fine, we won't go for a walk." When the lead was removed, the dog again ran upstairs and jumped on the bed, this time standing with her front paws on the bedside table.

She couldn't know what was in the drawer, surely, Sophie thought to herself. That's just nonsense, but perhaps I should see if she can smell anything in there that shouldn't be, like food, she wondered.

After a little shuffling around, in the small drawer Sophie didn't find even a crumb of food. "There's nothing in there for you," she said to the dog. But then her eye saw the edge of something very familiar.

The notepad was still shoved where Sophie had left it, beneath magazines, books and other bits and bobs in her bedside table. It looked duller than she remembered, the rainbow printed cover of the book was faded and tattered at the edges from being chucked in her handbag and looked at too many times.

She traced one of the cartoon rainbows with her finger before opening it to the first page, which read *SOPHIE'S BUCKET LIST*, in neat black block capitals.

Overleaf, the double page spread set out the first two items on the list – one to a page – and had notes beneath them with ideas of how she could potentially complete them. The tasks she'd carried out early on, such as *Go to a drag bar* had been crossed through with a single line of blue ink. Beneath she'd written: *Met Paris, a drag queen, who offered me a job at the club as a backstage manager. Don't know what that is, but quit my job today so am not really in a position to turn it down.*

Below that in another colour, she'd penned: *Paris and the other girls lovely, but don't think they like me. Have made sure they all got on stage at the right times. They seem friendly to my face and haven't heard them laughing at me or poking fun, but it won't be long until they do.*

Sophie thought on this for a little while, casting her mind back to every interaction she'd had with the queens at Sophisticats. Paris had only ever been kind to her. He'd taken her to Selfridges to have a makeover, treat her to a nice hotel room in Manchester and bought the outfit for her first and only date with Josh – or with any man for that matter.

Josh. What did the notebook say about Josh? She flicked the pages to find *Go on first date* and saw nothing. There was also no entry beneath *Have a whirlwind romance*, but where it read *Have a one-night stand* a few quickly scrawled lines in green biro said: *Met a man at Sophisticats. Talked all night and went home. Woke up the next morning and felt like a new woman, until mother walked in and caused a headache of embarrassment.*

She had no recollection in her mind of writing these things down after they had happened. It was possible she'd pushed it all to the back of her mind while trying to shove the whole saga from memory after the date with Josh went belly up.

But the words she read were exactly the opposite of how she'd felt at the time of the events. In the moment of the one-night stand, when she'd tried to crawl away and deny it was all happening the day after, she'd felt trapped and sacred. But clearly, when she'd reflected on it at some point later, that hadn't been the case.

The few other things she'd completed on the list also had some thoughts, including *Learn to cook*. What she'd written after wasn't the embarrassing failure she'd believed it to be at the time. The book told Sophie that it was fun spending time with her mother, being a class rebel and although her mission to become a whizz in the kitchen hadn't been completed, it was marked a success in the book, with one clean biro line through the task, as did *Have a one night stand* and *Eat alone in a restaurant.*

'You're a complete and utter idiot,' she told herself, now sitting cross legged on the bed with the book on her knees. In the pocket of her jeans her phone vibrated, but it was just a spam email when she'd checked. Now it was in her hand, though, she had an itch to speak to Paris. To apologise for being such a cow and see if she could somehow beg for his forgiveness.

Paris would have to wait though, she thought. There was someone else would probably be less forgiving of her recent behaviour, considering their relationship wasn't all that strong. She found the number in her phone and typed: *Sorry. I need to explain. Want to meet for a coffee in town?* She pressed send and waited for what felt like hours, although in reality it was only minutes, for a reply.

It read: *Hey you. Sure, I'm in the area, shall we meet in an hour at 3?*

That would be enough time to shower and make herself look somewhere near decent, so Sophie replied yes with a smiley face emoji.

***

Now clean and made up with some light cosmetics and wearing a floaty floral A-line summer dress, that cut an inch below her knee, and a pair of tan sandals, Sophie sat in the same coffee shop where she used to have lunch sometimes when working at the energy company.

She looked around and wondered if her hideous old next-door neighbour Amanda Barnes with the plastic surgery would come in again. What would she think of dull Sophie now, wearing a colourful outfit and makeup?

She'd decided to leave Gracie at home, considering the fuss she'd made last night and this morning. Her hands were trembling and her heart beating fast, why had she thought this was a good idea and what exactly was she going to say?

The door to the café opened and the familiar tall frame and dark glossy hair of Josh Geller walked in, looking around to try and spot Sophie, who had ducked down a little, suddenly having second thoughts about this. Too late, he spotted her.

"Were you trying to hide from me?" he said with a smile, taking his coat off and hanging it on the back of the chair before sitting opposite her.

"Of course not, I invited you here. It would be silly to invite someone for coffee and then hide."

"I suppose it would be. Anyway, it's lovely to see you, you look great. What did you want to talk about?"

The skin across Sophie's back and up her neck began to prickle with panic, it was happening again, even though she wanted to open up to Josh, she couldn't. She should have brought Gracie with her, at least she could have stroked the little dog to help calm down.

As the turmoil and arguments raged through Sophie's mind, Josh sat patiently. He'd managed to learn a little more about her since their date, talking to Paris about what had happened and he now understood that Sophie wasn't trying to hide things from him, so he was willing to wait and not put any pressure on her until she could come out with what she wanted to say.

Now Sophie had started to fight back the doubts that were racing around her brain. Images of Josh laughing at her if she told him about her life and the hopes and dreams she'd only just discovered were being banished one by one as they sat together. He couldn't see the battle waging in her mind, nor did he know how exhausting it was for her to put out every little doubt that sparked into flame.

Pull yourself together you silly woman, it's not like you're telling him you've got seven toes and a hairy back. They're just words, you use them every day. You can do this. The lid on the box of the gremlins was slowly being pushed down, she felt. One or two were escaping, but they were small and could be dealt with later, but at least the bulk were trapped.

"I'd like to start again."

"What?" Josh asked, wrinkling his brow with confusion.

"Go back out and pretend that you weren't in here just now."

His smile made Sophie's stomach summersault. He must think I'm a bloody idiot, but I want to do this right.

"Ok then. I'll go back out and start again."

He got up and began to walk away. "Wait!" Sophie shouted a little too loud, making the few other people in the café turn to look at them.

"Wait," she said quieter, "You forgot to take your coat, it won't be starting again if you don't take your coat."

He chuckled, put the coat back on and left through the front door, turned right and walked past the shop's window. I hope he comes back, Sophie thought, worried that she may have scared him off with the strange request. But a second later he was back, she saw him check his watch, come in, look for her and then smile and walk towards the table.

"Hello Sophie, you look great," he said, leaning in to kiss her on the cheek. "What did you want to talk about?"

"Hello Josh, thank you. I wanted to apologise for our date and to ask if you'd like to go out for a second one. My treat, but it won't be as fancy as yours, just dinner at mine and I'd love to tell you about myself."

"Well, I don't know… I've heard you're not really a cook."

"That's true, but I do have a recipe for Malibu chicken that my mother is infamous for."

"Malibu chicken. Hmmm. I'm tempted. How about I bring the food and you supply the wine and the plates? Message me with a date and I'll see you soon."

With that he got up, kissed her on the cheek and walked back out of the café. Sophie let a big sigh of relief empty from her lungs. She was going to do this. But now it was time to put another relationship right.

Paris would be at home at this time of the day and it would be better to go around uninvited, so he couldn't make any excuses to stop her from calling over. On her way to Paris's from town, she drove to the supermarket to pick up a bottle of Champagne from his favourite vineyard. If he didn't want to see her, then she knew there was no way he would let a bottle this stuff walk away.

She pulled up outside the Victorian townhouse Paris had lived in just outside the town centre for a few years. It was a large four-storey home with a basement and a long and neat front garden, which had been planted with flowers and shrubs. There had been a touch of rain that day, so the garden smelled fresh and some of the plants had glistening droplets on them.

For all his flamboyant tendencies, Paris's home was reserved and had been renovated in keeping with its character. The one thing that told you it was his house, however, were the topiary cats wearing top hats that sat in purple plant pots on either side of the front door.

Sophie lifted the doorknocker and tapped it against the door three times before stepping back. She waited for a minute before seeing through the stained-glass window on the door that someone was coming down the stairs.

The unmistakeable slender outline of Paris bobbed around on the other side of the glass. She could hear him fumbling with the lock before finally opening the door.

"Sophie, what are you doing here?" A look of shock rushed over his face, which was quickly repressed and exchanged for the more familiar unreadable expression he usually wore, 'so no one knows what I'm thinking and so I don't get wrinkles', he once told Sophie.

"Hey. I, err. Erm. I just wanted to say that I'm sorry, Paris." She stuttered, trying to keep eye contact and not look down at the floor. "I was a terrible friend to you. You and the girls, but especially you. You are really special to me and I was going through something and that all got lost. Please will you accept my apology?"

Silence wrapped itself around the pair as Sophie waited for a reply, it even felt like the wind had stopped rustling the leaves on the trees and the birds had gone quiet too. Only seconds had passed, but the quiet was making Sophie nervous and she had to break it.

"I've been seeing the psychologist every day this week, for two-hours a day actually, so she must think I'm really broken, but that's going down to once a week for shorter periods after today," she began to ramble.

"Oh shut up you daft bat, of course I forgive you. There's nothing even to forgive though. It was an argument. You don't think I've been spoken to worse than that? That was nothing, it was almost a compliment compared to some of the other dressing downs I've had over the years. Get in here, I've got a visitor you might want to meet... and I bloody need you back at the club on Monday, I'm sick of doing the bookwork."

Relief washed over Sophie like water in a warm bath. Perhaps she had over thought the situation in her mind, after all, Paris was right. It wasn't as though she'd done anything other than throw a few negative words at him in the heat of the moment.

She pushed it all to the back of her mind now and followed Paris through the house, first hanging her jacket on a coat rack in the bright and generous hallway. They went up the creaking carpeted stairs and onto a landing that led to his bedroom.

"Err, Paris, who exactly am I going to meet in your bedroom?"

"Don't worry about it, you'll love this. I think you may even know her, or at least seen her around."

The door to her friend's bedroom was open. A woman with her back turned to them sat on the bed, with just a little of her face visible in a mirror, which stood on a garish glittery dressing table, which Paris would no doubt have thought was so tacky he had to have it.

"Sophie, I'd like you to meet Glinda the Good Bitch."

With a name like that, she must be a drag queen, thought Sophie, waiting for her to turn around so she could see who it was.

"Sweetie, darling! I didn't know you were coming over today. I would have asked for a lift otherwise. Don't I look fantastic? Paris has been working on my character and aesthetic."

Sophie's mouth dropped. Had Beryl not spoken, she probably wouldn't have recognised her mother who was wearing a faded purple wig in a beehive style. Makeup had been trowelled onto her face, so thick it had filled in the deep crevasses across her forehead, around her eyes and above her top lip, which like the bottom one was now painted a vicious red.

Beryl stood to show the full effect. A dark purple sequin gown hung to just above her ankles, barley touching the black kitten heels that were on her feet. Over the top of it all was a black faux fur coat that hung over her shoulders like a cape, dusting the floor as she paraded in and out of the room.

"Don't I look stunning, sweetie!?" She shouted while shimmying her top half so the sequins on the dress rustled and the hair swayed dangerously like a tall building during an earthquake. "Well, darling, don't you think your mother looks stunning? Paris said I could go on stage in a few weeks after a little more rehearsal time... he thinks I could bring in an older clientele in the early evenings."

"I don't really know what to say, mother. I'm not surprised, but just a little taken aback is all. Why... why are you dressed as a drag queen?"

"Sweetie, I'm not dressed as a drag queen. I am a drag queen. I just thought it looked fun. You're always messing around in that place and having a good time, so I wanted in on the action too."

Beryl, or Glinda the Good Bitch, set her daughter with a look that said, 'I'm serious about this, don't you dare tell me it's a silly idea'.

"Well, I guess you look good."

"Good, darling?! Good. I don't think anyone in this family has ever looked as fabulous as I do now. I am more than good, I am grand. I am now of the House of Paris Le Grand."

Paris shrugged at Sophie, as if to say he had no choice, but cracked a grin at the same time letting her know there was no harm in it.

"Glinda looks stunning," Paris announced to the room. "Now, I think a celebration like this calls for Champagne, Sophie, where did you leave that bottle?"

"It's downstairs, but it's probably not chilled enough. And what are we celebrating anyway?"

"A returnee to the House of Paris Le Grand and a newcomer too, of course," he said pointing at Sophie and Beryl in turn. "Now, I said Champagne, perhaps you could also tell us what Josh and you talked about when I'm back with the glasses."

"How do you know I spoke to Josh?" Sophie, now confused as she hadn't spoken to Paris at all recently, nor had she shared anything with her mum.

"Well, me, your mum, Josh, and some of the other girls at work have been keeping an eye on you, how's Gracie? I can't wait to meet her?"

"You were spying on me?"

"Not spying, just making sure you were going to see Doctor Jane and also to make sure you still ticked something else off the bucket list."

"You put the flyer on my car?"

"I did, sweetie. I couldn't bare for you to miss out on a little puppy like Gracie. I'd told Sally at the kennels to make sure you took her for a walk. So, when's your next date with Josh?"

"And here I thought I had shut myself off from you all. Returned to my old hermit ways..."

Paris chimed in before she could finish: "There's no escaping me, Sophie. I told you, you're part of my family now. But enough of this, tell us about your date with Josh. He's been bugging me since the first one went belly up."

Chapter Twenty-Three: Bon Voyage

Sophie's bucket list lay on the dining table, which had now been pulled into the centre of her dining/living room, and all the other furniture pushed against the walls to make room for the near forty people who were calling round that afternoon.

The table had been filled with typical party food like crisps, quiche and sandwiches, while a slow cooker full of chilli, which had been made by Josh, had been plugged in. Ralph, Thomas and her mother had stayed over the night before, and so had Josh, who'd spent most of his time at Sophie's over the six months that had passed since they'd met in the coffee shop.

Everything was ready, she just needed the boys and her mother to come downstairs to help finish the decorating, and for Paris to come with the Champagne which he'd ordered through the suppliers at Sophisticats.

The club had continued to grow, with her mother's first appearance on the stage making the national press and bagging her interviews with red top newspapers and lifestyle magazines. 'Oldest Drag Queen is 68-year-old Grandmother' and 'Being old is a drag for this OAP queen' were just a few of the headlines.

But Sophie was about to take some time away from the business – she and Josh had a big announcement to make and they wanted to do it in front of everyone they knew.

"Come on you lot, people will be starting to arrive, and I've still got to put the banner up," she shouted from the bottom of the stairs.

Everyone had been invited under the partially true guise that Josh and Sophie were taking a sabbatical together. They'd saved up some money between them and had decided to tick the last thing off Sophie's bucket list.

Travelling around Europe was something she'd wanted to do when she was a child, having grown up hearing all about her mother's worldly adventures. Although the Continent wouldn't be as exciting as touring with a circus or meandering around India, China and other exotic places, it was by far the most exciting thing Sophie had ever planned.

Ralph and his boyfriend Jack were the first to come downstairs, the new couple were still infatuated with each other and barley went anywhere without holding hands, kissing or having some sort of physical contact.

It had taken her eldest son a few months after their meeting in Manchester to tell Sophie that he was gay. Even though he knew her best friend was gay and that she worked in a drag club, Ralph had still been very nervous saying that he was interested in men and not women.

Sophie just shrugged when he told her, gave him a cuddle and asked if he'd like to go with her to see his nan performing at Sophisticats that night.

A few weeks later, Ralph came back down from university with Jack, who he'd been seeing for a little while. He was just as nervous introducing Jack to his mum as he was coming out, but bringing a new boyfriend into a room with Beryl, Paris, Josh, Thomas, Sophie and her ex-husband Carl – plus a handful of drag queens – must be quite intimidating.

In Sophie's eyes, if Ralph liked Jack, then that was good enough for her and she welcomed him into the family. Carl had seemed apprehensive at first, which annoyed Sophie. She hadn't had him down as the sort of person who would be funny around gay people, especially not his own son. He was such a laid-back man, calm and understanding about everything. Sophie eventually confronted him and found out he was worried about not dressing well enough around Ralph and his boyfriend. That caused a laugh among them all.

But now it was time for Sophie's big news. She'd never had anything like this to tell anyone before. Although announcing to everyone she and Josh were going be hitting the road together, it wasn't on the same scale as the additional surprise she'd been keeping to herself.

The family were now beavering away, making the house look festive for the big bon voyage party Josh and Sophie had planned, even Carl and his new girlfriend Louise had come early to help. This was appreciated, as Beryl's idea of helping was to walk around the room in her kitten heels and purple beehive wig like she was on a runway, modelling haute couture.

In reality, she was wearing a cheap charity shop dress, which caused Gracie to snap and yap excitedly as the dress's fringed hem whipped this way and that with each turn Beryl made.

Guests started arriving one after the other over the next half-hour until the room was finally packed with Josh's and Sophie's friends and family. Josh's brother Felix had turned up with Paris and the Champagne, leading Sophie to corner Paris in the kitchen to find out what was going on between the two.

"Nothing," Paris squirmed. "His marriage didn't exactly work out the way he wanted it to, and he just needed someone to talk to."

This was clearly a lie, Paris was late to the party and looked a little ruffled, she knew something was going on between the pair of them, but she'd find out sooner or later. Her best friend was many things, but a secret keeper was not one of those.

Once all the guests had been gathered into one room, Sophie and Josh stood in front of them and tapped a knife against an empty wine glass to bring them all to silence.

Josh began to make a speech, as they'd both agreed earlier that he was the confident one and Sophie would probably get too nervous and embarrassed. "Thank you all so much for coming today, it really means a lot to Sophie and me. This is the last time we're likely to see you all for a little while as you already know we're going on a mid-life crisis gap year, but..."

He stopped his rehearsed speech as Sophie stepped forward to face him, holding both of his hands as she moved around in front of him. She crouched down on to one knee and began, causing Josh to stutter, "what are you doing, silly?"

"Josh Oliver Geller, you walked drunkenly one night into a gay bar and my life, somewhere I never thought I'd meet the man who I would want to spend the rest of my life with. But I've learnt over the last year that things don't always happen in real life as they do in my brain. That's why I want to ask you if you'll make me the happiest middle-aged woman and marry me. Josh, will you be my husband?"

The room erupted into a commotion, some people were whooping and cheering, others wolf whistled or clapped and some gasped. But Josh stood, still holding Sophie's hands and looking into her eyes as she waited for a reply.

Epilogue: From the Author

Depression is a terrible thing, which seems like an extremely light and empty statement considering the destruction it can cause to individuals suffering with it and those around them.

It has been described as a black dog that follows you around, constantly reminding you that something is not right. That is how former Prime Minister Winston Churchill described his depression.

In some ways it is like a black dog, but it can also be bigger or much smaller. Sometimes I imagine it in various forms – a cat, bear, or a nipping ferret. There's no one size or type. Many will be unfortunate enough to have experienced depression, be it in a mild form or a daily struggle. I'm one of those people. Although there is nothing to complain about in my life, other than the odd grumble around work or some other minor thing, it creeps in without an invite or cause.

If I sit back and look at what I have achieved, that I'm fortunate enough to call Matthew my partner and the fact we have built a lovely home together, with both of us having good jobs and great friends, there is nothing to be down about at all. So many people have it much worse.

But that doesn't matter. Depression seeps into your bones and every organ in your body, pulling you down physically and mentally. If you're not strong enough or feeling particularly weak one day, you've had it. The disease begins to seed a rot into every aspect of your life. Instantly, you can become unrecognisable.

Just as bad is experiencing other people's struggles. So easily we can cast them off and out away from ourselves and brand them weird, hopeless, attention-seeking or mental. Although I've suffered too, I'm one of those who has wrongly turned my back on people when they needed someone to listen to them.

Depression isn't something that came to me in later life. My own experience of it wasn't my first. I've watched someone struggle. There were many times when it got so bad that, like Sophie, this person made rash decisions that have gone on to define the rest of their life. They'll never be able to undo what they did in a bid to escape that cold, dark beast that hovered over their shoulder.

It all seemed so normal, watching as this person shattered into thousands of pieces time and again. At times they were confused, lost and unable to handle even the simplest situation.

Witnessing someone grab a bag of pills and walk out towards an empty beach has scarred me mentally, but it has also defined me, by giving me some sort of privileged insight into the horrendous torment that they struggled with. Their actions on that day were a cry for help and, luckily, they didn't do anything with the drugs and were brought back safe.

Over the years, this person has continued to struggle with their illness. I don't know how much or whether it ever got as bad as those dark suicidal times again. But I know they still struggle.

As someone who has struggled with bouts of depression myself, I should be more understanding and given them more time in the past. But I still decide to take the easier option of not talking about it or giving it the right amount of time because I know it is going to be less painful for both of us.

But writing this book, using some real-life experiences, has helped me to understand that, although depression isn't something we can one hundred percent control, we can make things easier for ourselves and those around us.

Sophie has her own struggles with depression, which she's put up with since being a child. It's not unique now for a child to be on antidepressants, nor is it out of the ordinary for someone to be on them for years at a time or for their whole lives, like Sophie.

But Sophie was also a victim of society and the popular culture around her. She envied people on social media who took snippets of the best parts of their lives and posted them for the world to see. The person behind those pictures, though, is far from perfect.

Just like magazines are criticised for giving an unnatural representation of life – showing the perfect celebrity lifestyle, airbrushing blemishes and printing gushing interviews about how happy someone's life is – the potency of social media should take a portion of blame for people's poor mental health.

I don't think depression was the only thing Sophie struggled with, though. She had tendencies to live in the safety of routine, which there's nothing wrong with. This made her yearn for and look up to some of the most basic things in life that she'd never dreamt being was capable of.

Going on a shopping trip, having a makeover or finding romance – these are the desires of a child aspiring to be a grown-up. Sophie's depression swiped away her childhood, she never experienced or allowed herself to do the things most 'normal' people take for granted.

It's not explicit in the book, but the fact her children don't live with her or spend that much time talking to her shows how depression drove them all away. She needed their support but grew used to handling things alone. In her forties, like when she was younger, depression wasn't really something that was spoken about, it was a bit of a taboo and it still is now.

Even in a society when we're told that talking about poor mental health is normal and good and that we shouldn't discount or discriminate against people who suffer, it is still the done thing. People don't understand or don't want to understand. It is easier to wash your hands of someone who has mental health problems than it is to try and discover how to help them and to know what might be causing an uncharacteristic outburst.

If an often happy, useful person one day becomes miserable and easily agitated, don't you think there is a reason behind that worth discovering? Talking to someone about their problems has always been the best prescription. But sometimes it's not that easy to get the information out of someone either. Still, there's a fear from people who have poor mental health that they will be branded as some sort of loony, that they will be turned down for things at work because their 'fragile state-of-mind' prevents them from tackling anything that could prove stressful.

But the one thing that people too easily forget is that we all have mental health. Just because someone's mind may be stronger or less affected by the environment around them, it doesn't make them a better or more valuable person.

Sophie got there though, and she discovered how powerful she was. She recognised that her depression had stopped her from doing the things she could do. I don't know whether she got off the antidepressants fully – I'm not a doctor. But I do know she managed her mental health better after speaking about it to the people she trusted.

The big question, though, is did Josh say yes to her proposal and allow her to tick *Whirlwind Romance* off her list? I don't know the answer to that yet, because to say yes could irresponsibly suggest that everyone has a happy ending, yet saying no would be like writing off happiness altogether.

But we will find out one day.

Dedication:

Thank you to my wonderful supportive partner Matthew, who I dedicate this book to. He has put up with a lot from me over the many years we've been a loving couple. He supported me through some of the biggest moments in my life. The life we have together is like a dream. We are so lucky. If it wasn't for him, I wouldn't have had the career in journalism I had dreamed of.

An even bigger thanks to Matthew because he told me to write this book one evening when we were sat watching tele on the sofa and Sophie popped into my mind. He is also the one who introduced me to the world of drag through an amazing series called Ru Paul's Drag Race.

From that show I learned that I can be myself, that I don't need to wear a disguise or act in ways I think people want me to. Being myself is the best person I can be and I continue to learn how to do that.

Thank you also to my little partner in crime Milo, our Working Cocker Spaniel who had his own mental health problems. He kept me company while I wrote most of this book, lifting his head every now and then to agree with my ideas, even when they were bad. Unfortunately, we had to say goodbye to Milo when his problems became too much for him and us.

I'd also like to pay tribute to those who inspired the characters in the book. Some of Beryl's past and her eccentricities come from Agnes Jackson, my mother-outlaw's mum. She was once a magician's assistant and we have a wonderful black and white picture of her wearing a toga and handling a python. Agnes, although I never met her, was an amazing wife, mother and grandmother. She still inspires the people she left behind.

Thanks to my family – my dad Peter and my mam Janet who have always done their best for me and my sisters and brother. No life is perfect, but my life made me who I am today, and I wouldn't change that. Ever.

Finally, my friends and colleagues at the magazine where I've worked for years. They didn't know I was writing this book and unfortunately probably felt the brunt of my creative frustrations on more than one occasion.

Printed in Great Britain
by Amazon